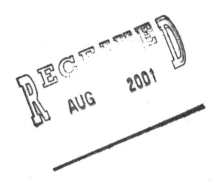

AUNT DIMITY'S DEATH

AUNT DIMITY'S DEATH

Nancy Atherton

PENGUIN BOOKS

PENGUIN BOOKS
Published by the Penguin Group
Penguin Books USA Inc., 375 Hudson Street,
New York, New York 10014, U.S.A.
Penguin Books Ltd, 27 Wrights Lane, London W8 5TZ, England
Penguin Books Australia Ltd, Ringwood, Victoria, Australia
Penguin Books Canada Ltd, 10 Alcorn Avenue, Toronto, Ontario,
Canada M4V 3B2
Penguin Books (N.Z.) Ltd, 182–190 Wairau Road, Auckland 10,
New Zealand

Penguin Books Ltd, Registered Offices: Harmondsworth, Middlesex,
England

First published in the United States of America by Viking Penguin,
a division of Penguin Books USA Inc., 1992
Published in Penguin Books 1993

PUBLISHER'S NOTE
This is a work of fiction. Names, characters, places, and incidents
either are the product of the author's imagination or are used
fictitiously, and any resemblance to actual persons, living or dead,
events, or locales is entirely coincidental.

ISBN 1-56865-525-8

Printed in the United States of America
Set in Sabon
Designed by Virginia Norey

For the Handsome Prince

AUNT DIMITY'S DEATH

1

When I learned of Aunt Dimity's death, I was stunned. Not because she was dead, but because I had never known she'd been alive.

Maybe I should explain.

When I was a little girl, my mother used to tell me stories. She would tuck me in, sit Reginald in her lap, and spin tale after tale until my eyelids drooped and I nodded off to sleep. She would then tuck Reginald in beside me, so that his would be the first face I saw when I opened my eyes again come morning.

Reginald was my stuffed rabbit. He had once had two button eyes and a powder-pink flannel hide, but he had gone blind and gray in my service, with a touch of purple near his hand-stitched whiskers, a souvenir of the time I'd had him try my grape juice. (He spit it out.) He stood nine inches tall and as far as I knew, he had appeared on earth the same day I had, because he had been at my side forever. Reginald was my confidant and my companion in adventure—he was the main reason I never felt like an only child.

My mother found Reginald useful, too. She taught third and fourth grade at an elementary school on the northwest side of Chicago, where we lived, and she knew the value of props. When the world's greatest trampoline expert—me—refused to settle down at bedtime, she would turn Reginald around on her lap and address him directly. "Well, if Lori doesn't want to listen, I'll tell the story to you, Reginald." It worked like a charm every time.

My mother was well aware that there was nothing I loved more than stories. She read the usual ones aloud: *How the Elephant Got Its Trunk, Green Eggs and Ham, The Bluebird of Happiness,* and all the others that came from books. But my favorite stories (and Reginald's, too) were the ones she didn't read, the ones that came from her own voice and hands and eyes.

These were the Aunt Dimity stories. They were the best, my mom's special treat, reserved for nights when even back-scratching failed to soothe me into slumber. I must have been an impossibly restless child, because the Aunt Dimity stories were endless: *Aunt Dimity's Cottage, Aunt Dimity in the Garden, Aunt Dimity Buys a Torch,* and on and on. My eyes widened with excitement at that last title—I was thrilled by the thought of Aunt Dimity preparing to set out for darkest Africa—until my mom reduced my excitement (and the size of my eyes) by explaining that, in Aunt Dimity's world, a "torch" was a flashlight.

I should have guessed. Aunt Dimity's adventures were never grand or exotic, though they took place in some unnamed, magical land, where a flashlight was a torch, a truck was a lorry (which made Reginald laugh, since that was my name, too), and tea was the sovereign remedy for all ills. The adventures themselves, however, were strictly down-to-earth. Aunt Dimity was the most mundane heroine I had ever encountered, and her adventures were extraordinarily ordinary. Nonetheless, I could never get enough of them.

One of my great favorites, told over and over again, until I could have told it myself had I wanted to (which I didn't, of course, because my mother's telling was part of the tale), was *Aunt Dimity Goes to the Zoo*. It began on "a beautiful spring day when Aunt Dimity decided to go to the zoo. The daffodils bobbed in the breeze, the sun danced on every windowpane, and the sky was as blue as cornflowers. And when Aunt Dimity got to the zoo, she found out why: All the rain in the world was waiting for her there, gathered in one enormous black cloud which hovered over the zoo and dared her to set foot inside the gate."

But did that stop Aunt Dimity? Never! She opened her trusty brolly ("umbrella," explained my mother), charged into the most drenching downpour in the history of downpours —and had a marvelous time. She had the whole zoo to herself and she got to see how all the animals behaved in the rain, how some of them hid in their shelters while others bathed and splashed and shook showers of droplets from their fur. "When she'd seen all she wanted to see," my mother concluded, "Aunt Dimity went home to warm herself before the fire and feast on buttered brown bread and a pot of tea, smiling quietly as she remembered her lovely day at the zoo."

I suppose what captivated me about Aunt Dimity was her ability to spit in life's eye. Take *Aunt Dimity Buys a Torch*: Aunt Dimity goes to "Harrod's, of all places" to buy a flashlight. She makes the mistake of going on the weekend before Christmas, when the store is jam-packed with shoppers and the clerks are all seasonal help who couldn't tell her where the flashlights were even if they had the time, which they don't because of the mad crush, and she winds up never buying the flashlight. For anyone else it would have been a tiresome mistake. For Aunt Dimity, it was just another adventure, one which became more hilarious floor by floor. And in the end she goes home to warm herself before the fire, feast on buttered brown bread and a pot of tea, and chuckle to herself as she remembers her day at Harrod's. Of all places.

Aunt Dimity was indomitable, in a thoroughly ordinary way. Nothing stopped her from enjoying what there was to enjoy. Nothing kept her from pursuing what she came to pursue. Nothing dampened her spirits because it was *all* an adventure. I was entranced.

It wasn't until I was in my early teens that I noticed a resemblance between Aunt Dimity and my mother. Like Aunt Dimity, my mother took great delight in the small things in life. Like her, too, she was blessed with an uncommon amount of common sense. Such gifts would be useful to anyone, but to my mother, they must have proved invaluable. My father had died shortly after I was born, and a lapsed insurance policy had left her in fairly straitened circumstances.

My mother was forced to sell our house and most of its contents, and to return to teaching much sooner than she'd planned. It must have been a wrench to move into a modest apartment, even more of a wrench to leave me with the downstairs neighbor while she went off to work, but she never let it show. She was a single mother before single mothers hit the headlines, and she managed the job very well, if I do say so myself. I never wanted for anything, and when I decided to leave Chicago for college in Boston, she somehow managed to send me, without a moment's hesitation. Around me, she was always cheerful, energetic, and competent. Just like Aunt Dimity.

My mother was a wise woman, and Aunt Dimity was one of her greatest gifts to me. I can't count the number of times Aunt Dimity rescued me from potential aggravation. Years later, when nearsighted old ladies ran their grocery carts over my toes, I would recall the very large man who had stepped on Aunt Dimity's foot at Harrod's. She guessed his weight to within five pounds. She knew because she subsequently asked him his exact weight, a scene which left me convulsed with giggles every time my mother recounted it. Remembering that, I found myself guessing the eyeglass prescriptions of my grocery-cart-wielding little old ladies. Though I never had the nerve to confirm my estimates, the thought made me laugh instead of growl.

By all accounts, I had a naturally buoyant spirit as a child and the Aunt Dimity stories certainly helped it along. But even naturally buoyant spirits sink at times. Mine took a nosedive when I found myself living the bits that never appeared in the Aunt Dimity stories: the bits when there was no wood for the fire and no butter for the brown bread, when all the lovely days turned dreary. It was nothing unusual, nothing extraordinary or exotic or grand, nothing that hasn't happened a million times to a million people. But this time it happened to me and it all happened at once, with no space for a breath in between. I was on one of those downward spirals that come along every once in a while and suddenly nothing was funny anymore.

It started when my marriage dissolved, not messily, but painfully nonetheless. By the time we sat down to draw up papers, all I wanted was a quick, clean break—and that was all I got. I could have stuck around to fight for property settlements or alimony, but by then I was tired of fighting, tired of sticking around, and, above all, I despised the thought of living *off* a man I no longer lived *with*.

I faced the Newly Divorced Woman's Semi-Obligatory *Wanderjahr* with no sense of adventure at all. About to turn thirty, I had little money, less energy, and absolutely no idea of what I wanted to do next. Before moving to Los Angeles, where my former husband's job with an accounting firm had taken me, I had worked in the rare book department of my university's library. I moved back to Boston, but by the time I arrived, my old position was gone—literally. The humidity control device, installed at great expense to protect the rare book collection from the ravages of time, had gone haywire, causing an electrical fire that no amount of humidity could extinguish. The books had gone up in smoke and so, too, had my prospects for employment.

Getting a new job in the same field was out of the question. I had no formal library degree, and the curator, at whose knee I had learned more about old books than any six library school graduates combined, was an opinionated maverick. A personal recommendation from Dr. Stanford J. Finderman tended to close doors rather than open them, and I soon discovered that the job market for informally trained rare book specialists was as soft as my head must have been when I'd first decided I could make a living as one. Had I known what the future held in store for me, I would have gone to motorcycle mechanics' school.

My mother wanted me to come home to the safe haven of our yellow-brick apartment building in Chicago, but I would have none of that. The only motherly assistance I would accept was a steady supply of home-baked cookies, mailed Federal Express and packed to withstand a nuclear blast. I never mentioned how often those cookies were all that stood between me and an empty stomach.

I stayed with a friend from college days, Meg Thomson, until the divorce was final. She introduced me to the wonderful world of temping and as soon as I'd registered with a reputable Boston agency, I struck out on my own. With high hopes, I joined the ranks of the urban pioneers—mainly because the only apartment I could afford was located in what real estate agents like to call a "fringe" neighborhood.

I can confirm the rumor about the poor preying upon the poor. Two weeks after I'd moved in, my place was ransacked. The intruder had apparently had a temper tantrum when he discovered that I was just as impoverished as the rest of my neighbors. I came home to an unrecognizable heap of torn clothing, splintered furniture, and a veritable rainbow of foodstuffs smeared decoratively across my walls.

That was pretty disheartening, but the worst part was finding Reginald. The boon companion of my childhood had been slit from cottontail to whiskers, his stuffing yanked out and strewn about the room. It took me three days to find what remained of his left ear. I interred him in a shoebox, too sickened to attempt his repair, knowing that my clumsy needlework could never match the beautiful stitches that had helped him survive an adventuresome bunnyhood. On the fourth day, shoebox in hand, I moved out, beginning what was to become a long sequence of moves in and out of apartments which, if not exactly squalid, were still a far cry from my predivorce standards of domestic comfort. In April of that year, an ad in the Cambridge *Tab* led me to share an apartment with two other women in a three-decker on a quiet street in West Somerville. I'd just settled in when my mother died.

There was no warning. The doctor told me that she had died peacefully in her sleep, which helped a little, but not enough. I felt that I should have been there, that I might have been able to do something, anything, to help her. Up to that point I had been able to bounce back from every blow more or less intact, but this one almost flattened me.

I flew back to Chicago at once. There was no need for me to arrange the funeral—my mother and Father Zherzshinski had taken care of that. The memorial mass at St. Boniface's was attended by scores of her former pupils, each of whom had a story to tell, a fond memory to share. In among the flood of flowers was an anonymous bouquet of white lilacs that had come all the way from England. I gazed at it and marveled at the many lives my mother had shaped, all unknown to me.

My mother had also arranged for the Salvation Army to pick up her furniture and clothing, knowing full well that her brilliant daughter had no place to put them and no means of paying for their storage. I spent a week at the old apartment, packing the rest of her possessions—mementos, photograph albums, books—and settling her accounts. She had left just enough savings to cover the funeral expenses, to ship her things to Boston, and to get me back there, with very little left over. I was neither surprised nor disappointed. Elementary school teachers are paid in love, not money, and I had never expected an inheritance.

I took on an overload of temp jobs when I got back, and not purely for financial reasons. Exhaustion is a great analgesic—it numbs emotion, silences thought—and I craved the release. The months passed in a blur. I stopped seeing my friends, stopped writing letters, stopped chatting with my roommates and co-workers. By the time April rolled around again, the only person I talked to was Meg Thomson, but that was because she kept in touch with me, not the other way round. And not even Meg could get me to open up about my mother's death. Did I mention a downward spiral? This is the point where I was about ready to auger in.

That's when I got the letter saying that Aunt Dimity was dead.

2

It was the perfect capper to a perfect day. April had roared in like an ill-tempered lion and I had just survived yet another week in yet another unfamiliar office, coping with yet another phone system (picture the control room at the Kennedy Space Center) and managerial style ("Are we up, up, up for another tee-rific day?"). I had been on the run since six that morning and had skipped lunch to get ahead on the filing, only to learn that I wouldn't be needed for the full day after all, since the office was closing at three in honor of the boss's birthday. Shrunken paycheck in hand, and dreading the empty hours to come, I dragged myself home through a bone-chilling drizzle, more sleet than rain, wondering how many more tee-rific days I could stand.

The apartment was deserted when I got there, pretty much the way it always was. One of my roommates was an intern, the other a premed student, and their Byzantine hours meant that I had the place to myself most of the time, which suited me just fine.

It was the best living arrangement I had found so far, but it wasn't exactly the Ritz. Not even the Holiday Inn. My furniture consisted of a mattress on the floor, a borrowed card table, a chair rescued from a life on the streets, and a wooden crate on which rested my one and only lamp. Reginald's shoebox lived in the closet, and I kept my clothes in the same cardboard boxes I had used throughout my many moves. It saved a lot of time packing. My mother's things, sealed in boxes, had stood along one wall since they'd arrived from Chicago.

I flicked on the hall light, slipped out of my wet sneakers and jacket, and grabbed my mail from the basket on the hall table. Changing into jeans and an oversized flannel shirt, I sorted through the mail, braced for the usual barrage of threats from various credit card companies who were unimpressed with my increasingly erratic payment schedule. Legalized hate mail is what I called it, and it was the only kind of mail I had received since my mother's death.

That and junk mail. The plain envelope nestled in among the bills was probably another promotional scheme, and I regarded it sourly. Just what I needed: an invitation to time-share in Bermuda, when the closest I would ever get to Bermuda was the pair of shorts I'd come across in the Salvation Army store last weekend.

Instead, it contained a letter from a law firm, the name of which was plastered (tastefully) across the letterhead: *Willis & Willis*. This is it, I thought, feeling a little queasy. The credit card companies are taking me to court. What were they going to do, repossess my mattress? With a sinking heart, I read on.

In polite, formal phrases, Willis & Willis apologized for the delay in reaching me, admitting to some difficulty in finding my current address (no surprise to me, since I'd moved six times in the past year). Willis & Willis went on to say that they were sorry to inform me of the death of Miss Dimity Westwood, whom I would recognize as Aunt Dimity. At which point, all thoughts of credit card companies and promotional campaigns vanished and I sat down, rather suddenly.

Aunt Dimity? Dead?

I was stunned, all right. In fact, I was downright spooked. As far as I could remember, I had never told anyone about Aunt Dimity. She belonged to my mom and to me and was far too special to share, except, of course, with Reginald. But he was in no position to be talking to law firms. Hurriedly, I skimmed through the rest of the letter.

Willis & Willis would be most grateful if I would stop by their offices at my earliest possible convenience to discuss some matters of interest. An appointment would not be necessary, as they would see me whenever I chose to appear on their doorstep. With sincere sympathy, they remained my most humble servants, William Willis, etc.

I spread the letter on the folding table and stared at it. The stationery was real enough. The words were real enough. The only thing that wasn't remotely real was their message. "Well, Reginald?" I said, glancing at the closet door. "What do you make of this? Pretty weird, huh?"

I didn't really expect an answer. I had decided long ago that the day Reginald started speaking to me was the day I checked myself into the nearest funny farm. Then again, a fictional character had just walked out of my earliest childhood and tapped me on the shoulder. Maybe, if I listened harder, I'd begin to hear Reginald after all.

I read the letter through once more, slowly this time, then examined it with a professional eye. The stationery was cream colored, stiff, and heavy. When held up to the light, the watermark and laid lines confirmed its quality. It hadn't been run off on a computer printer, either, but typed on a real typewriter and signed with a real fountain pen. I had the distinct impression that Willis & Willis wanted me to see this, wanted me to feel that I was worth more effort than computerized efficiency would allow. I wondered if the very best law firms employed scribes to handwrite correspondence in order to demonstrate their painstaking concern for the affairs of special clients.

Certain phrases seemed to stand out, as though in boldface. Miss Dimity Westwood. No appointment necessary. William Willis. And, most interesting, those "matters of interest" to discuss. Curiouser and curiouser. I glanced at my watch, glanced back at the letter, then looked once more at the closet door.

"What the hell, Reginald," I said. "It's not as though I had plans for the afternoon. As Aunt Dimity would say, it's an adventure."

*
**

As with many adventures, this one didn't get off to the start I had in mind. The law office was located a few blocks south of Post Office Square and I worked out a combination of bus routes to get there. It didn't seem like a bad trip: two buses and a short walk, no more than an hour, tops. Of course, I hadn't looked out the window yet.

I don't know what's worse about a blizzard in April: the fact that it's so wet and slushy, or the fact that it's in April. No wonder they call it the cruelest month. The two buses and the short walk turned into two hours of howling wind, driving sleet, and ankle-deep slush. Plus the heat didn't work on the second bus. I might have been able to shrug it off if I'd had proper winter clothing, but I had lived in LA just long enough to get rid of my nice warm woolen sweaters, down parka, and snow boots and I hadn't found the money to replace them yet. Most of the time it didn't matter, since I made it a point to be outside as little as possible.

This time, it mattered. My windbreaker and sneakers were no match for the storm, and by the time I found Willis & Willis, I was soaked to the skin, red-faced from the wind, and shivering uncontrollably. If I hadn't been afraid of dying from exposure, I would have been too embarrassed to approach their door. What a mess.

And what a door. Not that I saw it right away. I had to get past the gate first. The gate in the wall. The wall that rose up from the edge of the sidewalk and bore a brass plate engraved with the address mentioned in the letter. I checked and rechecked the numbers as carefully as I could, considering the velocity of the wind. It was the right place. I buzzed a buzzer, was scanned by a camera, and for God alone knows what reason, the gate unlocked and I let myself in. It wasn't until I was halfway down the path that I saw the door.

It was the exact door-equivalent of the elegant stationery: polished to a satin sheen and massive, with a lion-head knocker gleaming dully through the swirling snow. The storm seemed to abate for a moment so that I could admire the gleaming lion, and the building over which it kept watch.

3

Clearly, the law firm of Willis & Willis had no more use for glass and steel than they had for laser printers. They didn't have an office, they had a mansion, a gracious old mansion, surrounded and dwarfed, though not in the least intimidated, by office towers on every side. Don't ask me how it got there or, more incredible still, how it stayed there, but there it was, an oasis of charm and dignity in a concrete desert.

Great, I thought, Willis & Willis Meets the Little Match Girl. I staggered up the stairs and placed my hand on the lion's burnished head, knowing full well that I looked like something any self-respecting cat would refuse to drag in.

Two thumps brought a slightly rumpled looking man to the door. He was in his midthirties, had a short, neatly trimmed beard, and was wearing a well-worn dark tweed jacket and corduroy pants. If I'd had any sense of drama I would have chosen that moment to collapse into his arms— he was a big guy and looked sturdy enough to take it. He stood staring at me, while the snowflakes made little wet splashes on his glasses and the ice water dripped from the end of my nose. Then he smiled, so suddenly and with such radiance that I glanced furtively over my shoulder to see what he was smiling at.

"Hello," he said, with a warmth and intensity that seemed all out of proportion to the moment.

"Hello," I replied, a bit uncertainly.

"You must be Lori," he said, still beaming. My only response was another uncontrollable bout of shivering. It seemed to be enough. He threw the door wide and gestured for me to come in.

"I'm so sorry, standing around while you're freezing to death. Please, come in, come in and get warm." He took my elbow and guided me into the foyer. "Here, let me have your jacket. I'll see that it's dried. Please, have a seat. Can I get you anything? A cup of coffee? Tea?"

"Tea would be fine," I said. "But how did you know who I—"

"I'll be right back," he said abruptly, and hurried away.

Wondering which of the Willises he was, if indeed he was a Willis (did Willis &/or Willis answer their own door?), and baffled as to why *any* Willis would seem so happy to see me, I watched him disappear down the hall, then let my eyes wander around the room. I called it a foyer, but it was much grander, more like an entrance hall, with a high ceiling, oil paintings on the walls, and an enormous oriental rug that was more than capable of soaking up the sleet melting from my hair and shoes and jeans.

An ornate divided staircase curved up around the tapestry couch on which I sat, teeth chattering. There was a low table at my knees, and a tall vase filled with deep blue irises graced its flawless surface. I loved irises and the welcome reminder that, all evidence to the contrary, spring had to be just around the corner. An icy drop of water slithered down my neck, but I kept my eyes on the flowers, comforted by the thought that someday soon it would be warm again.

My host cleared his throat. I looked up and saw that he was carrying an armful of clothes—a hooded sweatshirt and some sweatpants, in crimson. Harvard, I thought.

"Here you are," he said, handing them over.

I looked at them blankly.

"I thought you might want to change into something dry," he offered. "I keep these on hand for the club, and trust me, they're clean." He patted his fairly ample midsection. "I don't use them as often as I should. I would've had proper clothes for you to change into, but I wasn't sure . . ." He looked me up and down in a way that wasn't remotely flirtatious. If it had been, at least I would have known what was going on. "Size eight?" he asked.

I nodded, not knowing what else to do.

His face lit up. "I'll remember that. But in the meantime, this is the best I can do. Will you take them for now, with my apologies? You can slip into them in the changing room. Right along here."

I hesitated. I didn't usually accept favors from strangers. Then I considered my blue-tinged fingertips and decided to force myself to make an exception this one time. I followed him down the hall, through a magnificent set of double doors and a sumptuous office, to what he had called the changing room. He set out a pile of towels and left, shutting the door behind him.

The changing room was to bathrooms what the Taj Mahal is to the Little Brown Church in the Vale. I would have gladly moved into it and lived there for the rest of my life. It was as elegantly appointed as the entrance hall and spacious enough to hold everything I owned, with room to spare. I had never seen anything like it: shower stall and whirlpool bath in gray marble, closet space galore, sleek reclining leather chair, massage table, full-length mirrors, telephone, stereo system, television, VCR, the works. But the best part of all was a carpet so thick and soft that my toes almost got lost in it. I took my time getting changed, savoring the sensation of being in a place designed to please the eye as well as the body. When I had finished, I tiptoed back into the office.

My host was sitting on the edge of the desk. He sprang to his feet when he saw me.

"Socks," he said.

"Excuse me?"

"Socks—I forgot dry socks. Here, take these, and give me those wet clothes. I'll be right back." We made our exchange and then he was gone again. The man was like a magic trick: now you see him, now you don't.

I pulled on the socks and popped back into the changing room to take a look at my new ensemble. It was about what I had expected, considering the fact that the donor was at least eight inches taller than I and a good deal heavier. The sweatpants were baggy enough for two of me, the sweatshirt, complete with its Harvard insignia, came down past my butt, and the heels of the socks reached well above my ankles. My hair was beginning to dry, and my short, dark curls completed the effect. It wasn't bad, if you go for the waif look.

"Comfy?" asked a now-familiar voice. I nearly jumped out of his socks. My host was looking in from the changing room doorway.

"Yes, thank you," I answered, "and I appreciate the dry clothes, but . . . do you think you could tell me who you are?"

"Whoops. Sorry about that," he apologized, "but you looked so damned wet and miserable that I thought introductions could wait." He began to chuckle. "I'll bet you thought I was the butler. . . ." He changed his chuckle into a cough when he saw the look on my face, which told him plainly that I didn't know *what* to think.

"I'm Bill Willis," he said hastily. "Not William. That's my father. We're partners in the firm. Do you mind if I call you Lori?"

"No," I said.

"That's great," he said. "Terrific, in fact. I can't tell you how happy . . . But please, come in here, sit down, and have your tea. I've let Father know you've arrived and he'll be here shortly. He's thrilled that you've come. We've both been looking forward to meeting you. You have no idea." His unexpected burst of enthusiasm hit me like a wave. I must have swayed on my feet because he was immediately at my side.

"Are you all right?" he asked.

"I'm fine," I said as I waited for the room to stop spinning. This had happened once or twice before on days when I skipped meals, but I was mortified to have it happen now, in front of this rich, Harvard-educated lawyer. Holding myself very erect, I walked past him into the adjoining office and sat in one of the two high-backed leather chairs that faced the massive desk. "I'm perfectly . . . fine."

"If you say so," he said doubtfully, crossing from the doorway to the desk. A silver tea service had been placed there. He poured a cup and brought it to me. "Maybe I should call for some food to go along with this." He reached for the phone, but I held out a restraining hand.

"Please don't," I said, in an effort to salvage what was left of my dignity. "There's no need. I said I was perfectly fine, and I meant it."

He stroked his beard thoughtfully, then nodded, once. "Okay. If that's what you want. But at least get some of the tea inside you. I don't want Father to think I've been inhospitable, and he'll be here any minute."

***

The sovereign remedy worked, as always, and by the time William Willis, Sr., entered the room, I was able to view him with something approaching equanimity. It was hard to believe he was related to Bill. A slight, clean-shaven man in his early sixties, with a high forehead and a patrician nose, he was impeccably attired in a black three-piece suit. Not only did Willis, Sr., dress better than his son, but while Bill had been almost too friendly from the moment I'd staggered through the front door, his father was as formal as an etiquette book, as though he knew the exact amount of pressure—in pounds per square inch—his handshake should exert, under these and any other circumstances. He was scrupulously polite, but he gave no indication of being thrilled about anything. What could Bill have been talking about? Sprawled comfortably in the leather chair beside my own, he had fallen silent at his father's entrance, and was watching him with an inexplicable gleam of excitement in his eyes.

After the punctilious handshake, Willis, Sr., seated himself behind the desk, unlocked the center drawer, and removed a file folder, which he placed carefully on the desk before him. He opened the folder and studied its contents intently for a moment, then cleared his throat and raised his eyes to mine. "Before continuing, young lady, I must ask you a few questions. Please answer them truthfully. Be advised that the penalties for misrepresentation are grave."

I felt a sudden urge to look to Bill for support, but I quelled it. Bill, for his part, remained silent.

"May I see your driver's license?"

I pulled my wallet from the sweatshirt pocket and handed it to him.

"I see," said Willis, Sr. "Now, will you please state your full name and place of birth?"

Thus began what I came to think of as the Great Q and A, with Willis, Sr., intoning the Q's and me supplying the A's. What was my mother's family name? Where had I gone to school? Where had my father been born? Where had I worked? Who was my godfather? On and on, with an almost sacramental regularity, for what seemed like a very long time, question after question after question. I could see Bill out of the corner of my eye the entire time and the look on his face continued to perplex me. He began with barely the ghost of a smile tugging at the corners of his mouth. As the questions went on, the smile settled and gradually became more pronounced, until he was grinning like a fool. Willis, Sr., seemed to share my puzzlement: the only time he faltered was when he happened to look up from his papers and caught sight of his son's goofy grin. Aside from that, Willis, Sr., showed no emotion whatsoever, never hurrying, never slowing down, pausing only to turn to the next page in the file.

My fatigue must have put me in a highly suggestible state of mind, because it never once occurred to me to fire any questions back at him. Like "What business is it of yours?" or "Who the hell are you to grill me like this?" The setting was so artificial that I felt like a character in a play. I even felt a touch of pride at knowing my lines so well. The hypnotic rhythm lulled me into a kind of semiconscious complacency, until Willis, Sr., asked what turned out to be the last question.

"Now, young lady, would you please tell my son and me the story entitled *Aunt Dimity Buys a Torch*?"

I sat bolt upright in the chair, sputtered a few incoherent syllables—and fainted. The shock of hearing those words on a stranger's lips did what a polar expedition on top of a hectic day without food had failed to do: awakened my sense of drama. I vaguely remember gaping in astonishment and then I found myself gazing blearily into Willis, Sr.'s face from a prone position on a couch.

"Miss Shepherd, can you hear me?" asked Willis, Sr., leaning over to peer closely at my face. "Ah, you are awake. Good, good."

I hardly recognized the man. The cool politeness in his eyes had given way to a look of warm concern, a lock of white hair had fallen over his forehead, and the hand that had shaken mine with such formality was now solicitously tucking an afghan around me. Suddenly I could see a clear resemblance between father and son.

"I am so very sorry about this," he said, with a worried frown. "I had no idea it would affect you so severely. But the terms of the will are quite clear and I had to be certain you were who you claimed to be. I was under strict orders, you see, but I never dreamt—"

"How did you know?" I murmured muzzily. "How did you know about Aunt Dimity?"

"I think we shall have a bite of supper first. You appear to be in need of sustenance," said Willis, Sr. "And then *I* will answer *your* questions for a change. A change for the better in my opinion, and in yours, too, no doubt." He beamed down at me. "I am so happy that you are here, my dear. I feel as though I have known you for years."

However much I disliked having my questions deflected yet again, I had to admit that food sounded like an idea whose time had come. I pulled myself into a sitting position as Bill entered the room pushing a supper-laden trolley.

"Feeling perfectly fine, are we?" he asked cheerfully, and I felt myself blush. He wheeled the trolley to within my reach and pulled up chairs for himself and his father. "If you'd felt any better, we might have had to call an ambulance."

"This is no time for levity, my boy," admonished Willis, Sr., gently. "If you had given Miss Shepherd a proper meal when she arrived, we might have avoided this unfortunate incident."

"You're quite right, Father. I stand corrected," said Bill, and I sank a bit lower on the couch.

"Please, Miss Shepherd, try some of the consommé," said Willis, Sr. "There's nothing like a good beef broth after an upset. And then, if you're up to it, a bit of the roast, I think . . ."

The two men fussed over me, filling my plate and keeping it filled, and between bites I told them the story of Aunt Dimity's quest for a torch. I felt awkward, hauling out a part of my childhood for these two strangers to examine, but Willis, Sr., assured me that it was a necessary part of the Great Q and A, so I went ahead and told it, word for word, exactly as my mother had told it to me. The only difference was that this time it put the teller to sleep instead of the listeners. Although it was barely eight o'clock, I dozed off with a dessert plate still in my lap.

I awoke in the small hours of the morning. The room was pitch-dark, but I didn't need light to know that I wasn't in my own bed. The mattress was firm and the pillows were soft—instead of the other way round—and when I stretched, my hands bumped into something which felt suspiciously like a headboard. Reaching to one side, my groping fingers found a nightstand, then a lamp. I turned it on.

Definitely not my room. A large, tweedy armchair sat in one corner, a small, graceful desk in another, the kind that sits in the front window of a fancy antique store and costs half the gross national product. A crystal carafe and a tumbler sat on the nightstand; the carafe was filled with water. The bed had a footboard to go with the headboard, and both were made of the same lustrous wood as the desk. The sheets and blankets were navy blue—very masculine—and the pillowcases bore a silver monogram in looping Florentine script: *W.*

For *Willis.*

I sat up as the rest of yesterday's events came flooding back, erasing my confusion and anchoring me firmly in . . . what? Yesterday morning I had been a struggling, semi-employed, ordinary person who slept on a mattress on the floor. This morning I found myself comfortably ensconced in an elegant bedroom, the honored guest of a venerable attorney. "What next?" I murmured, gazing about the room. "A glass coach and a Handsome Prince?"

The thought made me start as another memory settled into place, a sleepy memory of being carried up a long flight of stairs by the venerable attorney's son, the same son who had loaned me . . . I peeked under the covers and was relieved to spot the Harvard insignia. It was bad enough to know that I had been toted up to bed like a helpless child, but it could have been worse.

I still had plenty of questions, but they'd have to wait until the rest of the house had awakened. In the meantime . . . I swung my legs over the side of the bed. If I was careful and quiet, I should be able to take a look around. After all, it wasn't every day that I woke up with a mansion to explore.

Easing open a door at random, I discovered a spacious dressing room with empty shelves, empty hangers, an empty dressing table. The towels in the adjoining bathroom held the scent of fresh laundering, and everything else in it seemed to be brand-new: an undented tube of toothpaste, a toothbrush still in its wrapper, a dry bar of sandalwood soap placed between the double sinks. The shampoo and liquid soap dispensers in the shower were full, and an enormous loofah sat on one marble ledge, looking as though it hadn't touched water since it had first been wrested from the seafloor.

A second door opened on to a well-appointed parlor dominated by a wide, glass-fronted cabinet. Padding over, I saw that it held an assortment of trophies, plaques, and medals for everything from debating to Greek. There were a few sports awards, for odd things like squash and fencing, but most were for scholarly achievements. Each was polished and gleaming, and each was engraved with the name *William*

Willis. The dates indicated that they were Bill's, rather than his father's, and a young Bill's at that; the triumphs of childhood and young manhood memorialized quietly, in a very private room.

The cabinet reminded me of the steamer trunk I had found while sorting through my mother's things; a trunk carefully packed with the symbols of my own academic achievements, which had not been inconsiderable. It had been a crushing discovery, like encountering a trunkful of my mother's unfulfilled dreams for me. I looked at the trophies before me and envied Bill. He had lived up to the promise of his early years, while the schoolteacher's daughter was living out of cardboard boxes.

I turned away from the cabinet and was promptly distracted from my gloomy thoughts by the sight of my clothes from the day before. They had been placed neatly on the coffee table, cleaned, dried, and pressed. I was amused to see my well-worn clothing treated so respectfully, but I was also a little embarrassed. I doubted that Bill had ever seen such threadbare jeans before, or such shabby sneakers.

A piece of paper stuck out of one of the sneakers. I unfolded it and saw that the words on it had been printed in caps and underlined:

CALL 7404 AS SOON AS YOU GET UP
THE SOONER, THE BETTER!

I glanced at my watch, saw that it was coming up on four A.M., then looked back at the note and shrugged. Maybe I'd get those answers sooner than I'd thought. I picked up the phone on the end table and dialed the extension. Bill answered on the first ring.

"Lori? How are you feeling?"

"Fine," I said, "but—"

"Great. You're up? You're dressed?"

"Yes, but—"

"Terrific. I'll be right down."

"But what—" I began, but he had already hung up. I grabbed my sneakers and by the time my laces were tied, Bill was at the parlor door, rosy-cheeked and slightly out of breath, wearing a bulky parka with a fur-trimmed hood.

"I was hoping you'd be awake before dawn," he said. "Now, come with me, and hurry. I have something to show you."

"What is it?"

"You'll see." His eyes danced as he turned on his heel and took off down the hall. I scurried to catch up and we nearly collided at the first corner because I was so busy gawking at my surroundings. But how could I help it?

My suite opened on to a paneled corridor hung with hunting scenes, and the rug beneath my feet depicted a chase, the hounds bounding up the hall to bay at a smug-looking fox who perched out of reach at the farthest edge. A turn took us into another long passageway, this one devoted to still lifes, the rug woven with pears and peaches and pale green grapes glistening against a background of burnt umber. Another turn and we were racing up a staircase of golden oak, the newel posts carved with a pattern of grape leaves, the balustrade with the curling tendrils of trailing vines. The landings were as big as my bedroom. If Bill was trying to impress me, he was succeeding.

"Behold the House of Willis," I murmured.

Bill heard me. "Do you like it?" he asked. "It's what happens when you come from a long line of pack rats. We shipped all of our worldly goods over from England more than two hundred years ago and as far as I can tell, not one member of my family has ever thrown anything out. I wouldn't be surprised to learn that some of these pots were used in the ancestral caves." The "pot" he was referring to at that moment was a pale blue porcelain bowl spilling over with orchids. The flowers alone were probably worth more than my weekly paycheck.

He said nothing else until we reached the bottom of a narrow staircase with unadorned plaster walls and simple wrought-iron railings. There he turned and whispered, "Servants' quarters. People sleeping."

In silence, we climbed the stairs and made our way down a short passageway and into a small room. It was empty save for a rack hung with an assortment of jackets, and a table heaped with heavy sweaters. A spiral staircase in the center of the room led to a trapdoor in the ceiling. I rested against the wall while Bill rummaged through the pile of sweaters. He plucked up a tightly woven Icelandic pullover and handed it to me. "Size eight," he said. "Put it on." He stood with one foot on the bottom step of the staircase and looked at me closely. "Are you all right?"

"Yes," I said, wheezing. "It's just . . . all those stairs."

"We can stay here for a minute, if you need—"

"No, I'm okay."

"You're sure?"

"I'm *positive*," I said, with some exasperation. "Let's get going."

He climbed up the spiral staircase and through the trapdoor, then closed the trapdoor behind me as I emerged into the chilly predawn darkness of the mansion's roof. There was no moon, but the storm had spent itself, the clouds had flown, and the sky was ablaze with stars. I could vaguely make out the shadowy shapes of vents and chimneys and . . . something else. I knew what it looked like, but I couldn't imagine what it might be doing up there.

"Come." Bill led me directly to the strange shape that looked like, but could not possibly be, a dentist's chair. Except that it was. Piled next to it was what appeared to be a fitted waterproof cover.

"Had it since college," Bill said, giving the headrest an affectionate pat. "Saw it at an auction and snapped it up. Knew exactly where I'd put it. Have a seat."

I looked at Bill and I looked at the chair and for a brief

moment it crossed my mind that there might be an army of servants hiding behind the chimney pots, waiting for Bill's command to leap out and shout, "April Fool!"

"Hurry," he said. "It's almost over."

His sense of urgency was infectious—I climbed into the chair. It was upholstered in sheepskin, like the bucket seat of an expensive sports car, a welcome bit of customizing in this brisk weather. Bill levered it back until I was looking straight up into the star-filled sky.

"What am I looking for?" I asked.

"You'll know it when you see it," he replied.

I continued to gaze heavenward. With tall buildings towering on either side and the vastness of space stretched in between, I felt like a very small bug in a very big bottle. I didn't mind in the least when Bill placed his hand on my shoulder and whispered, "Be patient."

Then I saw them. Shooting stars. Not just one or two, but a dozen of them, silvery streaks that dashed across the velvet darkness, then vanished, as though the heavens were winking out at the end of time. I clutched the arms of the chair, dizzied by the sudden sensation that Bill's hand on my shoulder was the only thing keeping me from falling upward, into the stars. It ended as quickly as it had begun.

"There are very few things in this world that really can't wait," Bill said after a moment of silence, "and a meteor shower is one of them. I take it as a good omen that the clouds parted in time for you to see the end of this one."

The warmth in his voice brought me back down to earth, so to speak, reminding me that I was sitting in a dentist's chair on the roof of a mansion in the middle of Boston, with a complete stranger as my guide. And that the complete stranger was talking to me in a tone of voice usually reserved for very, very good friends. I eyed him warily as he levered the chair into an upright position.

"Do you do this with all of your clients?" I asked.

"No, I do not," he said, a hint of amusement in his voice.

"This is my private domain. There's something else I'd like you to see as long as we're up here—if you feel up to it, that is."

"If I feel . . ." I ignored his outstretched hand and clambered out of the chair on my own. "Look, Bill, in spite of my performance last night, I am not an invalid."

"Of course not." He pulled the fitted cover over the dentist's chair. "You're twenty pounds underweight, and a run up a flight of stairs leaves you puffing like a steam engine, but you're certainly not an invalid. Come on."

I stared at him, nonplussed, until he had almost disappeared in the shadows, then set out after him, ready to give him a piece of my mind. I made my way around chimney stacks and ventilators to a small domed structure in the center of the roof, but before I could say a word, he ducked through a low door, then stood back to let me enter. He shut the door, lit an oil lamp—and the walls sprang to life around us.

The entire interior, from the floor to the top of the dome, was covered with paintings—the Gemini twins, Orion with his belt and sword, and the regal queen, Cassiopeia, to name only a few. The paintings were inset with tiny faceted crystals that sparkled like miniature constellations, and the centerpiece was an old brass telescope that had been polished to within an inch of its life. Bill held the lamp high, clearly enjoying my wide-eyed amazement.

"Oh, my," I gasped at last, "this is *incredible*. Did you build it yourself?"

"The only thing I did was install a telephone. The rest"—he let his gaze wander across the glittering dome—"was Great-great-uncle Arthur's idea."

"Great-great-uncle Arthur?"

"Yes, well, every family has one eventually, and we had Arthur." Bill handed me the lantern, rummaged in a cupboard, and came up with a chamois cloth. As he spoke, he ran it across the smooth surface of the telescope. "He'd be considered eccentric in England, but here he was thought to be just plain nuts. He gave the family fits spending all that hard-earned cash on stargazing, but I, for one, am grateful to the old loon. Granted, it's not much good as an observatory now. Too many buildings, too much light from the city. But when he built it, the mansion was the tallest building around and the lights were fewer and farther between. Like this." He nodded at the oil lamp. "A softer light for a softer time.

"This is my bolt-hole," he continued. "I discovered it when I was a boy, and I've come here ever since, whenever I've needed to be by myself. Just me and the stars. And now, you."

There it was again, the warmth in his voice, and again it made me uneasy. "Thanks for showing it to me," I said, then tried to fill the uncomfortable silence by adding, "It's more than I deserve, really, after getting you in trouble with your father."

"After what?"

"What he said last night, about giving me a meal when I showed up. You did try, and I should have told him so."

"Oh, that." He folded the chamois cloth and returned it to the cupboard. "Don't worry about it."

"No, I mean it—I'm sorry I didn't say anything."

"It's okay."

"But it's not okay. I should have—"

"I understand, but there's no need—"

"Bill!" Did he think he had a monopoly on good manners? Here he was, showing me all of these lovely things, and he wouldn't even let me do something as commonplace as apologize for rude behavior. "If I want to say I'm sorry, I'll say I'm sorry, okay? I don't see why you won't—"

"Accepted," he said.

"What?"

"I accept your apology."

"Well . . . all right, then," I muttered, the wind leaking slowly from my sails.

"Good." He rubbed his hands together. "Now that we've settled that, let's go back to your rooms. There's one more thing I'd like to show you." He took the lantern from me, extinguished it, and opened the door.

***

I had hoped to see more of the mansion on the way back, so I was disappointed when we returned to the guest suite via the same route. Bill must have sensed it, because as we approached my door he said, "I'll give you a tour later, if you like. It's a wonderful place. You've seen some of the older parts, but we have an entire wing that would put IBM to shame. One of the reasons we've been so successful is that we're willing to take the best of both worlds: the gentility of the old and the efficiency of the new. Ah, good, they've arrived."

This last remark came as he opened the parlor door and I saw right away what had prompted it. During our absence, a vase had been placed on the coffee table, a slender crystal vase filled with deep blue irises. I gave a gasp of pleasure when I saw them.

"You like them?" Bill asked. "I hoped you might. I saw you looking at the ones downstairs and I thought—"

"They're my favorites. But how do you manage to find irises at this time of year? Isn't it a little early?"

"Where there's a Willis—" he began, but my groan cut him off. "The hothouse," he continued. "It's in the back. I'll be sure to include it in the tour." He jutted his chin in the direction of the one door in the suite I had yet to open. "Been in there yet?" When I shook my head, he frowned. "But that's the whole reason I put you in here! Come on." He opened the door, turned on a light, and stood aside as I entered a library as small and perfect as Great-great-uncle Arthur's observatory, though executed in a rather more sedate style.

"The big library is downstairs," Bill said. "This is Father's private stash."

I scanned the shelves, speechless. The collection was everything a collection should be. My old boss, Stan Finderman, would have approved wholeheartedly, and so did I. It wasn't full of showpieces. It was full of love and careful thought. The books were all related to polar exploration—Franklin's *A Journey to the Shores of the Polar Sea*, Ross's *A Voyage of Discovery*, and many others—some worth a small fortune, all priceless to the person who read and cherished them.

"And now for the grand finale," Bill said. He put a finger to his lips and tiptoed stealthily to a wall space between two of the bookcases. Pushing his sleeves up with a flourish, like some mad magician, he applied pressure to two places on the wall and, presto-chango, it swung open to reveal a staircase leading down.

"A mansion wouldn't be a mansion without a few secret passages, now, would it?" he said with a grin. "This one leads down to the changing room in Father's office. For all intents and purposes, you have your own private connection to all the comforts therein. You can lock the changing room door from the inside and use it anytime you like. But please—don't forget to unlock it when you're done."

"Wait a minute," I said as he closed the door in the wall. An appalling thought had just occurred to me. "If this is your father's collection, and if that staircase leads down to his office, then . . . Oh, Bill, this isn't his suite, is it? He didn't clear out to make room for me, did he?"

"Not at all. Father would have been happy to make way for you, but as it happens, he didn't. This used to be his suite—he used to live above the shop, so to speak—but he's on the ground floor now. We simply haven't gotten around to moving the books yet." Bill's gaze swept over the shelves. "It's ironic. All these stories about conquering the wilderness, and he's not allowed to climb the stairs in his own home."

"Not allowed?"

He glanced at me, then looked back to the books. "His heart," he said shortly. "Started acting up last spring. Hasn't been anything serious so far, but . . . I can't help worrying. My mother died when I was twelve, and aside from some desiccated aunts, it's been just the two of us ever since." He reached out to touch one of the books. "It's strange, isn't it? No one ever tells you that one day you'll worry about your parents the way they always worried about you."

I averted my eyes as my heart twisted inside of me. The fact was that I had never worried about my mother. She'd never been sick a day in her life. The only time she had ever been in a hospital had been to give birth to me. But Bill's words reminded me that I should have shown more concern for her, that I had failed her in that as I had failed her in so many other ways.

"But enough doom and gloom." Bill turned his back on the books. "As I said, there's no need to worry, not really. There's no reason Father shouldn't live to be a hundred, as long as he takes care of himself."

"You make sure he does," I said. "Because once he's gone . . ." I fell silent, hoping Bill hadn't noticed the tremor in my voice.

"Lori," he said. He touched my arm and I pulled away from him. I didn't need or want his sympathy, and I was annoyed with myself for provoking it.

"Breakfast is at nine," he said, after a pause. "The small dining room, downstairs, left, left, third door on the right. And Father would like to see you at ten. In his office." He walked to the door of the library, then turned. "And by the way—you're not my client. You're his."

It took a moment for his words to register, a moment more for me to realize that I had let him go without getting any of the answers I'd been looking for. What's more, as I returned to the small library for a closer look at Willis, Sr.'s books, I realized there was something else I wanted to know.

Why was Bill being so nice to me?

5

The small dining room made me wonder what the big dining room was like. The table at which Bill and I sat—Willis, Sr., having opted for breakfast in his rooms—was long enough to seat twelve, and anything above a sedate murmur caused muted echoes to reverberate from the domed ceiling. The food was set out in silver chafing dishes along a sideboard, except for a small mountain of strawberries that loomed over a stoneware pitcher filled with cream. Two servants, casually attired in khaki twills and crewneck sweaters, poured our orange juice, then sat down with us and engaged Bill in a heated debate over some obscure point of contract law.

"Law students," Bill explained when they had cleared the table. "Live-in staff."

"How convenient," I said. "Your own private supply of slave labor."

"Absolutely. That's why we have a waiting list as long as my arm." Bill looked at his watch. "My father, the capitalist tyrant, should be waiting for us now. Shall we?" He led the way to the office. "The students were his idea," he continued. "Room and board and a chance for hands-on experience in our clinics, not to mention the opportunity to learn from one of the finest legal minds in the country. I refer, of course, to my father's. In exchange for which they do everything but cook. Some things are best left to a professional, don't you agree? I'm sure they'd be much better off somewhere else, but what can we do? They're champing at the bit to be trodden underfoot." He opened the office doors. "Aren't they, Father?"

Willis, Sr., looked up from his desk. "Aren't who what, my boy?"

"Miss Shepherd was commenting on your unorthodox solution to the servant problem."

"Ah, the students. They have worked out marvelously well, Miss Shepherd. I don't know where we would be without them, and they seem to find the experience worthwhile. Bill, did you hear? Young Walters was made a judge last week."

"Sandy Walters? But he couldn't even wash dishes!"

"I doubt that he will be required to," Willis, Sr., observed dryly, then turned his attention to me. "Forgive our prattle, Miss Shepherd. How are you this morning?"

"She's perfectly fine," said Bill, and I sent a low-level glare in his direction. "I'll leave you to it, then, Father. And I'll see *you* later." He nodded pleasantly at me as he left the room.

"My son appears to be in a lighthearted mood this morning." Willis, Sr., stared thoughtfully at the door for a moment, then smiled at me. "But let us proceed, Miss Shepherd. I am sure you must be feeling very impatient by now. Please make yourself comfortable. This may take some time, I'm afraid." I took a seat in the tall leather wing chair facing him.

"Twenty-five years ago," Willis, Sr., began, "I was contacted by a colleague in England. A client of his, a mildly eccentric woman of comfortable means, wished to draw up her will. Further, she wished to have her will administered by an American law firm, since one of the legatees would be an American. She was quite concerned about finding the right people to handle the case and I am pleased to say that she found our firm satisfactory."

I smiled at this and Willis, Sr., raised his eyebrows in polite inquiry. "Don't take this the wrong way," I said, "but it's easy to see why Willis & Willis would appeal to an English-woman. I can't imagine a less 'American' law firm."

"You are quite right," said Willis, Sr. "She admitted as much when I traveled to England to meet her. She wanted a firm which hadn't 'succumbed to the rat race,' as she put it. We were anachronistic enough to suit her taste exactly."

His gaze returned to the doors through which Bill had exited. "I suspect that my son influenced her in our favor as well. I brought him with me, you see. My father, who was then head of the firm, disapproved of such unprofessional behavior, but my wife had just passed away, and to be so far away from the boy for any extended period of time was out of the question." He looked once more at me. "In the end, it proved fortunate. Bill's presence seemed to reassure my client that the firm wasn't completely ossified.

"At any rate, she told me that she had a friend, an American friend who had a daughter, and that the will concerned certain tasks that her friend's child was to undertake. The daughter, apparently, did not know of my client's existence, and my client wished to maintain her anonymity until the time came for the will to be administered. 'It's my last appearance in the story,' she told me, 'and I would like it to be a surprise.'

"As you have undoubtedly guessed by now, your mother, the late Elizabeth Irene Shepherd, was the friend and you are the daughter. What I am permitted to reveal to you now is that my client was Miss Dimity Westwood, founder of the Westwood Trust, which supported, indeed still supports, a great number of charitable institutions in the United Kingdom.

"During her lifetime, Miss Westwood was widely respected,

but something of a mystery—an invisible philanthropist, one might say, whose good works were better known than herself. She was also, if I may add a personal note, the most remarkable woman I have ever had the honor to know." Willis, Sr., leaned back in his chair and folded his hands across his waistcoat.

"I have practiced law for a good many years," he mused, "and I have seen every kind of scandal and battle royale imaginable. The cliché is true, I'm afraid: wills do frequently bring out the worst in those involved—the greed, the pettiness." He sighed. "I should not complain, I suppose, for I owe my livelihood to such disagreements. But I must say that it is a singularly pleasurable change of pace when a client such as Miss Westwood comes along.

"She was a voluminous correspondent, but I only met her in person that one time. Yet she was so generous, so kind, so . . ." he groped for the right word, "so good-humored," he concluded helplessly. "We stayed with her, you see, at her invitation, and not an hour passed during our visit when she didn't find something to laugh about, some incidental detail or absurdity that I would have overlooked completely. I felt quite renewed by the end of our ten days."

Willis, Sr., stared into the distance, lost in visions of the past, and I watched his face, entranced. One meeting, twenty-five years ago, and he was still under her spell. I could almost see Dimity Westwood welcoming him to her home. She had looked beyond the professional demeanor of the lawyer and seen a grieving widower who couldn't bear to be parted from his young son. This was the man she had chosen to look after my interests and it was clear that she had chosen with her heart as well as her head. Miss Westwood had to be Aunt Dimity. But why was this the first time I had heard that she was a real person?

Willis, Sr., returned to the present. "Forgive an old man his distractions, Miss Shepherd. Now, where was I? Ah, yes." Leaning forward, he continued, "My task was quite simple, really. I was to familiarize myself with certain of Miss West-wood's personal documents, draw up the will to her specifications, and keep myself apprised of your whereabouts. I was not permitted to contact you, however, until after Miss West-wood's passing. I regret to say that the sad event occurred eleven months ago."

"Just when I disappeared from the face of the earth," I said.

"Precisely," said Willis, Sr. "I had learned of your divorce, naturally, and managed to trace your first change of address, but after that?" He clucked his tongue. "Oh, my. I enlisted my son's help in the search, but it wasn't until last week that I believed I'd finally found you, here, living across town from us. You can imagine how surprised I was to learn that you were so nearby. It was an unexpected, though quite welcome, turn of events.

"I was very pleased when you appeared so promptly, even more pleased when you responded to Miss Westwood's questions with the appropriate answers. If you will permit me," he added, "I would like to apologize once more for the distressing climax of that particular interview. Had I not been constrained by the terms of the will to carry it out, I assure you—"

"That's okay," I said. "Really, I understand. You had to make sure you had the right person, so . . . To tell you the truth, I'm finding it hard to believe I'm me, too, if you know what I mean. I grew up thinking that Aunt Dimity was an invention, a fantasy. And now you're telling me that she was real." I shook my head. "It'll take a while for it to sink in. But what exactly are we talking about? What tasks am I supposed to undertake?"

"Ah, yes," continued Willis, Sr. "Having ascertained to my satisfaction that you are the Lori Elizabeth Shepherd so named in the will, I must now ask you to examine the contents of these envelopes." From a drawer in his desk, he withdrew two envelopes, one pale blue, the other buff-colored. He stood up and walked around his desk to bring them to me. "You

will, perhaps, care to read them in the privacy of your rooms."
He indicated the changing room door. "There is a staircase
that leads—"

"I know," I said. "Bill showed me."

"Did he?" Willis, Sr., said. His eyebrows rose in surprise,
but I had no time to wonder why. The entire room seemed
to fade as I saw what was written on the buff-colored envelope. It was my name, and it had been written in my mother's
hand.

*
**

I put my mother's letter aside to read last. Curled in an armchair in the parlor of the guest suite, a single lamp shedding
a pool of light around me, I slipped a letter opener beneath
the flap of the pale blue envelope, then paused to look at it
once more. My name had been written on the front of this
one as well, in neat, unfamiliar handwriting. I didn't need
subtitles to tell me whose it was, though. With great care, I
slit open the envelope, and Aunt Dimity's voice came through,
soft and clear.

> *My Dearest Lori,*
>
> *No, I am not your fairy godmother. Neither am I a
> witch. I may be dead now, but I assure you that, while
> I was alive, I was the most ordinary person imagina-
> ble. And before you get any more silly ideas, no, I do
> not plan to return from the grave! I'm looking forward
> to a nice, long rest and many pleasant chats with your
> mother.*
>
> *Yes, I just got word of Beth's death and I am so
> very sorry. I know how hard it will be for you. But I
> also know that you will weather this along with every-
> thing else. It may not seem so for a time, but it will
> come out right in the end.*
>
> *I am getting ahead of myself, however, and I must*

remember not to do that. You have been so much a part of my life that it is altogether too easy for me to forget that we have never met.

You must be very perplexed. I would apologize if I felt sorry, but I freely admit to feeling no remorse whatsoever. It's as though I'm watching someone open an oddly shaped birthday present. The intrigue is half the fun, especially when one knows how delighted the recipient will be when the contents are finally revealed. My wrapping paper is more elaborate than most, to be sure, but then, I've never wrapped something quite so oddly shaped before. How does one wrap the past? How does one wrap the future? I have done my best.

But enough riddles, Dimity, or Lori shall begin to tear at her hair with frustration. Get on with it! Are you comfortable, my dear? And have you a cup of tea? Very well, then, let us begin.

Your mother was the dearest friend I have ever had. We met late in the autumn of 1940, in London, when I was a humble clerk in the War Office and she was a humble clerk on the General's staff. I refer to General Eisenhower, of course, but lest you become overly impressed, let me reiterate the word "humble." We were very small cogs in that very large machine. What glamour there was was the glamour of being young and aware that we were living the great adventure of our lives. I consider myself blessed to have shared it with your mother. I could not have invented a more ideal companion. I suspect that the circumstances of our meeting will sound familiar to you.

I occasionally had a day free of duties and on one such day I decided to visit the zoological gardens. For some reason I had become intensely curious to know what the war had done to them, so intensely curious that I didn't mind the circuitous route I had to take to get there, nor the promise of rain that hung in the air, a promise that was fulfilled as soon as I'd entered the grounds.

In my mad dash for shelter, I ran straight into Beth. I mean that quite literally. I knocked her down. I was ready to sink into the ground with embarrassment when Beth did a most unusual thing. She blinked up at me for a moment—and then began to laugh. Suddenly the absurdity of the situation was brought home to me: how could a bit of rain and an accidental collision compare to the war raging on all around us? Laughter was the only reasonable response. When I had helped her to her feet, I invited her back to my flat to dry off. We chatted the evening away over what was to be the first of many shared pots of tea. We became very close very quickly, as one did in those days.

That was how our friendship began, with laughter. Beth knew where to look to find the humour in any situation and I learned how to find it myself after a short time in her company. As you can imagine, this was invaluable during the war, but it has stood me in good stead under "normal" circumstances as well. It was a great gift and I remain indebted to her for it to this day.

When the war was over, and your mother was posted home, I accompanied her to the ship. Somehow we knew it was the last time we would ever set eyes on each other. It wasn't easy to find the humour in that, but we managed. As we walked toward the gangplank, Beth threatened to start another war if I didn't write to her, and I vowed, for the sake of world peace, to be a faithful correspondent.

I was and so, too, was Beth. Long letters, short notes, postal cards—we became closer with an ocean between us than we had been while living in the same city. We often spoke of visiting one another, but we *never did. It seems strange to me now, but it did not seem strange then. Looking back on it, I suspect that we were trying to keep the world of our letters apart from the world in which we lived. Perhaps we had become so accustomed to the magic of words on paper that we were afraid a face-to-face meeting might break the spell.*

Our letters were our refuge. We looked to them for stability, for continuity, in a world of change. Beth regaled me with tales of married life while I spun the saga of spinsterhood and, through it all, our friendship became stronger, deeper than ever before. I believe that your mother needed these letters very much. Although she loved you and your father dearly, still, she needed one place that was hers and hers alone. To my knowledge, she never told another living soul of our correspondence, save your father, naturally.

Shortly after the joyous event of your birth, your mother faced a most difficult time. Your father's death was a terrible blow, as I am sure you know. Beth refused my offer of financial assistance, but it was clear that she needed something, some special way to remind herself that this difficult time would pass.

With that thought in mind, I began to include stories in my letters. I wrote them for you, but they were directed toward your mother as well. The stories featured a heroine who was, like Beth, blessed with the gift of easy laughter. They were tales of commonplace courage and optimism, for I knew from my own experience that everyday virtues endure best, and that quiet courage is worth more than the grandest derring-do. Thus "Aunt Dimity" was born, a heroine for the common woman.

By telling the tales to you, your mother told them to herself. They served as a steady reminder that she already possessed those qualities that would see her through whatever life held in store for her. It was a small thing, perhaps, but great changes begin with small things. Witness our friendship. Little by little the stories, and the healing power of time, helped restore Beth's tranquillity.

By anyone's measure, Aunt Dimity was a roaring success. You didn't outgrow the stories until you were nearly twelve, long after you had put away most other childish things. And during that time Aunt Dimity had given me a great deal of pleasure and Beth a great deal of comfort. By then, I felt that I knew you quite well. I had tried to tailor my stories to your tastes, you see, which meant learning as much about you as I could. And though you eventually tired of hearing about Aunt Dimity, I never tired of hearing about you.

I have followed the events of your life ever since and, though sorely tempted at times, I have never broken my promise to your mother to keep the identity of Aunt Dimity's creator a secret.

Even now, I am keeping my promise. Beth and I agreed many years ago that, without this chapter, the story would be incomplete—and nothing bothered us more than a story with gaps. We decided to fill those gaps by bequeathing to you our complete correspondence, from the first pair of letters to these, the last. With Beth's approval, I engaged the firm of Willis & Willis to carry out our wishes.

You will find the correspondence waiting for you in my cottage, near the village of Finch in England. I disposed of my other properties, but I could not bring myself to dispose of the cottage. I grew up there, you see, and returned to it occasionally even after the war. It has always held a special place in my heart.

There is a small task I would like you to perform while you are there. William Willis will explain it to you at the appropriate time. It is a favor I can ask of

*no one but you, and I am confident that you will find
it agreeable.*

*Please give my best wishes to William and to young
Bill. Your mother and I approved of them without res-
ervation, and you may trust them to look after your
affairs as though they were their own.*

*I hope you are not too put out with Beth and me
for keeping this from you for so long. I know that the
idea of being watched over from afar will pinch at
your independent spirit, but I assure you that it was
done with great respect and even greater*

love,

Dimity Westwood

I looked up from the letter and stared blindly across the
room as the words, and the images they evoked, settled over
me like drifting snow. It was difficult to accept the fact that
a woman I had never known had known so much about me,
but I no longer doubted her existence. She knew too much
to be a figment of anyone's imagination.

My mother had been in London during the war and she
had ended up on Eisenhower's staff. While there, she had
been an indefatigable explorer of the wartime city: she had
told me of seeing the Tate Gallery shrouded in blackout cur-
tains, St. Paul's Cathedral alight with incendiaries, the streets
cratered by bombing. She had met my father during that time
and she had often spoken of their first meeting. But she had
never spoken of this other momentous meeting, nor of the
forty-year friendship that had grown from it. As I turned it
over in my mind, though, I remembered the family ritual
known as Quiet Time.

Quiet Time came just after supper, when my mother retired
to her room, leaving Reginald and me engrossed in a story-
book or some other peaceful activity. She emerged from her
room looking so refreshed and invigorated that I had always
assumed she used that time for a nap. Since I had been a fairly

active—not to say rambunctious—child, it wasn't an unreasonable assumption.

Now it seemed obvious that a renewal of spirit had been taking place behind her closed door. I placed Dimity's letter beside me on the couch and took up the buff-colored one. Looking over the familiar scrawl, I pictured my mother at her writing desk, bending over these pages as she had bent over so many others, and after a few deep breaths, I opened the envelope.

Something fell into my lap. It was a photograph, a very old photograph, stained in places, the corners creased, one missing altogether; a photograph of . . . nothing much, as far as I could tell: a gnarled old tree in the foreground of a grassy clearing, a valley beyond, some distant hills. It was no place I'd ever been, no place I recognized, and there was nothing else in it: no people, no animals, no buildings of any sort. Baffled, I set it aside and unfolded the pages of my mother's letter.

> *Sweetie,*
> *All right, Sarah Bernhardt, dry your eyes and blow your nose. Your big scene is over.*
> *I know what you're thinking right now, just as surely as if I were sitting there looking at you. You've never been much good at hiding your feelings, not just from me, but from the world at large. It has always been one of your most endearing and exasperating traits. Your thoughts are on your face right now, and I can tell that they are U-N-H-A-P-P-Y.*
> *You feel as though Dimity and I have played a pretty mean trick on you and I can't blame you, because in a sense we have. But look at it this way: if I'd told you about everything, you'd know it all already and I'd be dead and that would be that. As it is, I may be dead, but you still have a lot to learn about me—*

the story continues, so to speak. I like the idea. I think you will, too, after you finish moping and feeling sorry for yourself.

You're probably wondering about the photograph. I am, too. That's why I'm giving it to you. This is serious, so I need your full attention. This is not something I can tell to Reginald.

Dimity said that she would tell you how we first met, and I'm sure she has. I'm equally sure that she hasn't told you the state she was in, that day at the zoo. Not to put too fine a point on it, she was a wreck. She looked as though she hadn't eaten a solid meal or slept a good night's sleep in a month. The reason she ran into me was because she was walking around in a daze, only half aware of her surroundings. I took her back to her flat, got some tea and dry toast into her, then stayed with her until she fell asleep. I talked myself hoarse that evening, and the next, and gradually, over the course of a few weeks, I managed to coax her out of her shell. She talked about a lot of things after that, but she never mentioned what it was that had knocked her for such a loop.

After I got to know her better, I asked her about it. It was as though I'd slapped her. The color drained from her face, she said there were some things she couldn't speak of, even to me, and she made me promise never to ask her about it again. You know how I am about promises. I never asked her again, but I never ceased to wonder.

Dimity took me down to her cottage once, to show me the place where she'd grown up. While we were there, two of her neighbors pulled me aside. They were elderly and not very coherent, but I got the impression that Dimity had suffered some kind of nervous collapse the last time she'd been home. Apparently, they'd found her in the cottage one day, with photo albums strewn about her on the floor, mumbling to herself and clutching—you guessed it—this photograph.

They were convinced it had something to do with her condition, so they took it from her, then didn't know what to do with it. They were afraid to give it back to her, but they didn't want to destroy it, either, so they decided to pass it on to me for safekeeping. They said I was "what Dimity needed" and seemed to think I'd know the right time to return the photograph to her. I tried to explain about my promise, but they wouldn't take no for an answer.

So here I am, all these years later, still pondering the question of how an innocent-looking photograph could cause a woman like Dimity to fall apart. And why someone who opened her arms to the world kept one part of her life in darkness.

I'd like you to find out for me. I don't know how. I don't know where the picture was taken or by whom. The neighbors who gave it to me are no doubt dead and gone by now, so they won't be able to help you. It may even be that the answers died with Dimity, but if not, I know that my unstoppable baby girl will find them.

Why is it so important to me? I'm not sure. It's certainly too late to fix whatever it was that went wrong. But I can't help feeling that, whatever it was, it needs to be brought into the light. It can't hurt my friend now, and I'll rest easier, knowing you're looking for answers to questions I was never allowed to ask. You can tell me all about it the next time I see you.

And that's about all for now, except to tell you to scratch Reginald behind the ears for me. And to tell you that I love you very much. You will always be my favorite only child.

Mom

She almost tripped me up with that last paragraph—I guarantee that nothing turns on the waterworks faster than a dead parent telling you she loves you—and her mention of poor old Reginald nearly sent me running to the nearest tissue factory. But the story of the photograph put a halt to that. I picked it up and looked at it again, then looked down at the letters nestled together on the couch. All those years of friendship, and not one word about . . . it.

What had happened in that clearing? I studied the tree, tried to imagine how it would look today, if it hadn't been struck by lightning or chopped down or knocked over by the wind or . . . I stopped myself. That sort of thinking would get me nowhere.

I would go to the cottage. I would take care of Dimity's task, then turn the place inside out, if need be, looking for clues. I'd ask around the village, show everyone the photograph, and if that didn't work, I'd . . . I'd think of something else.

I would find out what had happened to Dimity, if I had to conduct a personal interview with every tree in the British Isles. I would find the answers to my mother's questions.

It was my last chance to do something right.

6

I used the phone on the end table to call Willis, Sr., and he asked me to meet him in his office in half an hour. Standing at the tall windows in the parlor, I watched the gardener repair the damage from last night's unseasonable blizzard, kept an eye on the time, and tried to absorb what the letters had told me.

I suppose, somewhere in the back of my mind, there was a certain sense of disappointment. Surrounded as I was by the luxurious House of Willis, it was only natural to hope that my mother's wealthy friend had left me some small part of her estate. I certainly could have used it. Not that I was looking for a handout—Meg Thomson had tried to loan me money once and I had bitten her head off—but a small bequest for the daughter of a beloved friend? I could have accepted that.

Such minor regrets were overshadowed, however, by thoughts of the correspondence. That was a treasure beyond price. Where I would find a safe place to store forty years' worth of "long letters, short notes, and postal cards" from two voluble correspondents was a problem I'd solve when I got to it. For now, it was enough to know that, whatever else might happen, my mother's words would belong to me.

Sarah Bernhardt, indeed. My even-tempered mother had often teased me about being oversensitive and I was the first to admit that I sometimes let my emotions run away with me. So far, though, under what I thought were very challenging circumstances, I had kept them under control. I hoped she was proud of me for that, wherever she was.

I couldn't for the life of me imagine what kind of favor Dimity Westwood had in mind. A philanthropist had to be rich, after all, and if she could afford the long-term services of a firm like Willis & Willis, Dimity was surely rich enough to hire people to do whatever else needed doing. I had no special skills. I knew about old books, but there were all sorts of people who knew more about them than I did, especially in England. What could it be, then? Only time, and Willis, Sr., would tell.

I also counted on him to tell me how I was going to get to the cottage. The last time I'd looked, there hadn't been a huge selection of transatlantic bus routes, and the cost of flying over was more than my temp's wages could handle. But Dimity wouldn't have left me something I couldn't get to.

I wasn't sure if I should tell Willis, Sr., about the photograph. He might object to anything that took time away from carrying out Dimity's task. Then again, he might know something useful. I decided to wait and see. In the meantime, I'd wash my face and brush my hair and get myself ready for our meeting. I glanced down at my jeans and sighed—I was no doubt unique among Willis, Sr.'s well-heeled clientele. It was kind of him not to make me feel out of place.

I headed for the bathroom, got as far as the dressing room, and stopped dead in my tracks. The low shelves, empty that morning, now held shoes, women's shoes, five or six pairs of tasteful pumps and fashionable flats, and there were purses on the high shelves, tiny embroidered clutches, and shoulder bags in buttery leather. The racks were hung with dresses in dainty floral prints, silk blouses, pleated gabardine slacks, tweed blazers and skirts—all size eight.

I stared at them, open-mouthed, as my blood pressure began to rise. I could almost hear it, like the faint whistle of a teakettle just coming to boil. So *that* was Bill's game, was it? I understood it all now: the irises, the star show, his father's books—the whole nine yards. Prince Charming bestows gifts on the wide-eyed beggar girl, dazzles her with his castle, then sweeps her off her feet with . . . *Had he picked out new underwear, too?*

The pent-up emotions of the past twenty-four hours fueled my indignation. Who was he to tell me what to wear? Willis, Sr., might know a thing or two about tailoring, but Bill looked as though he slept in his clothes. I looked upon those lovely dresses and thought only of the audacity, the gall, the sheer, unmitigated . . . Did he expect me to be *grateful?* I had never been so embarrassed in my life, and I was seriously annoyed with him for causing my humiliation.

A muffled knock sounded at the parlor door and when I opened it I found the object of my wrath standing there with frayed cuffs and bagged-out trousers, compounding his sins by looking extremely pleased with himself.

"How *dare* you," I snapped.

The smug look vanished.

"Come in," I said, "and sit down. There are a few things we need to get straight."

Bill sat on the edge of the couch and watched as I paced the room. In a small voice, he ventured, "You don't like the clothes?"

"Oh, they're beautiful," I said. "Just beautiful. I'm all set for the Governor's Ball." I closed in on him. "*Bill.* I don't *go* to the Governor's Ball. Where am I supposed to *wear* that stuff? To the *grocery?*"

"Well, I—" but he never had a chance. My wounded pride was on a rampage.

"But *you* wouldn't know about places like that," I said. "*You* have servants. Well, let me fill you in. The grocery is the place where you go when you have enough money to buy maybe three cans of tomato soup, right? It's the place where the express register is always just closing when you get there, so you and your tomato soup wind up in the regular checkout line, where you're invariably stuck behind the illiterate lady with the coupons for things that are *almost* the same as the things she has in her cart. And you have to stand there juggling soup cans while she argues every ounce, pound, liter, and gram, and you don't want to be *rude,* because she has blue hair and she's probably living on dog food, but you also want to *scream,* because you'd think that just once she could manage to bring a coupon for the *right brand* of dog food. Heaven knows it's important to wear the proper dress for moments like that. That blue silk number in the back should be just right." When I paused to catch my breath, Bill made a brave attempt to rally.

"Now, Lori, I just thought that, when you went out, you might—"

"Go *out*? Like on *dates*? What makes you think I have time to go out on dates?" I took another deep breath and added, very evenly, "Thank you very much for your thoughtful gifts, but I'm afraid they don't suit my life-style." I strode to the door, then turned. "I'm going down to speak with your father. When I've gone, I'd be most grateful if you'd return everything to the shops. If it's all the same to you, Mr. Willis, I'd prefer to select my own wardrobe."

*
**

Willis, Sr., smiled at me from behind his desk as I entered the office, but his smile faded when he saw the look on my face.

"My dear Miss Shepherd," he said in alarm, "whatever is the matter?"

I closed the doors and strode restlessly over to the billowing fern in the corner. I plucked a small brown frond and crumbled it absently between my fingers. Keeping my back to the desk, I asked, "Do I look awful, Mr. Willis?"

"I beg your pardon?"

"Do I look like . . . like a wreck?"

"Miss Shepherd, I would never presume to—"

"I know," I said, holding perfectly still. "That's why I'm asking you."

When he failed to respond, I snuck a peek over my shoulder, then looked quickly back at the fern. His pained expression made me want to sink through the floor, but his voice was gentle when he began to speak.

"I would not put it quite that way, Miss Shepherd," he said. "I would say rather that you appear to have lived under a great deal of stress, and to have known too little joy as of late."

"That bad, huh?" Tears stung my eyes and I blinked them away.

"You misunderstand me, Miss Shepherd," said Willis, Sr. "Please allow me to make myself clear. My dear, to my eyes, you are lovely. Fatigued, yes, and under some strain, certainly, but quite charming nonetheless." He rose from his chair. "Please, Miss Shepherd, come and sit down." He gestured for me to join him on the couch, where he leaned back, tented his fingers, and stared silently at me for a few moments before going on. I kept my gaze fixed on his immaculate gray waistcoat.

"Miss Shepherd, I realize how unusual this experience must be for you. You have had quite a lot thrown at you in a very short period of time. You are no doubt feeling slightly overwhelmed by it all."

"Slightly," I agreed.

"It is only natural that you should. I confess, I can do little to remedy this. I can, however, assure you that I will fulfill my role as your legal advisor to the best of my ability. And, if you will permit me, I can do one more thing. I can offer the hope that you will someday look upon me as your friend."

He lowered his eyes and added, "A somewhat antiquated friend, to be sure, but a friend with your interests at heart nonetheless."

I bit my lip to keep my chin from trembling. It had been a long time since I had let anyone say that to me, and a much longer time since I had let myself believe it. It was weak, it was childish, and it went against my better judgment, but I thought I might risk believing it now. I needed a friend. I needed someone I could talk to, someone I could trust in this . . . unusual situation.

If Willis, Sr., noticed my distress, he had the decency to move smoothly on to other things. He gathered some papers from his desk and returned with them to the couch. "Here we are," he said. "I trust you are prepared to proceed to the next step?"

"I'm ready when you are," I said, grateful to him for the change of subject.

"Excellent. Please feel free to stop me at any point, Miss Shepherd. I greatly dislike haste in these matters. It so often leads to misunderstandings." He straightened his waistcoat, then folded his hands atop the papers. "Shortly before her death, Miss Westwood collected the Aunt Dimity stories into a single volume, which she intended to publish posthumously."

"She's going to publish the Aunt Dimity stories?"

"That was her intent, Miss Shepherd. Arrangements have been made with a reputable publisher, and the illustrations are nearing completion."

"You mean, other people have read them already?"

"A small number of people, yes. My dear, does this trouble you?"

The sound of my mother's voice drifted through my mind. "I guess it does. Until yesterday evening I thought I was the only one who knew those stories. I guess I've always thought of them as *mine*."

"That," said Willis, Sr., "is undoubtedly why Miss Westwood wanted you and no one else to write an introductory essay for the volume."

"She did?" I looked at him in surprise. "Is that the favor she mentions in her letter?"

"It is. She wished for you to write an introduction focusing on the origins of the stories, which, according to Miss Westwood, are to be found in the collection of private correspondence now housed in her residence in England, near the village of Finch. I believe she refers to the correspondence in her letter to you?"

I nodded.

"You are to read the letters written by your mother and Dimity Westwood, locate within them the situations or characters or events that inspired the Aunt Dimity stories, and write about what you find." Willis, Sr., paused, then added softly, "I think I can understand your reluctance to have these stories published, Miss Shepherd. They must have been a treasured part of your childhood. But, my dear, you shall not lose the stories by sharing them."

Willis, Sr., would have made a brilliant teacher. He had a way of showing you things you should have seen for yourself, without making you feel like a fool. I would lose nothing by the stories' publication, and many children would gain a great deal. Aunt Dimity would come to life for them, too, and that was as it should be.

"You're right, Mr. Willis," I said sheepishly. "It's a fine idea. And I suppose they couldn't really publish the thing without me in it somewhere. I must be the world's greatest authority on Aunt Dimity."

"You are indeed," said Willis, Sr., with a contented nod. He glanced down at the paper on top of the stack, then continued. "You shall have one month—that is, thirty days from the time of your arrival at the cottage—in which to do the necessary research and writing. I shall contact you periodically to confer with you and to ask certain questions Miss Westwood has prepared."

"Questions? About what?"

"The questions concern the contents of both the letters and the stories, Miss Shepherd."

"I should be able to answer questions about the stories right now."

"Undoubtedly, but we shall follow Miss Westwood's wishes nonetheless. At the end of the month, if you have answered those questions satisfactorily and completed the introduction in the manner described by Miss Westwood, you shall receive a commission of . . . let me see . . ." He ran his finger down the sheet. "Ah, here it is." He looked up and smiled pleasantly. "You shall receive a commission of ten thousand dollars."

"Ten thousand . . ." My voice cracked. "Isn't that a bit much?" I added faintly.

"It is the value Miss Westwood placed on the task. It was, I understand, very close to her heart."

"It must have been." My mind flew to the stack of bills that was threatening to engulf my apartment at that very moment. I had expected to be paying them off with my Social Security checks, but now . . . *ten thousand dollars.* For one month's work. I sank back on the couch and raised a hand to my forehead.

Willis, Sr., peered at me worriedly. "Great heavens, I've done it again. Please, allow me to pour you a glass of sherry. You've gone quite pale."

While Willis, Sr., poured the sherry, I tried to gather my wits. It wasn't easy, since visions of hundred-dollar bills kept them fairly well scattered. But by the time he returned with the sherry, I had at least calmed down enough to listen attentively.

"Here you are, my dear. Drink that down while I continue." He waited until I'd taken a sip, then referred once more to his notes. "You need not depart for England until you are fully prepared to do so. Miss Westwood felt that you might require some time to take leave of your friends, make the necessary arrangements with your employer, and so on." Folding his hands, he added, "Miss Westwood also hoped that you would accept our hospitality and reside here at the mansion until it is time for you to leave."

"Is that a condition of the will?"

"No, Miss Shepherd, but it coincides with my own wishes. I should be only too happy to welcome you as a guest in my home for as long as you wish to stay." He leaned toward me and added confidentially, "It brings me great pleasure to have a fresh face in the house, especially one belonging to someone who is neither studying nor practicing the law."

I laughed. "I can understand that, Mr. Willis. Thank you, I'll stay, as long as it's no trouble."

"None at all." He consulted the notes and continued, "Funds have, of course, been made available to pay for your travel and for any expenses incurred before or during your visit to the cottage. These expenses need not, I might add, relate directly to the writing of the introduction. Miss Westwood wanted you to be able to concentrate, you see, and felt that you would be able to do so only if your ancillary needs and desires were satisfactorily met. Anything, therefore, that ensures your comfort and well-being shall be considered a necessary expense."

A bottomless expense account. I could pay the bills, take care of the rent, buy some new clothes—of my *own* choosing—without even touching the commission. I was so dazzled that I almost missed Willis, Sr.'s next words.

". . . also for your convenience, Miss Westwood specified that the arrangements for your trip and the disbursement of funds be directed by my son."

A mouthful of sherry nearly ended up on Willis, Sr.'s immaculate waistcoat.

"Bill?" I gasped.

"Indeed. Miss Westwood did not wish to trouble you with the day-to-day details of travel and finance. My son, therefore, shall be responsible for looking after you from now until you have completed your task. He shall supply your transportation, oversee your expenses, and accompany you to England to act as your . . . facilitator, for want of a better term." The expression on my face must have alarmed Willis, Sr., for he added reassuringly, "His role shall in no way limit your access to the funds, Miss Shepherd. You have only to ask, and you shall be given whatever you require."

"By Bill."

"Miss Westwood is quite specific on that point, yes."

"You mean that, without Bill, I can't do anything else?"

"I fear not."

"But why *him?*" I asked. "I'd much rather work with you."

"That is very kind of you, Miss Shepherd. I should be only too happy to be of service to you, but . . ." Willis, Sr., sighed. "I fear, alas, that my health will not permit it. I have for the past year been beset by some minor difficulties with—"

"Your heart," I broke in. "Bill told me about it—"

"Did he?" said Willis, Sr.

"This morning. And, like an idiot, I forgot. Of course you can't go off globe-trotting. Please—forget that I mentioned it." I scowled at my shoes for a second, then asked, "How much does Bill know about all of this?"

"I enlisted his aid in locating you, but other than that, I have told him nothing. Indeed, I have not yet informed him of the part he is to play in Miss Westwood's plan. I felt it would be best to withhold that information until I was certain of your participation." Willis, Sr., hesitated. "I do not wish to pry, Miss Shepherd, but do I detect a note of dismay?"

"Oh, yes," I said, my chin in my hands. "I think you could put it that way."

"Might I ask why?"

I turned to face him. "Do you know what your son did?"

"I tremble to think."

"He bought *clothes* for me! A whole closetful!" It sounded

so trivial, now that I'd said it aloud, that I was afraid Willis, Sr., would laugh, but he seemed to understand exactly what I was getting at.

"Without consulting you? How very presumptuous of him." After a thoughtful pause, he added, "And how unlike him. If you will permit a personal observation, Miss Shepherd, my son has always been most reserved with the young ladies of his acquaintance."

"Reserved?" I said. "Bill?"

"I would go so far as to say he displays a certain degree of shyness in their company. I cannot imagine him selecting apparel for them." Willis, Sr., leaned toward me. "Tell me, has he done anything else you deem noteworthy?"

"He took me up on the roof this morning to look at a meteor shower."

Willis, Sr.'s jaw dropped. "He took you to Arthur's dome? Oh, but that is extraordinary. Unprecedented, in fact. The students have access to it, of course, but I have never known him to *invite* anyone up there, aside from myself. I cannot think why . . ." He frowned for a moment, clearly at a loss.

I wasn't at a loss. It stood to reason that Bill couldn't play Handsome Prince games with the rich and polished "young ladies of his acquaintance." What he needed was a Cinderella, a grateful orphan girl to mold as he pleased. Just thinking about it made my blood pressure rise all over again, but it wasn't something I could explain to his loving father.

"My dear Miss Shepherd," said Willis, Sr., finally, "I can offer no explanation for my son's curious behavior. I can only hope that you will believe me when I tell you that he has a good heart. I am sure he meant well, however clumsily he may have expressed himself.

"Be that as it may," he went on, "I am compelled to inform you that his actions do not constitute grounds for circumventing Miss Westwood's wishes. I confess that it saddens me, however, to think that my boy's presence has become intolerable to you—"

"That's not what I meant," I said hastily. "Your son isn't *intolerable,* Mr. Willis. He's just a little . . ."

"Rash?" suggested Willis, Sr.

"But in a thoughtful way," I assured him. "I'm sure that it's all a matter of . . . getting used to him."

Willis, Sr.'s face brightened. "I am so pleased to hear you say that, Miss Shepherd. You will proceed as planned, then? You will go to England and write the introduction? It meant so much to Miss Westwood."

"Of course I'll go," I said. "It means a lot to me, too."

"And you will accept my invitation to remain here as my guest?" he asked.

What could I do? Throw the old man's kindness back in his face? I nodded and he looked well pleased. He placed the papers on the coffee table and we sat in companionable silence. I was still somewhat dazed by the prospects that lay before me. The biggest decision I'd had to make lately was the number of books I'd allow myself to check out of the public library at one time. Now here I was, with an overseas trip, an unlimited expense account, and a chance to earn ten thousand dollars doing something I knew I would enjoy. I didn't know where to start. What did people *do* with expense accounts? I had no past experience to go on, but as I looked at Willis, Sr.'s patient smile, an idea began to take shape.

"Are you feeling okay, Mr. Willis?" I asked, twisting my hands nervously in my lap.

"How thoughtful of you to inquire," he said. "Yes, thank you, Miss Shepherd, I feel quite fit."

"Then would you . . . would you like to have dinner with me tonight?" I asked, adding hurriedly, "If you're not too busy, and if you don't have other plans, and if you're sure you're feeling—"

"Miss Shepherd," Willis, Sr., broke in gently, "I would be honored to accept your kind invitation." He placed a wrinkled hand on my fidgeting fingers, and I didn't have the slightest inclination to pull them away.

7

Willis, Sr., arranged for our dinner to be served in the large library on the ground floor, a room that might have been lifted, lock, stock, and bookplate, from one of the great English manor houses. "My great-uncle, Arthur Willis, saw an engraving of the library at Chatsworth," Willis, Sr., explained, "and decided to pattern his after it." The room was long and relatively narrow, with tall windows on one side and bookshelves on the other. A ladder and a narrow catwalk, resplendent in gold leaf, gave access to the highest shelves, and the ceiling was a marvel of sculpted plasterwork and medallion paintings.

We sat at a round table at one end of the room, I in my freshly laundered jeans and flannel shirt, and Willis, Sr., in a flawless charcoal-gray suit. He acknowledged my casual attire by slightly loosening the knot in his silk tie, and entertained me with talk of books and travel while the law students served our meal from the trolley Bill had used the night before.

Midway through the fish course it occurred to me that, before going down to the cottage, I might visit the places in London my mother had visited during the war, as a sort of preamble to reading the letters and writing about the stories. It wasn't until the second sorbet that I got up the nerve to present it for Willis, Sr.'s appraisal. It received his full support.

I decided against telling him about the photograph. As gracious as he was, Willis, Sr., obviously felt that his first duty was to Dimity Westwood, which meant seeing to it that the introduction was completed on schedule. The sobering truth—the truth I couldn't share with him—was that I might not finish the introduction at all. One month was all the time I would have at the cottage, and it might not be enough time to do everything. My first duty was to my mother, and I didn't want to put Willis, Sr., in the position of having to disapprove of something I was determined to do anyway.

For the same reason, I couldn't tell Bill, either. I would have to get rid of him once we got to Finch, of course, send him to stay at a hotel or a local guest house, but that would be easy enough to do without arousing suspicion. If anyone would be sympathetic to a plea of decorum, it would be Willis, Sr. And, partners or not, I thought I knew who called the shots in the family firm.

*
**

Bill's behavior took a new and even stranger turn during the week we spent preparing for the trip.

The dressing room was empty when I returned to the guest suite after my dinner with Willis, Sr., but I was awakened the following morning by a scuffling noise in the hall. When I investigated, I found Bill and four staff members walking off with sixteen pieces of the most beautiful hand-rubbed leather luggage I had ever seen.

"More gifts?" I asked.

"I meant to head them off downstairs," said Bill, "but I

was too late." He told the students to go ahead, then held up a particularly attractive garment bag. "You don't happen to like it, by any chance?"

"It's gorgeous, but no thanks," I said. "Every thief between here and Bangkok would find it irresistible."

"Right," he said, setting the bag on the floor. "What do you usually use, then?"

"Canvas carryalls," I replied. "Durable, lightweight, ordinary-looking, and when you're done with them, you roll them up and shove them in a drawer."

"Wouldn't nylon bags be lighter?" he asked.

"Yes, but they're harder to patch when they tear."

"Very practical," he observed.

"I'm a practical sort of person," I said.

"So I'm discovering." He shoved his hands in his pockets and rocked back on his heels. "Father told me about Dimity's plans, by the way. From this moment on, I am at your service. When would you like to get started?"

"Is ten too early for you?"

"Ten is perfect. Milady's carriage will await her at the appointed hour. Until then." He clicked his heels and executed a formal half bow, then picked up his share of the luggage and left.

I sighed and closed the door, wishing that someone would pull Bill aside and tell him that one simple offer of friendship was worth twenty Prince Charming routines.

* *
*

For the next five days, Bill did everything but walk ten paces behind me. He was meek, he was polite, he was the very model of docility, but I didn't buy it for a minute. There were too many times when I caught him smiling to himself—as though he found his own performance vastly entertaining.

My "carriage" turned out to be Willis, Sr.'s Silver Shadow. Bill insisted that he was following his father's orders in using it, but I was not amused. It wasn't the car I minded so much.

It was the little driving cap Bill wore, and the short woolen jacket, and the formal manner with which he opened the car door for me, as though he'd been rehearsing his role as chauffeur.

Our first stop was a local camping store, where I bought a pair of lightweight hiking boots—suitable for hill climbing—a durable down jacket, and a decent pair of jeans. I steered clear of anything fussy or feminine in order to demonstrate to Bill my idea of *useful* clothing. He kept his mouth shut and watched me like a hawk while I shopped, as though he were memorizing my every move. The salespeople treated him like a deaf-mute, nodding politely in his direction, but speaking only to me. It was mortifying, especially when he paid.

The next morning, I dropped by the temp agency to let them know that I would be unavailable for a while. They must have wondered why I'd bothered to give notice, once they'd ogled the Rolls, but I was burning no bridges. Bill continued to be on his best behavior, though he came close to going over the edge when he swept his cap off in a low bow to the women in the office and kissed my supervisor's hand.

That afternoon, when he introduced himself to my roommates as "Miss Shepherd's driver," I'd had enough. I made him hand over the checkbook and go wait in the car. I thought it was a perfect solution—I'd fill out the checks and he could sign them somewhere far away from me. Then I caught sight of him smiling his little smile and suspected that I had been outmaneuvered. It occurred to me—fleetingly—that he might be aware of how reluctant I was to have him see my humble digs.

I spent two hours at my apartment, writing checks with such gay abandon that I broke out in a cold sweat at one point and had to call Willis, Sr., to get his okay before I could go on. When I finished, I gave my roommates my share of the rent, outlined the situation for them, and asked them to forward any calls or personal mail to the mansion until I returned. Since I got about as many phone calls as a Trappist monk, it didn't seem a lot to ask.

It took me twenty minutes to pack. When I finished, I sat down on my mattress beside my beat-up old canvas bags. The late afternoon sun filtered through the blinds, bathing the room in a muted gray light. The apartment was very quiet and my room looked very bare.

I didn't want to come back here. I would never admit it to Bill or to anyone else, but I didn't want the fairy tale to end. I wanted that ten thousand dollars so badly I could taste it. It would give me a chance to escape from the grind, to look for a real job, maybe buy some decent furniture. But if it came to a choice between earning the money and fulfilling my mother's request, I knew what I would choose. Ah, well, I thought, with no conviction at all, I had gotten used to doing without. I could get used to it all over again.

My gaze wandered the blank walls and came to rest on the closet door. Instantly, I was on my feet. I rescued Reginald's shoebox from the floor of the closet and looked in fondly at the ragged bits of pinkish-gray flannel.

"Mom says hello," I said softly. I reached in to touch a hand-stitched whisker. "Yes, Reginald, you're right. Things could be worse. At least both of my ears are still attached."

I put the box in my carry-on bag and went down the stairs and out into the first golden rays of sunset.

*
**

I also made time for a visit to Stan Finderman, my old boss. He lived in a restored eighteenth-century town house near the Gardner Museum and I found him at home, where he'd been working ever since his university office had burned to a crisp.

"Lori!" he boomed, standing on the doorstep. "How the hell are you and how's that punk who kidnapped you?" Stan had not approved of my move out of state. "Who's this?" he added, catching sight of Bill. "You finally get rid of that lunkhead husband of yours?"

Dr. Stanford J. ("Call me Stan") Finderman wasn't what most people thought of when they pictured a curator of a rare book collection. He was smaller than Mount Everest, but not by much, and his white hair was cropped in a no-nonsense crew cut. Like Willis, Sr., he was in his early sixties, but he could have snapped Willis, Sr., in two with one thumb and a finger. Nothing tickled Stan more than the fear-glazed eyes of less robust scholars ("pasty-faced wimps") who were meeting him for the first time.

They soon found out that Stan's brain was as imposing as his brawn. He had served in the Navy during World War II, gone through college on the GI Bill, and left the rest of his class squinting in the glare of his brilliance. If people wondered why he had gone into the rare book field—instead of, say, weight lifting or alligator wrestling—they had only to see him cradle a book in his meaty paws, and they stopped wondering. Books were Stan's first, last, and only love.

He seemed in remarkably good spirits for a man who'd seen his life's work go up in smoke. As we followed him down the narrow hallway, I explained the change in my marital status—"Best damned decision you ever made!"—and introduced Bill, then asked him about the tragedy.

"Best damned thing that ever happened," he bellowed. "Sued the company that made the damned machine, the bastards settled out of court, and now I've got more damned money than you can shake a stick at! Look at this!" He waved us into his box-littered living room. "Been trawling all winter and hauled in some beauties. Should be able to move 'em onto the shelves by next spring—if the goddamned builders get off their goddamned asses."

He gave Bill a measuring look, then leaned in close to him. "What do you know about books?" he demanded.

"Not a thing," Bill replied cheerfully.

I held my breath, anticipating an explosion. My old boss had no use for nonbibliophiles, and no reservations about telling them so, emphatically. I tensed when Stan poked Bill in the shoulder, then watched dumbfounded as Stan's face broke into a wide grin.

"I like a man who knows his limitations," said Stan. "You want a beer?"

"Love one, Dr. Finderman."

"And you can cut that crap. Call me Stan."

"Whatever you say, Stan." To complete my amazement, Bill tapped Stan lightly on the shoulder, adding, "Within reason."

Stan's eyes narrowed, but all he said was, "I like this one, Lori." He put his arm around Bill's shoulders and walked him over to a partially opened box near the leather sofa. "Park yourself here and have a look at this while I grab the beers. Just got some goodies from Fitz in Japan. He's a helluva judge of rice paper, for a goddamned Scot."

It was an hour before I could get a word in edgewise.

I had wanted to speak with Stan privately, a difficult enough proposition if anyone was within shouting distance; an impossible one with a third party in the same room. When I finally got a chance to speak, I gave Bill a stern look and said, "What we're about to discuss is supposed to be a surprise. If your father gets wind of it, I'll—"

"Lay off the guy, Lori," Stan said. "He's a lawyer, for Christ's sake. He knows how to keep his mouth shut. What's the big secret, anyway?"

I explained what I wanted, and as I'd expected, Stan knew where to get it. He even phoned ahead to make sure it would be available before accompanying us to the front door.

"I think you picked a winner this time, Lori," he said.

"Stan, Bill isn't—" I began, but Stan was already clapping Bill on the shoulder.

"You look after her, Willis," he said, "or you'll have me to answer to."

Bill very wisely said nothing.

A short drive took us to a cramped and dimly lit shop owned by a Mr. Trevor Douglas, purveyor of antique maps. Stan's call had produced the usual results and Mr. Douglas had already unearthed a beauty for my inspection: a delicate and intriguingly incomplete depiction of the Arctic wilderness printed in 1876; the fruit of many daring gambles, broken dreams, and lost lives. Mr. Douglas agreed to have it framed and delivered to the mansion as soon as possible. The price was daunting, but I considered the map to be a very necessary expense. Nothing would ensure my peace of mind as effectively as the thought of Willis, Sr.'s pleasure when he opened this package.

*
**

We were breakfasting with Willis, Sr., in the small dining room the following day when Bill looked up from his toast and marmalade. "Lori, I've been thinking. You've been to your apartment and your agency and you've said good-bye to your old boss, but what about your friends?"

"My friends?"

"Don't you want to say good-bye to them, too? Or at least tell them what's going on?"

"Well, I . . ." I fiddled with my eggcup, not knowing what to say. I had lost track of most of my friends over the past year.

"Yes, Miss Shepherd," Willis, Sr., joined in, "you must not allow your natural diffidence to prevent you from visiting your friends before you leave. It is quite in keeping with Miss Westwood's wishes." Father and son stared at me, their heads tilted at identical angles, until I felt like an antisocial geek.

"There is one person I'd like to see," I admitted finally, "but she doesn't live in Boston."

"Doesn't matter," said Bill.

I looked to Willis, Sr., and he nodded.

"Okay, then," I agreed, "I'll give her a call."

*
**

Meg Thomson was a short, unrepentantly heavyset woman, with an abrupt manner and a mile-wide mothering streak. If Meg thought you needed to hear something for your own good, you would hear it, whether you wanted to or not. And she was fiercely loyal. She lived in Maine, in a small coastal town about a hundred miles north of Boston, where she and her partner, Doug Fleming, owned a strange and wonderful art gallery. Doug lived in an apartment above the shop, but Meg had a ramshackle old house overlooking the beach.

The gallery specialized in science fiction and fantasy art, and touring the maze of paintings and sculptures was like traveling through a world of dreams made real. The business was usually on the verge of bankruptcy, but that never seemed to bother Meg. She had found where she wanted to be in life and she regarded the occasional scramble for rent money as just another dash of the spice that kept her life from getting too bland.

"Meg?" I said when I heard her voice. "It's me, Lori. Think you could put up a couple of houseguests?"

"I'll drive down tomorrow and pick you up," she replied without missing a beat.

"No need. I have a car." I smiled to myself and added, "A Rolls-Royce."

That did slow her down, but only for a minute.

"Okay, Shepherd. But if this Rolls-Royce of yours crashes and I don't get to hear the rest of the story, I'll never speak to you again."

I told her I'd be up the next day, sent my best wishes to Doug, and packed my bag.

8

Between traffic jams, detours, and a scenic route designed by a civil engineer with homicidal tendencies, Bill and I didn't reach the gallery until late afternoon the next day. There was no answer when I rang Doug's bell and the gallery was locked up tight, so we headed out to Meg's beach house. Bill parked the Rolls in her driveway and unloaded our bags while I ran up the stairs and banged on the screen door. Meg opened it, and I pointed over my shoulder.

"Want to take a picture?" I asked.

"I never doubted you," she said. "But who's that carrying the luggage, your manservant? Does he do windows?"

"It's a long story, Meg," I murmured.

"I'll bet," she replied, elbowing me in the ribs. She turned and hollered over her shoulder. "Doug! They're here!"

Doug Fleming was slender, balding, bespectacled, and gay. He and Meg had been lovers in college, and when that hadn't worked out, they had become best friends and, eventually, business partners. Their partnership was a finely tuned balancing act: where Meg was blunt and bossy, Doug was tactful and diffident. When it came to compassion, however, they were evenly matched; I wasn't the only friend they had helped through tough times.

I gave Doug a hello hug when he appeared, introduced Bill, then followed Meg inside, pausing in the living room to say hello to Van Gogh, Meg's one-eared cat, who was perched in his usual place atop the bookcase. Bill put our bags beside the couch, reached up to give Van Gogh a scratch behind the ear, and we all ended up in Meg's kitchen.

Since Meg only did housework when she was in a grumpy mood, I was relieved to see dishes in the sink and art catalogs stacked helter-skelter on every horizontal surface. Bill cleared off a chair for me, then stood behind it while Doug and Meg filled me in on the latest gallery news.

"We closed up shop early today to celebrate your visit," Doug concluded.

"But not early enough to get any food in the house," said Meg. "You want to hit King's Café?"

"I've got a better idea," said Bill. All eyes turned to him. "Why don't you three talk while I make dinner?"

"Sounds good to me," said Doug, "but I'll lend a hand in the kitchen, if you don't mind. I think these two want to get down to some serious gossiping."

Bill scanned the kitchen, then fixed his gaze on Meg's portly form. "Linguini," he said. "Garlic bread. Caesar salad, heavy on the anchovies. Cheap red wine. A nice, light, chocolate soufflé for dessert. And . . . maybe some Amaretto with the coffee."

"Shepherd," said Meg, "you'd better marry this guy."

"Oh, she will," said Bill.

"*What?*" I squeaked. Meg grabbed my arm and Doug all but shoved Bill out the kitchen door.

"We'd better get to the grocery before it closes," Doug urged.

"The grocery?" Bill's voice came through the open window. "Is that where they have the tomato soup?"

If Meg had let go of my arm, I would have gone straight out the window after him.

"Deep breaths, Shepherd," she murmured. "Deep breaths. Come on out on the porch. I think you need some fresh air."

*
**

"So let me see if I've got this straight," said Meg.

It had taken her a while to get a complete sentence out of me, but when she did, the whole story had come tumbling out, everything that had happened since the letter from Willis & Willis had arrived. A sense of calm had settled over me once I'd off-loaded the story, and I sat in a chair on the covered porch, Van Gogh purring drowsily in my lap, listening to the surf crash against the rocks below, and watching the sky. Dark clouds were moving in, lit now and then by flashes of lightning. A storm was brewing out at sea.

"You're ready to throw away ten grand looking for a needle in a haystack," Meg summarized, "but it's a needle your mother wants found, so I can understand that. You two always were pretty tight. I like the stuff about the letters, too."

"They're in a cottage," I said, "near a place called Finch." A dreamy smile crept across my face. "A cottage in England. Isn't that a kick? I can't wait to see what it looks like."

"Maybe you already know what it looks like," said Meg.

"How could I? It's not in the photograph, if that's what you mean. I went over the thing with a magnifying glass and there are no houses in sight." Van Gogh yawned and began licking my hand, and Meg directed her next comment to him.

"She sure can be thick at times, eh, Van? In fact, if I didn't know better, I'd say she had the brains of a lungfish." She leaned toward me, her elbows on her knees. "Now, think, Shepherd. In all those Aunt Dimity stories, didn't maybe just one include a pretty little cottage? C'mon, now, think."

I didn't have to think. Meg was right. *Aunt Dimity's Cottage*. If I closed my eyes I could almost see the lilacs and the slate roof (which my child self had pictured as a blackboard tent) and the foul-tempered cat who had driven Aunt Dimity to distraction. Suddenly I knew exactly what the cottage looked like, right down to the cushions in the window seat.

"Lilacs," I murmured. "There were white lilacs at the funeral, just like the ones at the cottage."

"I thought so," said Meg, with a satisfied nod. "No surprise, really. Dimity Westwood wrote her life into the stories. It's been known to happen." Meg leaned back against her cushions and looked out over the ocean. The jagged bolts of lightning were almost constant now, and thunder competed with the booming surf. A freshening breeze ruffled the spiky hair on the top of Meg's head as she reached down beside her chair.

"It's cooling off—better cover up." She tossed one of her blankets to me.

Meg's "blankets" were her own personal works of art, hand-knitted afghans so soft and beautiful that I flinched whenever I saw them piled in haphazard heaps around the house. "I make them to be used," Meg growled at anyone who dared to comment. I just shook mine out and draped it over my legs and the drowsy lapcat.

Meg snugged her own blanket in place, then frowned. "What I *don't* get is why you're so ticked off at Bill. He'll do whatever you want him to do. He's well educated, polite, filthy rich, and not at all bad-looking." Meg curled her legs under her and rested her chin on her hand. "Gee, that's enough to ruin anyone's day. My heart goes out to you. I think you need your head examined, Shepherd."

"Thanks, Meg. I knew I could count on you."

"Sorry, Shepherd, but he just doesn't strike me as the Svengali type. I watched him back there in the kitchen. He never took his eyes off of you. Okay, so maybe he made a bad joke about the forbidden subject of marriage, but I'm sure that's all it was—a joke."

"I'm tired of being the butt of his jokes, Meg," I said heatedly. "I'm tired of having my leg pulled, and I am *sick* and tired of him playacting and goofing around and smirking behind my back and . . . What are you looking at?"

"You. I haven't seen you this riled up in a long time."

"So?"

Meg continued to stare at me intently. She opened her mouth as if to say something, then closed it again and shook her head. "Nope. Not this time, Shepherd. This time you figure it out for yourself."

Before I could respond, the porch door opened and Doug came out, accompanied by the delicious aroma of garlicky tomato sauce. "Sorry to interrupt," he said, "but I can't find the cheese grater."

"Have you checked the garage?" asked Meg. "Never mind—let me see if I can find it. I'll be right back, Shepherd."

Van Gogh decided the storm was too close for comfort and scooted in after them, leaving me alone on the porch. As soon as the door had closed, a few fat drops hit the roof overhead; then the rain came rushing down, enclosing the porch in flickering, translucent walls. I got up from my chair and stood with my hands on the railing, spellbound. I didn't hear the porch door open once more.

"I'm sorry," said Bill, and I came out of my reverie, startled to find him standing beside me.

"I'm sorry," he repeated. "What I said before—it was out of line. I embarrassed you in front of your friends and I should never have done that. I apologize."

For a moment—one short moment—it was as though I could see Bill, really see him, for the first time. He wasn't such a Handsome Prince, after all. He wasn't young and dashing. He had no jutting jaw, no aristocratic nose, no piercing blue eyes, and not even a hint of flaxen hair. His nose was far from aquiline, in fact, and although his beard disguised it, his chin seemed to be a bit on the receding side. His neatly trimmed hair was more gray than anything else and behind his glasses, his eyes were a warm brown. He wasn't handsome in a classic way; but then, I'd never trusted classic faces. In that brief moment, it struck me that his was a face I could trust. A Handsome Prince is in the eye of the beholder, I mused silently, and I'm having no difficulty picturing Bill in full armor. I gulped and chased the image from my mind at swordpoint.

"That's okay," I said stiffly, tightening my grip on the railing.

His shoulders slumped. He gave a soft sigh and looked out over the rain-swept sea.

"Really, Bill. It's no big deal." I glanced up at him and gently bumped his arm with my elbow. "I know how hard it can be to pass up a good opening."

"Do you?" said Bill. He reached over and brushed his fingertips across the back of my left hand. "I promise you, it won't happen again."

Between the rush of the rain and the pounding of my heart, I scarcely heard Doug's voice from the doorway. "I've tossed the salad," he announced. "And Meg says that if we don't eat pronto, she's going to chew a leg off the kitchen table."

***

For the rest of the evening, Bill behaved like a normal human being. He bantered with Meg, discussed the art market with Doug, played cat games with Van Gogh, and stopped treating me like visiting royalty. He even went to bed early so that my friends and I could have some time to ourselves. When we left the next day, he went so far as to let me forget my bag. Meg came puffing out to the car with it at the last minute.

"Look, Shepherd," she said, "I know you don't want to sully your gorgeous vehicle with this crummy piece of canvas, but I don't want it cluttering up my immaculate domain, either." She dumped it in the backseat behind Bill as Doug ran down the stairs.

"You be sure to write to us from England," he said.

"Waste of time," said Meg.

Doug and I looked at her in surprise.

"With your expense account," she explained, "you can afford to call."

I hugged the two of them, climbed into the car, and began the drive home.

*
**

It wasn't until we were stuck in a long line of cars waiting for a truckload of fertilizer to be cleared from the interstate —which Bill had taken to avoid the tortuous scenic route— that I began to consider what Meg had hinted at. Was I riled up over nothing? I could see that I had been a bit defensive with Bill, but defense mechanisms hadn't evolved because it had been a slow Thursday afternoon. Fear was essential to self-preservation. It had worked for our caveman ancestors, and who was I to argue with history?

Still, it was possible that Bill's intentions had been good all along, and it did seem odd to be afraid of kindness. It was definitely not a survival trait.

As we crawled past the aromatic accident scene, Bill touched a button on the dashboard and my window hummed shut. I glanced at him, then closed my eyes and leaned back, feigning sleep. I had some serious thinking to do and I wanted no distractions.

*
**

Willis, Sr.'s map was waiting for me in the guest suite when I got back. It had been well padded and securely wrapped in brown paper, and a note from Trevor Douglas had been placed beside it on the coffee table. I dropped my bag on the floor and picked up the note, expecting it to contain the usual polite business phrases. Instead, Mr. Douglas had written:

*Please thank Bill for directing me to that woodcarver
friend of his. The man is a genius. I'll be sure to send
more work his way.*

Woodcarver friend? I put the note back on the table. Worried,
I propped the package on the couch, tore off the wrapping
paper, removed the padding, and stood back to see what Bill
had done now. I stood there for a long time.

Trevor Douglas had not spoken lightly. Whoever had done
this work *was* a genius. In almost no time at all, he had created
a frame that was as subtle and intricate as the map itself: a
two-inch band of polished wood carved with a frieze of
animals—beavers, squirrels, raccoons, and other small creatures of the North American woods—linked by oak leaves
and acorns, pine cones and needles. When I ran my fingers
over the surface I could feel the care that had gone into its
creation.

The phone rang.

"Hello," said Bill. "Thought I'd call to let you know that
Father has planned a farewell luncheon for us tomorrow at
two, in the small dining room. 'Fortification,' he called it,
'against the trials of airline fare.' Can you make it?"

"Sure, I can make it," I said. "And, uh, Bill—the map has
arrived."

"Has it?"

"I'm looking at it right now," I said. "The frame is . . . it's
beautiful, Bill. It's perfect. I'm . . ."

"I've come up with a scheme for giving it to Father. I can
put it on his desk in the office tomorrow while you're saying
good-bye, so he'll find it after we've gone. I think he'd prefer
it that way. He's not fond of public displays of affection, you
know."

"Then that's what we'll do," I agreed. "And Bill, I . . . I
just want to say that . . ." I took a deep breath, then chickened
out completely. "Trevor Douglas asked me to thank you for
telling him about the woodcarver."

There was a prolonged silence on the line.

"Thanks for the message, Lori," Bill said at last. "I'll see you at lunch." And he hung up.

Unsettled, I cleared up the wrapping paper, then carried my canvas bag into the bedroom to unpack. "Why couldn't you just thank him?" I muttered fretfully, then paused in surprise as I opened the bag. A sheet of sketching paper was lying where my sweater had been. A single sentence from Meg was scrawled across it: *Your clothes are in the mail.* I flashed back to her lugging the bag to the car before I left. Sneaky, sneaky, I thought, then caught my breath when I saw what lay beneath the sketching paper.

There, folded with uncharacteristic care, was one of Meg's blankets. It was one I'd never seen before, done in rich, muted shades of gold and green and lilac and deep purple, like the hills of Scotland in full heathery bloom. I pulled it out and held it to my face and it was as soft as a baby's kiss, scented with salt air and the whisper of rain. How she had achieved that last effect, I had no idea, but it sent me spinning back to that stormy evening on her porch.

Almost without thinking, I touched the back of my left hand. It seemed to be tingling.

9

I spent the next morning browsing through Willis, Sr.'s books and packing my few bags. There was no need to hurry. The only thing left on my agenda was our bon voyage luncheon. I reread the letters from Dimity and my mother, paused to examine the photograph once again, then put them all into my carry-on bag along with Reginald.

I wasn't sure what to do with Meg's blanket. It was too bulky to fit in my carryon and too precious to pack with my clothes; I quailed at the thought of some overworked baggage handler sending it to London, Ontario. I didn't want to leave it behind, either, but I didn't know what else to do. I presented the problem to Willis, Sr., when we met in the small dining room that afternoon, and his solution was simplicity itself.

"Leave it upstairs for now," he suggested. "I'll have one of the staff fetch it later and we'll send it to London by courier. It will be at the cottage when you arrive.

"I'm sorry to say that my son will be unable to join us,"

he continued. "He is rather busy, I'm afraid, putting his work in order before his departure. Please, sit here, Miss Shepherd, and I shall ring for the first course. Do you care for asparagus?"

It was a leisurely meal and Willis, Sr., was a charming host, as always. I brought up the subject of the Northwest Passage and he took it from there, regaling me with stories of the bravery—and foolishness—of the men who had risked their lives in search of it. Two hours later, as we lingered over the raspberry tarts, he returned to more familiar terrain.

"You may be interested to know, Miss Shepherd, that I have contacted the cottage's caretakers, Emma and Derek Harris, to let them know you are coming. The Harrises are a most pleasant couple. They knew Miss Westwood, of course, and were quite helpful during the renovation of the cottage. A few minor improvements," he added, "undertaken by Miss Westwood some time ago, to bring the cottage into the twentieth century."

I pictured a white-haired couple keeping a watchful eye on the cottage and became suddenly alert. "Do they live nearby?" I asked.

"I believe so," said Willis, Sr. "If I recall correctly, theirs is the next house up the road."

That made them Dimity's neighbors. Could the Harrises be the kindly old couple who had come to Dimity's aid? It seemed unlikely. If they had been elderly forty years ago, they'd be tombworthy by now. I would have questioned Willis, Sr., further, but Bill chose that moment to burst into the room, looking harassed.

"Change of plans, Lori," he said. "We're going to have to leave sooner than I'd expected." He glanced at his watch. "Immediately, in fact. Our flight isn't until seven, but Tom Fletcher tells me that the new security procedures for overseas flights can eat up a lot of time. Father, I'm bringing Tom out to the airport with me so I can finish some memos on the Taylor case. Aside from that, my desk is clear."

"You'd best be off, then," said Willis, Sr. "I shall meet you at the front entrance in, let us say, ten minutes?"

"Fine," said Bill. "What a day. . . ." He ran a hand through his already disheveled hair as he left the room.

Willis, Sr., folded his napkin and placed it beside his plate, then withdrew a flat, rectangular package from the inside pocket of his suitcoat. It was wrapped in gold foil.

"It seems that I must give you this now, Miss Shepherd. I do hope you will find it useful."

"Oh, but you shouldn't have. . . ." Taking the package from him, I peeled away the gold foil. "Honestly, you've already gone out of your way to . . ." I faltered when I saw what he had given me. "A map," I said, a bit unsteadily.

"A topographic map," corrected Willis, Sr. "My son happened to mention your purchase of walking shoes, and I thought you might be considering a foray into the local countryside during your stay. If so, you will find this map most helpful. Have you ever used a topographic map?"

"No," I said, "I've always hiked along posted trails."

"You'll pick it up in no time. You see, it shows the natural features and the elevations of the land surrounding the cottage. Here, I'll show you where the cottage is. . . ." Willis, Sr., opened the map and gave me a crash course in how to read it. When he finished, I reached out and squeezed his hand.

"This is a lovely present," I said. "Thank you."

"Not at all. I am very pleased that you like it." He sighed contentedly. "I have a great fondness for maps."

*
**

I raced up to the guest suite, hoping to catch Bill before he descended the hidden staircase with Willis, Sr.'s map. I wanted to show him what his father had given me—the irony was too delicious to keep to myself—but he had already come and gone by the time I got there, taking my bags as well as the map. I put Meg's blanket on the coffee table in the parlor, then went back down to meet Willis, Sr., at the front door.

"Do you have everything you need, Miss Shepherd?" he asked.

"I do now," I said, brandishing his gift.

"I shall telephone you regularly with Miss Westwood's questions—though I confess I should probably do so in any case."

"We'll be happy to hear from you," said Bill, joining us in the doorway. "You take care of yourself while I'm gone, Father. No wild parties, no rowdiness, or I'll have to come home and give you a stern lecture." He gripped his father's hand, hesitated, then leaned over and hugged him. Willis, Sr., stiffened for a moment, then raised a tentative hand to pat his son's back. Before either one of them could say a word, Bill turned and made his way to the car.

"Extraordinary," Willis, Sr., murmured.

"Thank you for everything," I said. "I'm going to miss you, you know. I'll talk to you soon."

"Soon," he agreed. I started down the steps. "And Miss Shepherd," he added, "I shall miss you, too."

**
*

Bill dictated memos until the last boarding call and by the time I'd stowed my carry-on bag under the seat in front of me, fastened my seat belt, and declined the free champagne, he'd fallen asleep. I was more than a little disappointed. I had spent a restless night gearing myself up for a heartfelt expression of gratitude for the exquisite frame, I'd waited all day to deliver it, and now it looked as though I would have to go on waiting.

Still, he did seem exhausted, as though he'd been on the go since dawn. He had spent so much time with me during the past week that I had forgotten about his other responsibilities. Apparently he had, too, and had tried to cram them all into a single marathon day. Once we were airborne, I called a flight attendant over and asked for a blanket. Bill didn't stir so much as an eyelid when I tucked it in around him.

I was much too keyed up to sleep, so I spent the time leafing through magazines and reading the novel I had brought along. After a while, I simply gazed out of the window at the moonlit clouds. I imagined Willis, Sr., examining his map, perhaps asking a law student to fetch a book or two down from the small library. I smiled again when I remembered his going-away gift to me. The smile grew broader when I thought of his characteristically precise description of it: "A topographic map . . . It shows the natural features and the elevations of the land surrounding the cottage."

The natural features and elevations . . .

With a sharp glance to make sure Bill was still asleep, I reached into my bag and pulled out the photograph, kicking myself for not having thought of this sooner.

A small clearing on a hill overlooking a broad valley. Beyond the valley, a series of hills, all of them of uniform height and shape. Excited now, I took out the topographic map. It would be child's play to locate the clearing if it was anywhere near the cottage.

Except that the cottage was smack-dab in the middle of the Cotswolds, which meant that it was *surrounded* by hills and valleys, and I hadn't learned enough from Willis, Sr.'s short lesson to be able to distinguish one hill from another. As soon as I opened the map, I saw that there were at least a dozen places that seemed to meet my requirements. I pored over the maze of curving lines, as though staring at it would force it to yield up its secrets, until Bill's voice broke my concentration.

"Planning a walking tour?" he asked, peering at the map with great interest. A scant two days ago, I would have bristled and told him to mind his own business. Now I tilted the map so he could see it better.

"A bon voyage present, from your father," I explained.

"You're kidding." He shook his head in disbelief. "Did you manage to keep a straight face?"

"More or less. Well, I mean, you're supposed to grin when you get presents, aren't you?"

"I wish we'd hidden a camera in the office. I would love to have seen his face when he saw *his* map."

"Thanks for remembering to smuggle it down." I refolded the topographic map, trying to recall the words I'd rehearsed the night before. "And, Bill, about the frame. I just want to say that—"

"What's this?" Bill was folding the blanket I had put over him, but he stopped and reached for something on the floor. When he sat up again, he was holding the photograph. "Is it yours?"

I nodded, too shocked by my own carelessness to speak.

"It must have fallen when you moved the map. Very pretty. Where is it?"

"England," I said. "It's . . . a place my mother visited. During the war."

"It must mean a lot to you," said Bill. "I have my mother's photo albums up in my rooms, and I go through them every once in a while. Do you do that?" He handed the photograph to me. I put it and the map in my carryon and zipped the bag securely before answering.

"No," I replied, in a tone that persuaded most people to drop the subject.

"It was hard for me at first, too," he said. "I'd just turned twelve. I was away at school when the news came—she'd been hit by a bus and killed instantly. That's one of the reasons Father doesn't care for public transportation." He gave me a sidelong look. "I wasn't making that up, you know.

"It's never easy to lose a parent," he continued, "but at that age . . ." He creased the folds of the blanket carefully between his finger and thumb. "That's when I claimed Arthur's dome for my own. I think part of me believed that if I looked hard enough through the telescope, I'd be able to find her." He unbuckled his seat belt. "Thanks for covering me up, by the way. I'd hate to arrive in London with the sniffles." He stood up and stashed the blanket in an overhead bin.

"You're welcome." I hoped the interruption might turn his mind to other things, but when he sat down again, he picked up where he'd left off.

"When I went back to school after the funeral I felt like a freak. The faculty had briefed the other boys not to say anything that might upset me, so they ended up not saying anything at all. It confused the hell out of me, as though my mother had done something that couldn't be mentioned in polite company."

"You didn't want to talk about it, did you?" I said.

"No, but I didn't want a hush to fall over the room every time the word 'mother' came up. It was a relief when Father pulled me out of classes to go with him to England."

"That's when you met Dimity." I began to pay closer attention.

"We stayed at her town house in London. It was a fantastic place, and I had the run of it. I spent most of my time in the attics, going through dozens of dusty crates. I found gramophone records, kaleidoscopes—even an old cat's-whisker radio that still worked. And Dimity was . . . I don't know what I'd have done without her. She didn't tiptoe around the subject. We'd be in the walled garden and she'd ask what flowers my mother liked best. Then she'd fill baskets with them and put them all around the house, just like that, as though it was the most normal thing in the world. And every night, she told me stories."

"Aunt Dimity stories?"

"No," said Bill, with a brief smile. "As far as I know, those stories were created exclusively for you. Mine had a different heroine entirely."

"But they helped, those stories?" I was intrigued in spite of myself.

"Yes. They helped." He was silent for a moment. "I'd like to read your stories someday. Perhaps we can work an exchange. How about it?" He nudged my arm. "I'll tell you mine if you'll tell me yours."

"Only if you behave yourself," I said.

"I am a paragon of good behavior," he replied. "Father would have sent a chaperone to stand guard over you at the cottage otherwise. I was planning on staying there, if it's okay with you. There's plenty of room, apparently, and it'll be that much easier for me to run errands for you. Father suggested that I check into a local hotel, but I convinced him that his ideas of propriety weren't exactly au courant. We're hardly a pair of teenagers, are we?"

The challenge in his eyes was more than I could resist— and if necessary, I could send him on some extremely time-consuming errands. With a toss of the head, I replied, "Fine with me, as long as I can get my work done."

"You won't know I'm there." He took a fountain pen and a small, leatherbound notebook out of his pocket. "As long as we're discussing details of the trip, there are a few questions I'd like to ask before we land. Father said that your mother met Dimity Westwood in London during the war. Is that right?"

"Yes," I said. "My mother was sent over with a team of advisors before we'd even declared war on Germany, and she stayed on until VE Day."

"What did she do?"

"She was a clerk, a secretary—a paper-shuffler, as she put it. Now that I know about Dimity I'd like to see the city the way they saw it, go to the places they went."

"Such as?" He uncapped the pen and opened the notebook.

"Such as . . . Well, some of this may not make sense to you," I said. "They aren't places usually associated with the Second World War."

"But they *are* places you associate with your mother."

"She tried to see everything. You remember the story I told you and your father the night I arrived at the mansion? The one about the torch?" Harrod's went into the notebook, along with the zoo, the Tate Gallery, St. Paul's Cathedral, and several other museums and monuments that didn't require explanation. When I had run out of places, Bill capped his pen, then returned it and the notebook to his pocket.

"We'll see what we can do," he said.

I stifled a jaw-cracking yawn. "We may have to wait until tomorrow to start. I can feel jet lag setting in already."

"This isn't your first trip overseas?" Bill asked.

"Hardly," I replied. "But don't get me started on that. I've been known to bore strong men to tears with my hitchhiking stories."

He pulled a large white handkerchief from his breast pocket and regarded me expectantly.

*
**

"So this will be my fourth visit to London," I concluded. "The first was during the summer after my freshman year in college. I spent a week there that time, crashing in my sleeping bag on the floor of a flat belonging to two guys I'd met on the road. The second time was with my former husband. By then I'd had enough of sleeping on floors, so we booked a room at a B & B. It turned out to be an Earl's Court special, though, complete with an uncloseable window overlooking a train yard, and a mattress that sagged to the floor, so I ended up sleeping on the floor again anyway."

"You're joking," said Bill. "Exaggerating, at least."

"I am not. I had to hook my leg over the side of the bed to keep from rolling down into the middle. But we learned. The next time we went, we booked a room at a clean and quiet guest house in Sussex Gardens. Even with a bath up the hall, we thought it was heaven." I rested my head against the back of the seat.

Bill went through the motions of wringing out his handkerchief, then tucked it back into his pocket.

"Where are we staying this time?" I asked, closing my eyes.

"A hotel," he said. "Father and I stay there when we're in town. Dimity recommended it to us, in fact. It's a nice place. Clean. Quiet."

10

When the liveried doorman trotted out to open the door of our limousine, I began to suspect that Bill had indulged in some serious understatement. When I found myself standing beneath the venerable forest-green awning of the Flamborough Hotel, I knew it, and succumbed to momentary panic. There I was, wearing jeans which, although new, were still *jeans,* for pity's sake, about to walk into one of the world's most genteel hotels. The regular residents would probably strain their eyebrows.

"Clean and quiet, huh?" I said under my breath.

"Private baths, too," Bill murmured.

"Oh, goody. Now I feel right at home." I averted my eyes when my decrepit canvas bags were pulled from the limo, and stared when they were followed by an unfamiliar set of royal blue canvas carryalls. Bill saw what had caught my attention.

"Like my new luggage?" he asked as we entered the lobby. "Wonderful stuff, canvas. Durable, lightweight, easy to repair . . ."

I groaned inwardly. Evidently Bill had changed hats again. The amiable traveling companion was gone, the joker was back, and there was nothing I could do about it—except gird myself to face whatever other surprises he had in store in London.

Bill escorted me to a chair and I sank into its depths, peering timidly at my surroundings as he walked to the front desk. The lobby was all brass and wood, tall ferns and taller doorways, with writing desks tucked discreetly into alcoves, islands of comfortable chairs, and bellboys in spotless dove-gray uniforms. Elderly women sat or stood, draped in ancient fur stoles, pearls at their throats, tiny hats nestled in their silver hair, chatting with equally elderly gentlemen. I felt like a dandelion in a grove of stately oaks, a drooping dandelion at that, and I was relieved when Bill returned; his wrinkled tweed jacket was at least as disreputable as my jeans. He arrived in the company of a dignified, middle-aged woman, and I stood up as they approached, wishing I had a forelock to pull.

"Lori," said Bill, "this is Miss Kingsley. She takes care of Father and me when we're staying here."

"Miss Shepherd, how nice to meet you," said Miss Kingsley.

I shook her hand and nodded dumbly. She must have wondered if I understood English.

"If you will excuse me," said Bill, "there are some arrangements I need to make. You take it easy, Lori, and get some sleep. Why don't we meet here tomorrow morning, at ten o'clock? I'll see you then." Bill went back to the desk and I was left alone with Miss Kingsley.

"Shall I show you to your suite, Miss Shepherd?"

"Yes, please," I said. "And . . . would it be all right with you if you called me Lori? Bill's father is the only person in the world who calls me Miss Shepherd."

"Of course." Miss Kingsley summoned a porter to carry my bags and led the way, explaining that she would be at my disposal while I was in London. If I had any questions, problems, or special requests, I should feel free to contact her. She couldn't have been friendlier, but I found myself restraining the urge to curtsy when she left.

The suite consisted of a sitting room, bathroom, and bedroom, with windows that opened on to a courtyard garden. It was charming, but I was pooped. After a brief tour, I made a beeline for the bedroom, peeled off my clothes, dumped them in a heap on the floor, and fell into bed. The last thing that passed through my mind was the memory of my mother's voice telling me that the best way to deal with jet lag was to fight it. "Good idea, Mom," I murmured. Then I faded into sleep.

I awoke at three in the morning, of course, wide-awake and raring to go. Miss Kingsley, or some of her elves, had visited the room while I slept. The heap of clothes had vanished and a fluffy white robe had been placed on a chair near the bed. I slipped it on and noticed that my bags had been unpacked and my gear stowed in the wardrobe.

Wandering into the sitting room, I saw a tray of sandwiches on the table near the windows. Beside it was a lovely, floral-patterned tea service, complete with an electric kettle. And next to that was a guidebook, several London maps, and the current issue of *Time Out*. "Good grief," I muttered. "They could have ridden the Horse Guard through here and I wouldn't have noticed."

I thumbed through the guidebook and saw that someone had marked it in red ink. A handwritten list, keyed to the page numbers in the book, had been taped to the inside of the front cover. The list had been written on a page torn from a small notebook. Just like Bill's.

*
**

He was waiting in the lobby at ten o'clock, along with Miss Kingsley and a small, white-haired man in a dark blue uniform, whom Bill introduced as Paul.

"Paul will be our driver while we're in London," Bill explained, "and I can testify that he knows the city inside out."

"That's very kind of you, sir," said Paul. "And you, miss —young Mr. Willis here tells me that you'd like to see places having to do with the Second World War. Is that correct?"

"Yes," I replied.

"Did you know that you're standing in one?"

"The Flamborough?" I looked around the lobby with renewed interest.

"Paul is quite right," said Miss Kingsley. "The Flamborough was a famous watering hole in those days, or so I've been told. The young airmen thought of it as their unofficial headquarters. They used to come here to relax, to have a drink, to dance with their wives and girlfriends—"

"They came here to gossip," Paul put in with an authoritative nod. "Talked like there was no tomorrow, they did, miss, bragging and poking fun at one another. If there was any news to spread, it came to the Flamborough first. The Flamborough Telegraph, they used to call it."

"Please, come with me," said Miss Kingsley. "I think you might find this interesting."

She took us into the hotel lounge, a large, rectangular room with wine-red banquettes along the walls and a small dance floor. The focal point was a glorious traditional English bar, with mahogany framework that went right up to the ceiling. The bar was ornamented from top to bottom with carved scrollwork and brass fixtures, and an oval mirror etched with fruit and flowers stretched across the back of it. The room was dim and silent, not yet open for business.

"The Flamborough was fortunate to escape the Blitz," Miss Kingsley said, "and the nature of our clientele precludes extensive renovations. The room appears now very much as it did during the war. Here, this is what I wished to show you."

The walls at the far end of the room were hung with photographs. They were snapshots rather than professional portraits; framed, black-and-white pictures of men in uniform or in flying gear, standing beside their aircraft or sitting at camp tables, grinning.

"They're so young," I said, looking from face to face.

"And they stayed that way," said Paul.

Miss Kingsley frowned slightly at him, then turned to me. "These are the boys who didn't come back," she explained. "Their comrades put the pictures here, in tribute. We keep them here, to remember."

The faces of those boys remained with me throughout my time in London. My mother had always spoken of the war as a great adventure, a time of unforgettable sights and sounds, of strong friendships quickly made. She had never mentioned the friendships that had been even more quickly ended.

*
**

Bill seemed to hold the keys to the city. He got me into the building where my mother had worked—now just another maze of modernized corridors—and out on the roofs of St. Paul's, where she had seen the incendiaries fall. He found an elderly general to give us a private tour of the Cabinet War Rooms, the underground bunkers from which Churchill had conducted the war during the Blitz, and he somehow got permission for me to view Imperial War Museum photo archives that were usually reserved for scholars.

Bill was so solicitous, in fact, that he made me edgy. There was nothing I could point to, no overt act that embarrassed or annoyed me, but there was something in his manner. . . . Perhaps it was the return of the same secret, knowing smile he had tried to hide during his tenure as my chauffeur in Boston. In London it gave me the feeling that something was up, that he was planning some monumental prank that would leave me flabbergasted.

As far as I could see, however, he only put his foot wrong once in London, and even that wasn't his fault. It was pure bad luck that brought us together with a guy who had frequented the rare book reading room at my university in Boston; a genuine, bona fide, one-hundred-percent-guaranteed creep named Evan Fleischer. Evan was in his late twenties, with stringy, shoulder-length black hair, thick glasses, and a hairy little potbelly that peeked out between the lower buttons of his ill-fitting shirts. I might have found him endearingly scruffy if it hadn't been for the fact that he was the single most egocentric individual I had ever met.

I was never able to pin down Evan's area of expertise because he claimed to know everything. The word "important" was frequently on his lips, but he defined it rather more narrowly than the rest of the English-speaking world. If anyone else had a deadline to meet, it was inconsequential, and the same went for ideas: only Evan's were "important." One day in the reading room, when he referred to his laundry as "important," I laughed in his face. It didn't faze him. He simply explained, in little words that even I could understand, why doing *his* laundry was a service to humanity. Looking pointedly at his grease-stained tie, I conceded that he had a point, but the jibe was lost on him. He merely assumed I'd seen the light.

And how he loved to enlighten people. He gathered around him a coterie of emotionally disturbed undergrads who hung on his every word, which reinforced his self-image as an altruistic mentor. He led them on in order to feed his own ego, and that, when all was said and done, was what made him a creep rather than just another obnoxious jerk. I had no time to explain any of this to Bill when I heard Evan call my name in the lobby of the Tate.

"Lori? Lori Shepherd?"

I would have tucked my head down and sprinted for the exit, but Bill was already shaking Evan's hand, eager to meet another one of my friends.

"What a pleasant surprise," said Evan.

"You're half right," I muttered.

"I don't believe we've met before." Evan blinked owlishly at Bill. "I am Dr. Evan Fleischer. You may call me Evan, if you wish, although naturally I prefer Dr. Fleischer. Lori and I are old friends."

"It's very nice to meet you, Dr. Fleischer," said Bill. "I'm Bill Willis. Lori and I are—"

"I'm sure Evan doesn't have time for small talk," I interrupted.

"Only too true," said Evan. "I'm delivering an important paper on Dostoyevski's use of patronymics this coming Saturday at the British Museum. I'm sure you would find it instructive, though perhaps a bit esoteric. I find it difficult to write for a general audience, you see, because—"

"What a shame," I said. "We're leaving London on Saturday."

"Where are you off to?"

In full Mr. Congeniality mode, Bill piped up: "We'll be staying in a cottage in the Cotswolds, near a place called Finch."

"What about our change of plans?" I asked Bill urgently.

"What change of plans?"

"Oh, but you mustn't change a thing!" Evan exclaimed. "It's a fascinating area. I'm sure I can find the time to visit you there. I'm always eager to give foreigners the benefit of my extensive knowledge of the sceptered isle." Since Evan had been born and raised in Brooklyn, New York, his use of the word "foreigners" was highly suspect.

"I'd rather you didn't," I said. "Really, Evan, I'm going to be awfully—"

"It would be my pleasure." He checked his watch. "I'd love to tell you about my paper, but I have some important appointments."

"Picking up your laundry?" I asked.

"No, I had that seen to this morning," he replied. "Now I've really got to run. Where are you staying?"

"The Flamborough," said Bill.

"I'll be in touch." He strode off toward the exit, leaving me to glower at Bill.

"What's wrong?" he asked.

"Nothing much," I said. "Only that you've saddled us with a visit from one of the most obnoxious human beings on the face of the planet. Once he moves in, we'll never get rid of him. Oh, God," I groaned, "he'll probably try to read his paper to us."

Bill had the grace to hang his head. "I thought he was a bit of a pill, but—"

"I know. You also thought he was my friend." I sighed and took his arm. "Oh, come on. I'll tell you all about him while we look at William Blake's visions of hell. After a brush with Evan, they'll seem soothing."

*
**

Bill redeemed himself by showing up at my suite the next day with enough of the finest Scottish wool to keep Meg's knitting needles flying for a good long time. Impressed, I had to admit that he noticed far more than I gave him credit for.

I bought a few things I couldn't resist—a couple of sweaters, a book or two—and others I didn't even try to resist. A flashlight, for instance. From Harrod's, of all places. And I made sure to have a brand-new brolly handy when I went to the zoo. Even when I was caught up in shopping, Dimity and my mother were never far from my thoughts.

I kept seeing them in my mind's eye, sharing a bag of chips, riding bicycles, running for shelter during an air raid. I touched the shrapnel-gouged walls of buildings along the Embankment and tried to imagine what it had been like to hear the rumble of German aircraft overhead, to feel the sidewalk shake as the bombs struck home. There was one moment, driving past Hyde Park, when I thought I saw the greensward scarred with trenches, sandbags piled high, conical canvas tents staked out in rows across the fields. The image was startlingly vivid. I called out for Paul to stop the car, but before he could pull over to the curb, the vision was gone, the helmeted Tommies replaced by the usual lunchtime throng of trench-coated Londoners. When Bill started to question me, I only shook my head and asked Paul to drive on.

Because the zoo had gained an almost mythic status since I'd read the letters—I guess I subconsciously expected to find a brass plaque commemorating the day Beth Shepherd met Dimity Westwood—I'd saved it for last. Needless to say, it was a bit of a letdown to see it bathed in sunlight and crowded with noisy families.

Bill had arranged for me to speak with one of the keepers who'd been there during the war, a pink-faced, elderly man named Ian Bramble. We sat with him by the Grand Union Canal, and he sighed when I asked him what the zoo had been like in those days.

"A sad place," he said. "Terribly sad. Hated to come to work, myself. No children around, and the place all boarded up." He pulled a handful of corn from his pocket and tossed it to some passing ducks. "It was a strange time. People were afraid there'd be lions in the streets if a bomb fell in the wrong place, and they had enough to worry about without lions. So we put them down, the lions, and others as well. Perfectly healthy they were, too. It's not something we tell the kiddies, you understand, but perhaps we should. I sometimes think they'd be better off knowing it's not all crisps and candy floss during wartime."

11

Paul had been too young to enlist. "Not that I didn't try, mind you," he told us. "Lied like a rug, I did; used boot-blacking to give myself whiskers. Board told me to go home and wash my face." We were speeding along a narrow, twisting lane, on our way to the cottage. We had left London very late in the afternoon the day after our visit to the zoo. I had wanted to leave earlier, but Bill had gone off to make some more of his mysterious arrangements and hadn't surfaced again until after tea.

"That's why I went to the Flamborough," Paul continued. "The bartender there was a chum of mine, and I liked to listen to the lads. We were taking such a pasting in London that it was good to hear the Jerries were getting some of their own back. Finch should be coming up shortly, miss." I had tried to break him of the "Miss Shepherd" habit, but he had been trained at the Old Servant's School of Etiquette and "miss" was as far as he would unbend. "The cottage lies about two miles beyond the village."

It was too dark and we passed through Finch too quickly for me to see much of it, but as we pulled into the drive, I could see that lights had been lit in every window of the cottage. It was exactly as I had pictured it. And it seemed to be waiting for me.

"Here we are," said Paul, switching off the engine. An absolute silence settled over us. We climbed out of the limo to stand on the gravel drive and I shivered as the cold night air hit me.

"Touch of frost tonight, I'd say." Bill blew on his hands and I could see his breath.

"A bit nippy for this time of year," Paul agreed. "You two run along in and get warmed up. I'll see to the luggage."

Paul unloaded the limo and Bill headed for the front door, scrounging through his pockets for the keys Willis, Sr., had given him. I started to follow Bill, then stopped on the path to confirm my initial impression that the cottage looked . . . as it was supposed to look.

It was just as my mother had described it in her story, a two-story stone house with a broad front lawn, sheltered from the road by a tall hedgerow. The yard light glinted from diamond panes of leaded glass and hinted at the golden glow the walls would have in sunlight. The slate roof, the flagstone path leading from the drive to the weathered front door, all was as I had envisioned it, down to the bushes that were already heavy-laden with white lilacs.

"Lilacs in April," I murmured. "They must bloom earlier here than they do at home."

Paul came to stand beside me. "Lovely old place this is, miss."

"Too good to be true," I said, searching the facade for some flaw that would jar it, and me, back into the real world. I didn't like the sense of belonging that was seeping into my bones. It made it too easy to forget that I was only a visitor.

But the yard light revealed no imperfection. With a shrug,

I joined Bill on the doorstep. He seemed to be having difficulty with the lock.

"Let me try," I offered. I turned the key, and the door swung open to reveal a brightly lit hallway.

"Look at the place," said Bill. "It's lit up like a Christmas tree."

"The Harrises probably came by today to get things ready for us," I said. "They must have forgotten to turn off the lights."

"I'd talk to them about that if I were you, miss," said Paul, Old Servant's School disapproval in his voice. "The electric doesn't come cheap these days."

"Cheap or not, I'm glad they turned on the heat," said Bill. "Let's get inside before we all catch colds."

Paul set the bags in the hall and returned to the car for the last of them. As I stepped across the threshold, the cottage seemed to pull me into its warm embrace, and when the door swung shut behind me, I thought: I may be only a visitor, but I sure do feel like a welcome one.

There was a gentle knock at the door. The Old Servant's School again, I thought, rolling my eyes.

"For heaven's sake, Paul, you don't have to knock," I called out. "Come on in, it's open."

His muffled voice came through from the outside. "Sorry, miss, I can't budge it."

"What do you mean, you can't—" The door opened at my touch. Paul stood on the doorstep, a bag in each hand and a perplexed expression on his face.

"These old places do have their quirks, miss." He set the bags beside the others while Bill fiddled with the door handle.

"There doesn't seem to be anything wrong with it," Bill said, "but I'm not a locksmith. I think I'll ask the Harrises to have this checked out."

"Fine," I said. "Now, how about a cup of tea before you go back to London, Paul? Or would you like to stay here for the night? You're more than welcome."

"Thanks very much all the same, miss, but I'd best be getting back, if it's all right with you. Up early tomorrow, you know, can't keep the ambassador waiting." He offered to carry our bags upstairs, but we assured him that he had done more than his fair share of work for the day and walked him to the limousine. After he'd driven off, I turned in the still night air for another long look at the cottage.

The feeling of familiarity was uncanny. There was the shadowy oak grove and, there, the trellis ablaze with roses. Each item was in its proper place and the whole made a picture I remembered as clearly as the apartment house in which I had grown up. I probably would have stood there all night, lost in the déjà vu, but the crunch of Bill's shoes in the gravel reminded me that I was not alone. He held out his jacket and I pulled it around my shoulders, grateful for the warmth.

"You seem to be a million miles away," he said softly.

"More like a million years," I said. "One of my mother's stories has a cottage in it, exactly like this one. I feel as though I've been here before."

"It's a strange feeling," said Bill, "to see a legend from your childhood come to life."

"Mmm." I nodded absently. "I was a little worried, after the zoo. She told a story about that, too, and she made it sound like . . . like Disney World. And it wasn't like that at all—not during the war, at any rate. But the cottage is just as it should be."

"As she promised it would be," Bill murmured.

It was an odd comment, but I wasn't paying attention. I was already walking toward the door, curious to see if the inside of the cottage would be as true to the story as the outside was. Bill followed me into the hall, then stopped. He pointed to the ladder-back chair beside the hat rack. "I'll wait here. You go on ahead, get acquainted with the place."

"You don't mind?"

He shook his head. "It's your story."

I searched his face for a trace of mockery, but there was none to be found.

"I'll be right back." I handed him his jacket and started up the hall.

The two front rooms on the ground floor were the living and dining rooms. A study was just beyond the living room, to the rear of the cottage, and there was a pretty little powder room just beyond that, complete with lavender-scented hand soap and ruffled towels. I wasn't big on ruffles, as a rule, but here I couldn't imagine anything else.

Having completed a quick once-over, I returned for a more leisurely examination of the living room. I saw no sign of the renovation Willis, Sr., had mentioned until I found a television and a snazzy sound system hidden in the cabinetry along one wall. The room had to have been enlarged to accommodate these additions, but even so, I had no trouble picturing Aunt Dimity eating brown bread and drinking tea before that fireplace.

The room was spacious yet snug, with deeply upholstered chairs and a beamed ceiling. Bowls of lilacs had been placed here and there, filling the room with the scent of early summer. A bow window overlooked the front garden, and its window seat was fitted with cushions straight out of my mother's story.

Or were they? If I remembered the story correctly, Aunt Dimity's cat had spilled a pot of ink on one of the cushions (having already chewed the fern to bits, scratched the legs of the dining room table, and tipped over the knitting basket). Aha, I thought, feeling extremely clever, I've caught you. Surely, that had only been part of the story. Surely . . .

The inkstain was there. Someone had tried many times to remove it, and it had faded over the years, but it was still there, a defiant blue patch in the back corner near the wall. I gazed at it, then crossed the hall to check the legs of the dining room table. They bore the claw marks of a cantankerous cat. I glanced over my shoulder, half expecting him to stalk through the doorway, demanding a bowl of cream. No such thing happened, of course. The cat had undoubtedly gone on to harass his mistress in another world.

Even without the cat, the dining room was recognizably Aunt Dimity's. It mirrored the living room, with its fireplace, bow window, and cabinetry, though here the cabinets were glass-fronted and filled with delicate bone china and crystal. A door in one wall opened on to the kitchen and it was there that I found the first big discrepancy between the cottage of my mother's story and the one in which I stood. I also discovered that Willis, Sr., shared his son's fondness for under-statement.

This was no "minor improvement." This was the most fully equipped modern wonder of a kitchen I'd ever seen, with everything from a microwave oven to a set of juice dispensers in the refrigerator door. As I opened doors and drawers and examined countertops, my first coherent thought was: This is a kitchen for someone who can't cook.

In other words, a kitchen designed with me in mind. It was a farfetched notion, to say the least. My former husband had been as good a cook as my mother, and I had been too intimidated to learn, but even if Dimity had known of my culinary incompetence, she couldn't have revamped the kitchen for my benefit. I was only going to be here for a month, after all. The truth had to be that Dimity Westwood had been a lousy cook, too. It would certainly explain why Aunt Dimity seemed to subsist on brown bread and tea.

I wasn't one bit disappointed to find that the kitchen bore no resemblance to the primitive one of *Aunt Dimity's Cottage*. I loved the idea of an open hearth, but if I'd been forced to cook on one, I would have starved.

A second door led into a well-stocked pantry and a roomy utility area, and the third and last door led into the hallway. Directly across the hall was the book-lined study, and a white-painted, fern-bedecked solarium stretched across the back end of the cottage.

I paused to survey the study. A stack of papers sat on the desk that faced the ivy-covered windows, and I crossed the room to investigate. I thought it might be miscellaneous bits and pieces of the correspondence—selected letters, perhaps, related to the stories—but it proved to be the stories themselves. They had been written in longhand on fine, unlined paper, and the title page brought me up short.

"*Lori's Stories,*" I whispered. It was as though Dimity had foreseen my reluctance to share my heroine with the masses, and had offered this title to reassure me: no matter how far afield these tales might travel in years to come, they would always be mine. I straightened the edges of the manuscript with hands that were none too steady, glanced idly at the bookcases—and found the correspondence.

Books filled several vertical sections of shelves, but the rest of the wall was reserved for row after row of neatly labeled archive boxes. Talking about the letters, reading about them, even thinking long and hard about them, hadn't prepared me for the impact of seeing them. More than forty years of my mother's life had been captured in those boxes and the sight left me feeling slightly dazed. Stan Finderman had once mentioned something called "the mystique of the manuscript" and I finally understood what he had meant. My mother had touched these pages, and in their presence, I felt hers. I wanted to pull down a box right away, but I held off. Not now, not yet. Not with Bill cooling his heels in the hall. After a moment's thought, I picked up the manuscript and headed for the front door.

Bill stood as I returned.

"That good?" he asked.

"Better," I replied with a grin.

"And there's still one more floor to go."

"You can come up with me, if you want," I offered. "Aunt Dimity never went upstairs in the story, so it won't change anything to have you there. Here, you can put this on your nightstand." I handed him the manuscript, grabbed my bags, and started up the stairs.

Bill stayed where he was. He looked down at the manuscript, then up at me on the stairs. "You're sure you want me to read these?"

"I'm sure," I said; then, more gruffly, "Well, don't just stand there. They're bedtime stories. They belong upstairs, next to your bed."

A full bath was at the top of the stairs, and two cozy bedrooms occupied the front of the cottage, each with twin beds, wardrobes, reading chairs, and fireplaces. I put my bags in one and Bill put his and the manuscript in the other.

"You wouldn't think they'd need so many fireplaces," Bill remarked as he emerged from his room. "The central heating seems to work well enough."

"But central heating doesn't warm the soul the way an open fire does. It's so"—I skirted around the word "romantic" and finished lamely with—"old-fashioned." Bill was about to reply when the sight of the master bedroom silenced him.

The master bedroom took up the entire back half of the second floor. A sliding glass door opened on to an outside deck, and another sliding door led to a bathroom that brought to mind the changing room in the Willis mansion. The main difference was that, instead of a simple whirlpool bath, it had a strange-looking Jacuzzi/steam-bath installation. Bill, of course, knew how it worked and showed me how to use it. A good thing, too—I would have parboiled myself if I had tried it on my own.

This room seemed to combine bits and pieces of all the other rooms in the cottage. Aside from the wardrobe and bureau, there were bookshelves, glass-fronted cabinets, and a desk, all of which appeared to be empty. Two overstuffed chairs were in one corner and a tea service had been placed on a round table between them.

The bed was the size of a small football field, and another grin broke across my face when I saw Meg's blanket folded atop a wooden chest at its foot. Seeing it there was like seeing an old friend. I began to say something about it to Bill, then noticed that he'd left me alone again so I could enjoy my discoveries in private. The bed faced yet another fireplace, in which a fire had been laid, but I was too distracted to contemplate that pleasure. For there, on the mantelpiece, was a vase filled with deep blue irises. My knees buckled and I sat, stunned, on Meg's blanket.

Bill reentered the master bedroom, carrying my bags. He placed them on the bureau, folded his arms, and declared: "*This* is your room."

"Bill," I said, "did you come here today?"

"No. Why?" He walked over to stand in front of me.

"I was wondering how those got here." I pointed to the flowers.

Bill glanced over his shoulder. "So that's where they put them. With so much to look at, I nearly missed them. The Harrises must agree with me—about this being your room, that is."

"The Harrises?"

"I called them today and asked them to put some irises in the cottage for you. I thought they'd add a nice welcoming touch."

"So you've really never been here before?"

"Lori, I may have an odd sense of humor, but I've never lied to you. I have never set foot in this cottage before this evening."

I twisted a strand of the fringe on Meg's blanket. "I didn't mean to sound so . . ."

"Suspicious? Paranoid?" Bill suggested helpfully.

"It's just that, for a minute there—"

"You thought someone else had opened your birthday present."

I ducked my head. "It sounds pretty childish when you put it that way."

"What's wrong with that? I'd feel the same way if I found

out that someone had been snooping around Arthur's dome. By the way"—he stepped aside to give me an unobstructed view of the flowers—"do you like them?"

"You know I do." I stood up. "But you haven't seen the rest of the place yet. Come on, I'll give you a guided tour." We were halfway down the stairs when I heard tires crunching on the gravel drive.

"Who on earth—" I backed up a step. "Oh, no . . . not Evan."

"You stay here," said Bill, squaring his shoulders. "I'll take care of this."

12

If Bill had his heart set on giving Evan the boot, he must have been disappointed when he opened the door. I know I was, but for very different reasons. Our unexpected guests turned out to be Emma and Derek Harris, and one look was enough to tell me that they couldn't possibly be the couple who had given my mother the photograph. They weren't the doddering, white-haired caretakers I had envisioned. In fact, unless my ears deceived me, Emma wasn't even English.

"You're American?" I asked, coming down the stairs.

"Yes, I am," said Emma, looking up from the doorway. She was shorter than I, a bit plumper and some years older, wearing a bulky hand-knit sweater beneath a lightweight parka, and a gorgeously mucky pair of Wellingtons. Dishwater blond hair hung to her waist and she peered shyly at me through a pair of wire-rim glasses. "But my husband is the real thing. Harrow, Oxford—he even plays cricket when he has the chance."

"Which is none too often." Derek Harris had eyes to kill

for, the kind of deep, dark blue eyes that casting directors dream about and the rest of us don't really believe exist. Emma would have been justified if she had married him for his eyes alone. He was tall and angular, with salt-and-pepper curls framing a weatherworn face. Like Emma, he wore a light-weight parka and appeared to be in his late forties. "I scarcely have enough time to run my business, let alone practice my bowling." He eyed Bill speculatively. "I don't suppose you . . ."

"Sorry," said Bill, "speed-reading is my game." He gestured for the Harrises to come into the hall, closed the door, and made formal introductions. "By the way, Harris, my father wanted me to express his gratitude to you for keeping an eye on the cottage."

"Only too happy to help." Derek turned his blue eyes toward me. "Hope we haven't interrupted anything. Bill rang this morning to let us know you were coming out today. We spotted a car in the drive when we were coming back from town, so we thought we'd drop yours off."

"My what?" I asked.

"Your car," said Emma. "Bill asked us to lease one for you locally. It was no trouble," she added. "Our house is just up the road. We can walk back."

"Do you have to get back right away?" I asked. "If not, you're welcome to stop in for a cup of tea. It's the least I can do to thank you."

"An Englishman never turns down a cup of tea," said Derek with a smile. "Here, Em, let me help you with those." Emma took his arm and stepped out of her Wellies while Bill hung their jackets in the hall closet.

"I assume I have you to thank for stocking the pantry?" I said to Emma.

"I didn't want you to find the cupboards bare," she replied. "I hope I haven't forgotten anything."

"I don't think you have to worry about that. I doubt that

we'll get through half of it before we leave. How about helping us tackle the crumpets tonight?"

Derek and Bill were all in favor, so I set them to work lighting a fire in the living room while Emma and I repaired to the kitchen to put the kettle on. She helped me locate a sturdy brown teapot and four stoneware mugs—"No need to use Dimity's best china with us," she assured me. She filled a tea ball with loose tea from the tin tea caddy in the pantry, then brought out a white ceramic sugar bowl, a squat cream jug, and four dessert plates, arranging them with the rest of the tea things on a polished wooden tray with brass handles.

"So this is a toasting fork." I was fascinated. "I've read about them, but I've never used one before. I hope you know something about the fine art of crumpet toasting."

"With a ten-year-old daughter and a fifteen-year-old son at home I've become something of an expert on crumpets. Oh, and before I forget . . ." Emma reached into the pocket of her brown woolen skirt. "I borrowed this yesterday and I wanted to return it. Peter and Nell prefer these even to crumpets and I can't say that I blame them." With a cheerful smile, Emma handed me a recipe for oatmeal cookies.

It was unmistakably my mother's. An index card, browned with age and stained with use; her looping scrawl—I could almost smell the nutmeg.

"Where did you get this?" I asked.

"The usual place." Emma went into the pantry and came back with a fat old dog-eared cookbook. "I used to borrow recipes from Dimity all the time. I've copied this one, though, so I won't be needing the original again."

I paged through the cookbook, culling card after card, until I held a fan of my mother's old standbys: tuna casserole, meat loaf, onion soup, cookies, cakes, even the champagne punch she had made to celebrate my college graduation. She had gotten that one from Mrs. Frankenburg downstairs, who was fond of fancy touches.

"Should I have waited for your permission?" asked Emma in a small voice.

I had forgotten she was in the room.

"No, no," I said. "It's not that. It's . . ." I tapped the fan into a pile and tried to collect myself. "These are my mother's recipes. All of them. I mean, she wrote them herself. She must have exchanged recipes with Dimity Westwood. And she . . . she passed away last year."

Emma looked stricken. "I'm so sorry, Lori. I didn't mean to spring it on you like that. I had no idea."

"Of course you didn't. It's all right, Emma, really. To tell you the truth, it's a . . . a pleasant surprise. I knew that her letters were here, but I—"

"Is that what those are? In the boxes in the study?"

"Yes—hers and Dimity's. I'm going to be reading through them while I'm here. Didn't Bill tell you?"

"Bill told us that he was bringing someone to the cottage, and that it had something to do with Dimity's will. Period. Derek and I have been referring to you as 'the Westwood Estate' all day " Emma took a bottle of milk from the refrigerator and with a steady hand began to pour off the cream into the squat jug.

"I'm not the Westwood Estate," I said firmly. "I wish I were. It'd be nice to take up permanent residence here, but I'm only staying for a month. I'm going to be . . . doing a research project. You know—exploring Dimity's old haunts."

Some drops of cream spattered the wooden surface of the table, and Emma wiped them up with a spare napkin. "Are you? That sounds interesting."

"You knew her, didn't you?"

"Oh, yes," said Emma. She put the milk bottle back in the fridge. "We knew Dimity. That's the main reason we came over, in fact. We thought . . . That is, Derek and I thought you might want to know—" A shriek from the teakettle broke in on her words and as I was warming the pot, Bill put his head in the doorway.

"We can't get the fire going, Lori," he said. "Derek thinks you should have a try."

*
**

"You've checked the flue?" I knelt on the hearthrug while Emma put the tea tray on a low table. Bill stood behind me, and Derek sat on the couch, his long legs crossed, very much at ease.

"It's open," said Bill. "The wood is dry, the tinder is in place, and Derek says that everything is in working order."

I struck a match. "I used to be pretty good at this back in my hosteling days. . . ." It was like flipping a switch. The match touched tinder and the fire caught on contact. I tossed the spent match into the flames. "Maybe you hit some rot or something. Wood can be funny that way."

Emma glanced at Derek, then picked up a pair of toasting forks and knelt beside me. "Watch closely and I'll show you how it's done."

She was a good teacher and we soon had a respectable pile of beautifully browned crumpets to butter and munch. I hadn't burned a single one, a first in the annals of my cooking experience.

"My father told me that you helped with the renovation work here," said Bill.

"We did a lot more than help," said Emma. "Derek was in charge of it. He's an independent contractor."

"I specialize in dying arts," Derek elaborated. "Thatched roofs, stone walls, stained glass—"

"Everything that makes a place like this so special," Emma finished proudly. "I think the cottage is my husband's finest achievement."

"I can see why," Bill agreed, dabbing butter from his beard with a napkin. "It's magnificent. And you, Emma? What did you do?"

A self-deprecating smile played on her lips. "Dimity let me work in the garden."

" 'Let you'?" Derek echoed indignantly. "Emma, she begged you to work on it."

"Oh, Derek . . ."

"You're a gardener?" Bill asked.

"Well . . ." When Emma faltered, Derek smoothly stepped in.

"My wife trained as a computer engineer at Caltech," he explained. "She was working as a project manager for a Boston firm when we first met and she feels compelled to describe herself along those lines, although she's nothing of the sort anymore. Oh, she still does the odd consulting job in London, but most of the time she's rambling round the countryside or tending her gillyflowers. Emma is a gardener through and through. Cut her and she bleeds sphagnum moss."

"It's true," admitted Emma. "When I'm working in a garden, I'm at peace with the world."

"Then you're in the right place," I said, refilling Emma's cup.

"What do you mean?" Derek asked, and his blue eyes were suddenly alert.

" 'This other Eden, demi-paradise,' " I quoted loftily.

"Oh," said Emma, patting Derek's knee, "you mean *England*. Well, it's true enough. The English do love to dibble and hoe, but Dimity's garden is unusual, even for here." A faraway look came into her eyes. "Working on it has been quite an experience."

"The cottage, as well," Derek added. "Quite an experience." Waving away my offer of more tea, he returned his cup to the tray, contemplated the fire, then sat back, looking vaguely uncomfortable. "Actually," he went on, "we didn't come over tonight solely to deliver the car."

"Although we wanted to do that, certainly," said Emma.

"Yes, of course," said Derek. "But we were also wondering if . . ." He cleared his throat.

". . . if you had noticed anything," Emma put in. "Since you arrived, that is."

"Like what?" I asked.

"Oh . . . anything unusual," Derek said casually.

I thought for a second. "The lock's not working on the front door. I mean, it works sometimes, and sometimes it jams."

"Have you had any trouble with it, Lori?" asked Derek.

"No, but—"

"Anything else out of the ordinary?"

I shrugged. "All of the lights were on when we got here, but I assumed that you—"

"We didn't," said Emma. "You see . . . well . . . I'm not quite sure how to say this. It's not something I've had much experience with."

"There was the lady chapel in Cornwall," Derek pointed out.

"Yes, but that didn't involve someone we *knew*, Derek. This is completely different." Emma turned back to me. "Besides, we didn't know anything about you and we were afraid you might be . . . disturbed by it."

"Disturbed by what?" I asked warily.

"We simply wanted to tell you not to worry if you notice any peculiar things happening in the cottage," said Emma.

"Such as the front door lock," said Derek. "We've never had trouble with it before, but as you said, it will only open for you now. It stands to reason, of course. She had the whole place done up for you. She must feel protective."

"I'm sure that's why the lights were on, too. And the lilacs blossoming so early . . ." Emma gestured at the bowl of fragrant flowers on the piano. "She was always very fond of lilacs. There's the fire as well, but you saw what happened with that."

"Wait a minute," I said, as gently as I could. I put my cup on the tray and looked dubiously from Emma's face to Derek's. "Let me see if I've got this straight. By 'she' you mean Dimity?"

"Oh, yes," said Emma. "We're not sure why, but we're certain it's Dimity."

"You're telling me that the cottage is *haunted?*"

"I'm afraid so," replied Derek, and Emma nodded her agreement.

"Not that there's anything to be afraid of," Emma added.

"Bill, did you hear that?" But there was no reaction from Bill. Instead, a strange stillness had fallen over him, the stillness of a hunter waiting for his prey to step into the trap. I felt a pang of disappointment so intense that I nearly groaned aloud.

This was it, the monumental prank I'd been waiting for ever since we'd touched down at Heathrow. And I had to admire how carefully he had set it up. He'd drawn me out during the flight and behaved like a perfect gentleman in London, all in order to win my trust, to lull me into complacency, so that when the time came, I would . . . what? Scream and run out of the cottage? Fall fainting into his arms? What kind of a fool did he take me for? I had no doubt that Emma and Derek were in on the game, but I couldn't blame them. I knew how charming Bill could be.

"Thank you," I said, with a touch of frost in my voice. "I'll keep that in mind."

"As I said, it's nothing to worry about," Emma repeated earnestly. "It shook me a bit at first, but you'd be amazed at how quickly you get used to it." She looked uncertainly at Derek.

"Yes. Well." Derek drummed his fingers on the arm of the couch, then stood up. "Thank you very much for your hospitality. We'd best be going, Em. Vicar's roof tomorrow."

"First thing in the morning," said Emma. "They're forecasting heavy rain for the rest of the day."

We stayed with the safe subject of the weather until Derek and Emma walked out into the cold. I closed the door and leaned my head against it, willing Bill to admit that the whole thing had been his idea of a joke. If he had, I think I could have shrugged it off.

"Strange story," he said.

I straightened slowly.

"I can't imagine why they'd make it up, though," he added.

"Can't you?" I asked, still with my back to him.

"No. I'll have to speak to Father about it. He's not going to like—" He broke off as I swung around to face him. "Lori? You don't think I—"

"You don't want to hear what I think," I said. I darted past him and fled up the stairs to the master bedroom, where I slammed the door and locked it. I was not going to give Bill the satisfaction of seeing me cry.

13

Some people are lucky enough to look like Bambi when they cry. I look like Rudolph. I woke up the next morning with a headache and a shiny nose, and promptly blamed Bill for both.

I took a long, hot shower, then pulled on some jeans and a Fair Isle sweater I'd bought in London. When I slid open the door to the deck, a blast of wind nearly knocked me back inside. One glance at the overcast sky told me that this would not be my day for hill climbing, and as my breath condensed in the cold air, I wondered how often it snowed in the south of England in late April.

The back garden almost made up for the gloomy sky. It was spilling over with bright blossoms and the cold didn't seem to affect them at all—a pair of redbuds were just coming into leaf in the meadow beyond the stone wall. I recalled what Emma had said about the lilacs, but dismissed it when the first windblown splashes of rain sent me back inside to unpack.

I put my books on the shelves, set Reginald's shoebox in the bottom of the wardrobe, and stowed the rest of my gear in the bureau. I only had enough for three of the large drawers, so I decided to put the emptied canvas bags in the fourth one, and that's how I found the box. It had been shoved way back in the corner of the bottom drawer, and I would have missed it if it hadn't shifted forward when I jerked the drawer open.

I carried it to the windows, where a sickly gray light was beginning to leak into the room. Covered with smooth, dark blue leather and die-stamped with a curlicued W, the box fit easily in the palm of my hand, and when I saw a tiny keyhole on one edge, my heart fell. I didn't want to damage it, but I wanted very much to find out what was inside. If it held a picture of Dimity, it would be the first I'd ever seen.

"Damn," I said; then, "Oh, what the hell." I tried the lid and it opened without hesitation. The box held a locket, a gold locket in the shape of a heart, with flowers incised on the front. It hung from a fine gold chain. I lifted it gently from the box, slipped a thumbnail into the catch, and opened it.

It was empty. There were places for two small pictures, one in each heart-shaped half, but they held nothing. I closed the locket and regarded it thoughtfully. According to my mother, Dimity had been looking at albums of photographs when the neighbors had found her alone in the cottage, in a state of nervous collapse. Where were those albums now? What if the photograph that had been given to my mother had come from one of those albums, and what if the page had been labeled, and what if . . . I hung the chain around my neck to remind myself to search for Dimity's albums, then went to listen at the hall door.

The wind rattled the windows and the rain pounded the roof, but there was no other sound. I hadn't heard a peep out of Bill since the night before. With any luck, he'd have the good sense to move in with the Harrises for the rest of the month.

*
**

The lights had been turned off throughout the cottage, and a fire burned cheerfully in the fireplace in the study, proof, I thought, that Bill had given up on the ghost hoax. If he hadn't, he would have called upon my alleged magical powers to start the fire for him. I wondered if he had stayed up all night in the study, reading the Aunt Dimity stories and—I hoped—feeling ashamed of himself.

My experience with the crumpets, and the absence of witnesses, gave me the confidence to try an omelette for breakfast. To my great delight, and even greater amazement, the result was light and fluffy and oozing with melted cheese. I ate in the solarium, watching the rain cascade down the glass panes and hoping that the poor vicar's repairs had been finished in time. When the telephone rang, I went to the study to answer it.

"I do hope I've gotten the time change right." The line crackled with static from the storm, but Willis, Sr.'s thoughtfulness came through loud and clear. "I haven't disturbed your sleep, have I, Miss Shepherd?"

"No," I replied, "and it wouldn't matter if you had. It's wonderful to hear your voice."

"Thank you, Miss Shepherd. It is pleasant to speak with you as well. I take it that you have arrived in good order?"

"Paul drove us to the doorstep last night."

"And the cottage—it meets with your approval?"

"I'd like to wrap it up and bring it home with me," I said. "I'm in the study right now, looking out through the ivy with the rain pouring down and a fire in the grate. It's so beautiful . . . I wish you could see it. And we had a wonderful time in London, too. Bill was . . . um . . ."

"Yes, Miss Shepherd? You were saying?"

"Bill was fine," I said quickly, too quickly to fool Willis, Sr. I could hear his sigh even through the static.

"Would I be correct in assuming that my son has done something objectionable, Miss Shepherd?"

"Well . . ." I toyed with the phone cord. "Does trying to convince me that the cottage is haunted count as objectionable?"

"Pardon me, Miss Shepherd. Did I hear you correctly? Did you say *haunted*?"

"Hard to believe, isn't it?"

"Where my son is concerned, I no longer know what to believe. I really am going to have to speak with the boy."

"I don't think he meant any harm by it," I blurted, wishing I'd kept my big mouth shut. I didn't like the agitation I heard in Willis, Sr.'s voice.

"Nonetheless, this has gone far enough. He can have no excuse for such unprofessional conduct. If he cannot be trusted to carry out Miss Westwood's wishes, I shall order him home and appoint a suitable substitute. I am beginning to regret my failure to accompany you myself."

"You mustn't do that." Now I was thoroughly alarmed.

"I am Miss Westwood's executor, Miss Shepherd. It is my responsibility to—"

"It was just a joke," I insisted, "a silly practical joke. It didn't even scare me. Not for a second."

"You are quite sure?"

"Do I strike you as someone who believes in ghosts?"

"No. . . ."

"Then please don't give it another thought. I'll talk to Bill myself."

"Very well. But if he continues to—"

"I'll let you know, Mr. Willis."

"I shall count on you to do so." There was a moment of silence on the line and when Willis, Sr., spoke again, his voice had regained its customary calm. "Now, Miss Shepherd, if I might turn to a more pleasant subject before I go?"

"Yes, of course."

"I would simply like to express my heartfelt gratitude for your most thoughtful gift. I attempted to contact you in London, but you were out much of the time, and I did not like to convey my thanks through Miss Kingsley. I am most grateful. I have seldom seen such a fine example of cartographic art and I have never seen such a splendidly appropriate frame. My dear, it quite took my breath away." His warm words sent a rush of pleasure through me. I twirled the phone cord around my finger and turned a slow pirouette, like a little girl being lauded for a flawless piano recital.

And stopped.

Because there, looking up at me from the arm of one of the tall leather chairs near the fire, was Reginald.

Not *my* Reginald. *My* Reginald was upstairs in the master bedroom, in the wardrobe, in the shoebox, in pieces, and *this* Reginald was here, in the study, in the chair, sitting up as pretty as you please, with every stitch intact, two button eyes gleaming, and both ears on straight, as powder-pink as the day he'd been born.

Except for the purple stain near his hand-stitched whiskers.

"I have to go," I said abruptly.

"Pardon me, Miss Shepherd?"

"I really have to go," I said. "Right now. I'll call you back in a little while."

"Is there anything wrong?"

"I'll call you back," I repeated. I dropped the phone on the cradle, tore out of the study, pounded up the stairs, flung open the wardrobe, grabbed the shoebox, and flipped the lid onto the floor.

The shoebox was empty.

***

There was no way Bill could have known about Reginald. Not even Meg knew about Reginald. Having a stuffed bunny as a confidant isn't something a thirty-year-old woman readily admits to.

But someone had known about him. Someone who needed to get my attention.

I put the shoebox back into the wardrobe and gently closed the door. I descended the staircase in slow motion, stopped at the doorway of the study, and peeked in. The fire was snapping, the rain was drumming, a book of some sort was lying on the ottoman, and Reginald was sitting beside it. He had *moved.*

"Reg?" I called softly. "Is that you?"

His eyes glittered in the flickering firelight. I walked over to pick him up. With a trembling finger, I traced his whiskers and touched the purple stain on his snout, then cradled him in one arm and bent to pick up the book. It was bound in smooth blue leather, with a blank cover and spine; a journal, perhaps.

Slowly, I sat down with it in the chair and, even more slowly, I fanned through the pages. All were blank except for the first one, on which a single sentence had been written.

Welcome to the cottage, Lori.

Before I had time to digest that, another formed below it as I watched.

I'm so glad you are here, my dear.

I'm not sure how long I stopped breathing, but it was long enough to make my next breath absolutely essential.

"Dimity?" I whispered. "Is that you?"

Yes, of course it is, my dear. And let me say what a joy it is to make your acquaintance after all these years.

I clapped a hand over my mouth to suppress a quavering giggle. "It's nice to meet you, too." I cleared my throat. "Uh, Dimity?"

Yes, Lori?

"Do you suppose you could tell me what's going on here? I mean, I know what's going on here, but what's *going on* here, if you catch my drift. I mean . . . what I mean is . . . I don't even know what I mean."

Perhaps you could be more specific?

"More specific. Right. Um . . ." My mind raced through the events of the night before. "Did you do the lock and the lights and the lilacs and the . . . the fire? Did you light the fire in here this morning?"

Why, yes, my dear. As Derek indicated, I wished to celebrate your arrival. You really should trust what he says about the cottage, Lori. He and Emma know it better than anyone. And you must stop blaming young Bill. I assure you, he had nothing to do with my arrangements.

"Well, thank you, Dimity, it was . . . lovely." I was reluctant to voice the other suspicion that had occurred to me. It was rather deflating, but it was also staring me in the face. "I should have known it'd take supernatural intervention to turn me into a good cook."

NO! I had nothing to do with the omelette!

"You mean it?" I asked. "You're not say—er, writing that just to make me feel better?"

I am telling you the truth. I did lend a hand with the crumpets, but that was only to build your confidence. You may take full credit for the omelette. You might try the oatmeal cookies next. I do so love the scent of cinnamon.

"Me, too," I said, with a nostalgic smile.

I had become so caught up in the give and take of our "conversation" that I had temporarily forgotten what was actually taking place. In fact, I had pretty much lost touch with reality altogether. When a log fell on the fire, I jumped, then looked slowly around the room, realizing the picture I would present to anyone peering in through the windows. I was sitting in an isolated cottage, the wind was howling, the rain was roaring, and I was communicating with the dead. I tightened my grip on Reginald and glanced nervously back at the journal as a new sentence took shape.

I know how strange this must seem.

"Now that you mention it, this is a little . . . no, this is a *lot* strange. I mean, you did say something in your letter about not coming back from the grave. And what about all those long chats with my mother?" I paused, almost afraid to ask the next question. "Dimity—how is she?"

I haven't seen Beth yet.

"You haven't? Why not? I mean, you're both in . . . the same place, aren't you?"

Not precisely. She's gone ahead.

"Oh. Well, she . . . went first, I guess. But you'll catch up with her, won't you?"

I hope so. A sigh breezed through the room. *You see, Lori, things are a bit muddled.*

A bit muddled? Was that what they meant by British understatement? My suspension of disbelief was about to snap.

It's my own fault, of course.

"What is?"

Oh, everything. I've known all along that I would never be forgiven.

"Forgiven for *what*?"

I simply don't deserve forgiveness. And this isn't such a terrible way to spend eternity, is it? I could think of much worse

The handwriting stopped.

"Hello?" I said. "Are you still there? Can you hear me?"

Nothing more. I stared at the page until my head swam, then looked up, round-eyed, to see Bill standing over me.

14

"Don't let me interrupt." As his eyes traveled slowly around the room, he held out the manuscript of *Lori's Stories*. "I finished reading it this morning, up in my room, and thought I'd return it before . . . Lori? Lori, what is it? What's the matter?" He put the manuscript on the desk, then knelt before me. "You look like you've seen a—"

"Don't," I said. "Please, Bill, no jokes."

"But I'm not—" His eyes widened. "You mean, you actually *have* seen—"

"Not *seen*, exactly."

"Oh, my. . . ." Bill sat back on his heels. "Dimity?"

I gave a barely perceptible nod.

"So the Harrises were telling the truth." He pulled the ottoman over and sat on it, leaning forward, his elbows on his knees. "I thought they might be. When you first stepped into the cottage, I . . . I don't know how to explain it, but I sensed something. That's why I let you go on ahead without me. I felt like an intruder." He shook his head. "Sounds crazy, doesn't it?"

"No," I said. I let the journal fall shut in my lap. "I felt it, too. But I—I thought it was the central heating."

"That's what comes of being such a practical sort of person," said Bill. He brushed away a tear that had rolled down my cheek. "Tell me about it?"

Struggling to keep my voice level, I introduced him to Reginald. "I've had him since I was a kid, Bill, since I was really little, you know? I'd recognize him anywhere. But last year a burglar left him in pieces all over my apartment. I brought him to England in a shoebox and now—" I gulped for air.

"Now he's fully recovered." Bill took out his handkerchief and wiped away a few more tears that had managed to escape. "The burglar didn't hurt you, did he? Oh, now, Lori, come on, don't cry like that. There's no need to be frightened."

"I'm not f-frightened," I said, taking Bill's handkerchief and burying my face in it. "For Pete's sake, Bill, it's not as though headless horsemen are galloping through the living room. How could I be afraid of Dimity? I'm—I'm *ashamed* of myself. Here you are, being so nice to me after I behaved like such a jerk last night. I didn't even give you a chance to explain."

"I don't think I could have explained," said Bill. "And even if I had, there was no reason for you to believe me."

I caught my breath and blinked at him through my tears.

"Well, I *might* have tried rigging the cottage," he said. "In fact, I kind of wish I had. It might have been fun. Give me one good reason why I shouldn't have been your prime suspect."

"Because you promised," I said bluntly, twisting his handkerchief into a knot. "When we were at Meg's. You promised that you wouldn't . . . step over the line again."

"You have a point. And yes, it would have been nice if you'd remembered it sooner. Consider yourself castigated. But

I refuse to stalk out of here in a huff, because if I do I won't get to hear what else happened this morning to convince you of my innocence. So let's skip over the recriminations and the apologies and go straight to the good stuff." Bill leaned closer and whispered, "Did she . . . manifest herself to you?"

"She *wrote* to me," I said with a sniff and a quavery laugh. I held up the journal. "A new form of correspondence. All the pages but one were blank when I opened it. Now look at it." I showed him the first page. "It's her handwriting, Bill. I'm sure of it."

"Does that mean it wasn't ghostwritten?" he murmured. He studied the page, then said, with great reluctance, "I know you don't want to hear this, Lori, but I have to confess that I—"

"You can't see it?" I took the journal from him. The sentences were still there, plain as day. I fought down a sudden surge of panic.

Bill took hold of my shoulders. "Calm down, Lori, and think about this. She's writing to you, not to me. I doubt if anyone else can see what you're seeing."

"But—"

"That doesn't mean I don't believe you," Bill stated firmly. "That doesn't make it less real. It doesn't make it less anything, except, well . . . less visible. Who knows? Maybe it's some sort of security system. A private line, open only to you. That would make sense, wouldn't it?"

"I suppose. . . ."

"Well, all right, then." Bill released his grip on my shoulders, took the journal from my hands, and opened it. "Please, Lori. Calmly and clearly and in the correct order, tell me what Dimity—" He glanced down at the journal and his eyes remained on the page, moving from left to right, as a ruddy glow rose from his neck to his hairline. He blinked suddenly, then snapped the book shut.

"What?" I said eagerly. "What did she write?"

"Nothing important," he said.

"Then why are you blushing?"

"You couldn't see it?" he asked.

"Private line," I replied.

"She was . . ." He averted his eyes. "She was complimenting me on my appearance."

I looked at him doubtfully.

"She *was*," he insisted. "She said that my teeth are nice and straight, as she always knew they would be."

"And what else?"

He looked away again and said, with studied nonchalance, "And that she was right in telling Father not to worry about my thumb-sucking."

"You were still sucking your thumb at *twelve?*"

"No," said Bill, "I *started* sucking my thumb at twelve. It's a common reaction to bereavement."

"Oh." The room grew very still. Bill watched the fire and I watched his profile until he turned in my direction.

"I don't anymore, if that's what you're wondering."

"What I was wondering," I said softly, "was why I didn't try it. A little thumb-sucking might have helped."

"It helped me."

"And your teeth are very straight," I added.

"Thank you."

"Bill," I said, "you know about Reginald, and I know about your thumb. I think that makes us even."

Some of the starch went out of his spine. "It's a start." Tapping the journal, he returned to the subject at hand. "She thinks of everything, doesn't she? It's a strange effect, though—how the words . . . appear. What did she say to you?"

I read through Dimity's half of the dialogue and supplied my side of it as best I could remember. When I finished, he let out a low whistle.

"Deep waters," he said.

"It's a metaphysical swamp, if you ask me. I don't even want to think about what her return address might be."

"What was all that about forgiveness?" Bill asked. "Forgiveness for what?"

"I don't know. That's when you came in."

"Why don't you try asking her again?"

"You mean just . . . ask?" With a self-conscious glance at Bill, I opened the journal once more. "Uh, hello?" I said. "Dimity? Are you there?" I touched Bill's arm as a new sentence appeared on the page.

Yes, of course, my dear.

"Good," I said, "because I want to ask you about what you said before, about needing to be—"

Do you like the cottage?

"Like it? I love it, Dimity. Derek did a fantastic job."

There are few craftsmen as gifted as Derek. I was fortunate to find him. Have you see the back garden yet?

"Only from the deck."

Oh, but it's no good gazing down on a garden. You must stroll through it in order to see it properly.

"I'll do that," I promised, "as soon as it stops pouring. But, to get back to what I was saying before, could you explain what you meant when you said—"

It's nothing for you to concern yourself with, Lori.

"But I am concerned, Dimity. I mean, it's great to have a chance to talk with you like this, but—"

There's nothing you can do, you see. I want you to enjoy your time here. I want you to read the correspondence.

"I will, Dimity, as soon as—"

You must read the letters. Read them carefully. But please, take the time to make a batch of cookies for young Bill. You could find no better way to make amends. Oh, dear, it seems I must go now. Once more, Lori, I welcome you with all my heart.

I tried a few more questions, but when nothing else appeared, I closed the journal and leaned on the arm of the chair, lost in thought.

"She's stonewalling," I murmured.

"She's what?"

"She's shutting me out, just like she shut out my mother."

"What has this got to do with your mother?"

I handed the journal to Bill and got to my feet. "You stay right here," I said. "I have something to show you."

✻✻

". . . So Dimity bottled something up all these years and now it's blocking her way to heaven?" Bill took off his glasses and rubbed his eyes. "The things they don't teach you in law school . . ."

He was sitting at the desk in the study, with the manuscript, the topographic map, the letters from Dimity and my mother, the tattered old photograph, and the journal arrayed before him. Reginald sat beside the journal, watching the proceedings with an air of benign detachment, while I paced the room, filled with nervous energy. I stopped at the desk and pointed to the photograph.

"And it must have happened here, in this clearing. The photograph reminded Dimity of it and that's why she keeled over. That's my working hypothesis, anyway. There's this, too." I pulled the locket from the neck of my sweater and showed it to Bill. "I found it upstairs this morning, in a box marked with the letter *W*—for Westwood. It's empty. See? No pictures. Where are they, Bill?"

"Maybe she never put any pictures in it."

"Not just *these* pictures." I perched on the edge of the desk. "Don't you remember? My mom said Dimity was looking at photo albums when the neighbors found her. I snooped around while you were in here reading the letters and—" I hopped off the desk. "Come upstairs and see what I found."

Bill put on his glasses and followed me up to the master bedroom. I moved Meg's blanket from the old wooden chest to the bed, then opened the lid of the chest. A row of photo albums bound in brown leather had been packed inside it, their spines facing upward. Like the archive boxes in the study, they had been labeled with dates.

"Neat little ducks, all in a row," I said, then pointed to a gap in the sequence. "Except that one has flown the coop, the one covering the years just before Dimity met my mom." I let the lid fall back into place. "So what did she do with it? And don't try to tell me that she stopped taking pictures all of a sudden, because—"

"Wait, Lori, back up a step." Bill sat on the chest. "What do you think happened in that clearing? What could be so terrible that it would follow Dimity into the afterlife? Are we talking about murder? Suicide? Are we going to find a body buried under that tree?"

"Don't say things like that," I said, suppressing a shudder.

"You've been thinking them, haven't you? I don't mean to sound ghoulish, but it has to have been something fairly drastic to cause Dimity this much grief. If we're going to go digging into the past, we should be prepared to uncover some unpleasant things."

"But . . . murder?" I shook my head. "No. I can't believe that. It's got to be something else—and don't ask me what, because I don't know I'm going to call the Harrises again." I started for the telephone on the bedside table, but Bill blocked my way.

"You've already left four messages on their machine," he reminded me.

"But where can they be?"

"Still bailing out the vicarage is my guess. The storm hasn't let up." Bill patted the space next to him on the wooden chest. "Come here and sit down. The Harrises will call when they call, and not one minute sooner. You can't help Dimity by running in circles." He waited until I was seated, then went on. "We have no idea where the missing photo album might be. For all we know, Dimity might have burned it."

"A depressing possibility," I conceded.

"On the other hand, she may have kept it somewhere else—a bank vault, a safe-deposit box—somewhere special. Maybe it got mixed up with the rest of her papers. I'm sure that Father would be—"

"Your father!" I clapped my hand to my mouth. "Oh, my gosh, Bill. I was talking with him when I saw Reginald. I slammed the phone down on him. He must be worried sick." I rose halfway to my feet, then sat down again. "But he'll want to know why I hung up on him. What am I going to say?"

"That's easy," said Bill. "Tell him that you were distracted by another one of my stunningly clever stunts."

I shook my head. "No way. When I told him you were haunting the cottage, he threatened to recall you and fly over himself."

"I hope you talked him out of it," Bill said quickly.

"I did, but I don't want to risk stirring him up again."

"Definitely not. Tell him . . . tell him that you were distracted by one of my stunts, but that you've had it out with me. You've taught me the error of my ways and I've promised never, ever to do anything so childish again." He looked at me brightly. "How's that?"

"Will he believe it?"

"It's what he wants to hear."

"That always helps." I went over to dial the number on the bedside phone and Bill stood beside me, listening in. Willis, Sr., answered on the first ring.

"Ah, Miss Shepherd," he said. "So good of you to call back. I was beginning to become concerned. Was there an emergency of some sort?"

"No, no, Mr. Willis," I replied airily, "no emergency. Just another one of Bill's silly jokes. The last one, as a matter of fact. I've given him a . . . a stern lecture and he's promised to behave himself from now on." Bill signaled that I was doing fine, but I felt sure Willis, Sr., would hear the deception and guilt in my voice.

But he began to chuckle. "Well, well, Miss Shepherd, if my son has stubbed his toe on your temper, I've no doubt he'll watch his step in future."

I put my hand over the receiver and whispered, "Is he saying I'm bad-tempered?" but Bill waved the question away and hurried to the foot of the bed to point at the wooden chest. He mouthed the word "Photos."

"Uh, Mr. Willis?" I continued. "While I have you on the line, do you think you could answer a couple of questions for me?"

"I am at your service, Miss Shepherd."

"It's just that I found some old photo albums here in the cottage and one seems to be missing. I was wondering what could have happened to it. Did you come across anything like that when you were going through Dimity's papers? It's an old album, from around 1939. . . ." I listened to Willis, Sr.'s reply, said a polite good-bye, and hung up.

"Well?" said Bill.

"He doesn't think so. He'll check, though, and get back to me."

Bill nodded, but his mind was somewhere else. "Let's go back to the study," he said. "It just occurred to me that the answers we're looking for might be right under our noses."

I trailed after him. "If you're thinking of the correspondence, Bill, you're way off base. My mother had her antennae out. If Dimity had dropped the slightest hint, she would have told me."

Bill entered the study and approached the shelves. "True, but what if Dimity didn't mail all the letters she wrote to your mother? What if she couldn't bring herself to send some of them?"

I hadn't thought of that. Scanning the crowded shelves, I felt a flicker of hope. If Bill and I worked together, we could read through the letters in a matter of hours. If there were any clues to be found—to Dimity's past, or to the origins of the stories—we would find them. With Bill's help, I might be able to keep everyone happy. Still, I hesitated.

"Bill," I pressed, "have you thought this through? Looking for answers to my mother's questions could take a lot of time, more time than I have. I may not be able to write Dimity's introduction. Bill . . ." I tugged on his sleeve and he looked down at me. "Your father has gone to a lot of trouble to see to it that Dimity's wishes are obeyed. Won't he be furious with you for helping me disobey them?"

"He'd be dismayed, certainly. But I'm not helping you."

"You're not?" I blinked up at him, confused.

"No." He reached for the first box of letters. "I'm helping Dimity."

15

I don't know what made me think we could rush through the correspondence. There were sixty-eight boxes full, for one thing, letters from my mother interfiled with those from Dimity in strict chronological order, but it wasn't the quantity that slowed us down. It was the quality. I had expected the letters to be moving, fascinating, enlightening—and they were—but I had not expected them to be so entertaining. I found myself pausing frequently to reread certain passages, to translate my mother's handwriting for Bill when he had trouble with it, and to read the best parts aloud.

I also found myself watching Bill. He never caught me at it—the slightest movement on his part would send my eyes scurrying down to whatever I was supposed to be reading—but it happened time and time again. Of all the strange things that had happened that day, his presence in the study was perhaps the strangest. Only that morning I had been ready to throw him out of the cottage, and now he was sitting peacefully across from me, his jacket and tie thrown carelessly over the back of the chair, his collar undone and his shirt-sleeves rolled up, calmly stroking his beard while he read his way through this most intimate correspondence, as though he belonged there. With each passing hour, it became more difficult to imagine journeying into my mother's past without him.

The seeds of the stories were scattered everywhere we turned. I think Bill was even more thrilled than I was each time a familiar situation or setting surfaced. He crowed in triumph less than an hour after we'd gotten started.

"I've found Aunt Dimity's cat!" he exclaimed. "Listen to this:

> *"My Dearest Beth,*
> *"My cat is terrorizing the milkman.*
> *"You didn't know I owned a cat, did you? That's because I didn't, until a week ago. I do now. The only trouble is that I'm not quite sure who owns whom.*
> *"He showed up on my doorstep last Monday evening, a ginger tom with a limp and a very pitiful mew. A bowl of cream miraculously cured the limp, and after a night on the kitchen hearth, the mew was replaced by a snarl that caused the milkman to shatter a fresh pint all over my kitchen floor. I strongly suspect premeditation, since the cat promptly lapped it up.*
> *"There's not a plant in the house that's safe from his depredations and he's learned to sharpen his claws on the legs of my dining room table. I've lost my temper with him a dozen times a day. I know I should put him outside to fend for himself, Beth, but I like him. There hasn't been a dull moment since he walked through my door, and he keeps my feet warm in bed. Surely that's worth the loss of a few houseplants. Or so I keep telling myself.*
> *"I have dubbed him Attila."*

Bill chuckled as he jotted the date of the letter in his notebook for future reference.

"Wait," I said. "Don't close that notebook."

"Why? What have you found?"

I shushed him and read aloud:

> "My Dearest Beth,
>
> "My dear, why do we put ourselves through Christmas? If the Lord had known what He was about, He surely would have announced His son's birth privately to a small circle of friends, and sworn them to secrecy. Failing that, He might at least have had a large family and spaced their arrivals at decent intervals throughout the year. But no. In His infinite wisdom, the Almighty chose to sire but one Son, thus setting the stage for a celebration only a merchant could love.
>
> "I have just returned from the vale of tears which is London the week before Christmas. Should I ever suggest such a venture again, you are encouraged to have me bound over for my own protection. Only the weak-minded would willingly enter the holiday stairwells at Harrod's, of all places.
>
> "Picture a trout stream of packed and wriggling humanity; picture the rictus-grins of clerks exhausted beyond endurance; picture my foot beneath that of a puffing and alarmingly well-fed gentleman.
>
> "And picture, if you can bear to, my chagrin at having survived it all, only to depart empty-handed. [Enter Greek chorus, cursing Fate.] The torch, my sole reason for braving the savage swarm, was not to be had, and I shall have to make do with candles until March, or perhaps June. Please God, the crowds will have thinned by then. . . ."

"No wonder your mother treasured this friendship," Bill said. "Can you imagine getting letters like that all the time?"

I told him the date of the letter and kept on reading. It was fun to run across those familiar-sounding passages, but I was even more captivated by the unfolding story of their everyday lives, and by their frequent references to the time they'd spent together in London.

"How do you like that?" I said at one point. "Dimity the matchmaker."

Bill started at the sound of my voice. "What's that?"

I glanced up. "Sorry," I said, "but I just found out that Dimity introduced my mom to my dad."

Bill blinked a few times, then grinned. "You don't say."

"It's right here in black and white: '. . . that night in Berkeley Square when I introduced you to Joe.' I knew they had met during the war, but not that Dimity was behind it. Well, they were a great match."

"Do you believe in that sort of thing?" Bill asked.

"What, matchmaking?" I paused to consider. It wasn't something I'd given much thought to. "I guess there's nothing wrong with it. If you know the people well enough, if you think it might work—why not bring them together? What harm could it do?"

"None that I can think of," said Bill.

"Why? Has your father tried it?"

"No," he said, going back to his reading. "He'd consider it impertinent, bless him."

It must be the "desiccated aunts," I thought, the ones he'd mentioned that morning in the guest suite. Did they parade their favorite nephew before a bevy of suitable females? It might explain why his father thought he was shy around women. I felt a touch of pity for him, but the temptation to tease got the better of me. "Bill?"

"Yes?"

"Does your matchmaker consider you a tough assignment?"

He put down the letter he was reading and pushed his glasses up the bridge of his nose. "Why do you ask?"

"Well, you're not married yet. Do *you* have something against matchmaking?"

Bill tilted his head to one side, as though debating whether to joke or give me a straight answer. I was a little surprised when he chose the latter.

"Not at all," he said. "There have been a few romances along the way, but nothing that stuck. It's a matter of time as much as anything. First college, then the Peace Corps—"

"You were in the Peace Corps?" I was impressed.

"For four years. I re-upped twice. Then came law school, then learning the ropes at the firm. No breaks for the son of the house, I'm afraid. And my job entails a lot of traveling, which makes it difficult to maintain any sort of ongoing relationship. But now that you mention it, maybe I am a tough assignment." He held up a frayed cuff and shrugged. "Let's face it. I'm not movie star material."

"But I think you're—" I broke off midprotest, realizing that I was on the verge of telling him that he was more attractive than any movie star and that the women who had rejected him had probably been shallow, vain, and dumber than doorstops. "I think you're forgetting," I said carefully, "that you were busy establishing yourself in your career."

"Mmm, maybe that was part of it. Anything else you'd like to know?"

"No, no, I was just, uh, wondering. . . ." I returned to my reading, but a short time later, I couldn't help looking up again. "Bill?"

"Mmm?"

"What did you do in the Peace Corps?"

"I gave puppet shows," he replied, still concentrating on the letter in his hand.

"Puppet shows?"

He put the letter down. "Yes. I gave puppet shows. I was sent to Swaziland—that's the place in southern Africa, by the way, not the place with the Alps—to teach English and after two years of using more traditional teaching methods, I added puppet shows."

"What a great idea." My mother had tried the same thing in her classroom.

"They were a big hit, education and entertainment in one neat package. I ended up traveling around the country in a Land Rover, giving shows in schools, churches, kraals, anywhere they sent me." He lifted his hand and began to talk with it, as though it were a puppet. *"Sahnibonani beguneni."*

"What does that mean?" I asked, delighted.

"Roughly? 'Good evening, ladies and gentlemen.' That's about all the SiSwati I remember after all these years. Oh, and: *Ngee oot sanzi, Lori."*

"What's that?"

Bill smiled. "Let's get back to work, Lori."

**

The news about my parents' meeting was the biggest revelation, but even the small ones fascinated me. After demobilizing, Dimity had remained in London: busy, happy, and unexpectedly up to her elbows in children.

> *My Dearest Beth,*
>
> *You will think me quite mad, for I have decided not to return to Finch. Moreover, I have taken off one uniform and put on another. No, I have not taken holy orders—perish the thought!—but I have signed on with Leslie Gordon at Starling House, a quite sacred place in its own right.*
>
> *I believe I told you of my friend, Pearl Ripley. She married an airman, young Brian Ripley, who was killed in the Battle of Britain. She was a bride one day, a widow the next, and a mother nine months later. I once questioned the wisdom of wartime marriages— even you waited until after the Armistice to marry Joe*

—but I have since come to admire Pearl greatly for making what I now feel was a very courageous decision. Surely Brian was fortified and comforted as he went into battle, knowing that he was so dearly loved.

Starling House is meant to help women like Pearl, war-widows struggling to support young children on a pittance of a pension. The kiddies stay there while their mothers work. Isn't it a splendid idea? Leslie asked only for a donation, and I have made one, but I think I have more to give these little ones than pounds sterling.

To be frank, I am not cut out to be a lady of leisure. Although I now have the means, I lack the experience. In fact, it sounds like very hard work. I suppose I could sit with the Pym sisters knitting socks all day, but I'd much sooner change nappies and tell stories and give these brave women some peace of mind.

Mad I may be, but I think it a useful sort of madness, a sort you understand quite well, since you suffer from similar delusions.

My mother's "useful sort of madness" had sent her back to college in pursuit of a degree in education. Despite exams, term papers, and long hours at the library, she managed to write at least twice a month.

D,

Midterms! Yoicks! And you thought D day was a big deal!

I can't tell you how much I'm enjoying all of this. Joe says that I'm regressing and I do hope he's right. After all of those gray years in London, I think I've earned a second childhood, don't you?

I've put student teaching on hold while I study. I'm not happy about it, but there are only so many hours in the day and I have to spend most of them in the library. I miss the day-to-day contact with kids, though. Makes me wonder when on earth Joe and I are going to have our own. We're still trying, but nothing seems to work, up to and including the garlic you forwarded from the Pyms. Thank them for me, will you? And just between you and me—how would a pair of spinsters be acquainted with the secret to fertility?

The two friends talked about everything that touched their lives. As my mother grew increasingly despondent over the lack of a family of her own, Dimity wrote to her about "Mrs. Bedelia Farnham, the greengrocer's wife, who delivered healthy triplets—Amelia, Cecelia, and Cordelia, my dear, if you will credit it—shortly after her forty-third birthday" and exhorted her not to lose hope. When Dimity wondered how she could bear to see another war-torn family, my mother responded with characteristic common sense:

Does the word "vacation" mean anything to you? How about "holiday"? I've copied the dictionary defi-nitions on a separate sheet of paper, in case you have trouble remembering. Take one, and write me when you get back.

I'm serious, Dimity. It's no good, wearing yourself down like this. It's not good for you and it's certainly not good for the children. I know I'm stating the ob-vious, but sometimes the obvious needs to be stated.

So take some time off. Paddle your feet in a brook. Read a pile of books and eat apples all day. Remind yourself that there's joy in the world as well as sad-ness. Then go back to work and remind the kids.

*
**

I fixed sandwiches for a late afternoon lunch, and Bill's dis-appeared so rapidly that I thought I had scored another culinary coup, until he happened to mention that he hadn't had any breakfast. I hastily made him another, a thick slab of roast beef on grainy brown bread, and sent him into the living room to eat it, ordering him to leave me alone in the kitchen until I called for him. The letters could wait. It was time for me to heed Dimity's advice and start making amends.

In no time at all, I produced a truly scrumptious double batch of oatmeal cookies. I was so proud that I was tempted to go upstairs and fetch my camera, to record the historic moment. It sounds foolish, I know, but if you'd burned as many hard-boiled eggs as I had, you'd understand.

I could almost hear my mother humming in the warm, cinnamon-scented air, and I hoped Dimity was around to enjoy it, but the best moment came when Bill took his first bite. A look of utter bliss came to his face and he closed his eyes to concentrate on chewing. Then, without saying a word, he picked up the cookie jar and carried it back with him to the study.

**
**

Later that evening, I tried my hand at onion soup and a quiche lorraine, and Bill seemed more than happy to test the results. He had three helpings of the quiche. Sometime after we'd finished our dinner break and gone back to our reading, he leaned forward and held a letter out to me. "Here's one I think you should read." He shook his head when I looked up expectantly. "Nothing to do with Dimity."

"Go ahead and read it aloud, then," I said.

"I think you'll want to read this one to yourself. Here, take it."

"But what's so special about—"

"The date, Lori. Look at the date."

The letter he was holding had been written by my mother on the day after my birth. I took it from him, bent low over the page, and inhaled the words.

D,

She's here! *and she's a* girl! *We got your cable, so I know you got ours, but I couldn't wait to write you a proper letter. Eight pounds twelve ounces, eighteen inches long, with a fuzz of dark hair, and ten fingers and ten toes, which I count every time she's within reach. Since you wouldn't allow us to use Dimity—I repeat, it is* not *an old-fashioned name!—we've named her Lori Elizabeth, after Joe's mom and me. She has my mouth and Joe's eyes and I don't know whose ears she has, but she has two of them and they're* perfect.

We got your package, too. What can I say? You are a whiz with a needle, but you know that already. How about this: Lori took one look at that bunny's face and grinned her first grin. Love at first sight if I ever saw it. He reminds Joe of Reginald Lawrence—remember him? that sweet, rabbit-faced lieutenant?—so guess what we've named him. On behalf of my beautiful baby girl: Thank you!

Gotta run. It's chow time for little Lori and I'm the mess hall. I'll write again as soon as I'm home. In the meantime, here's a picture of my darling. Joe snapped it with the Brownie and it's a little out of focus, but so was he at the time. Yes, he's still working too hard, and yes, he still smokes like a chimney—the nurses made him open a window in the waiting room!

Are we proud parents? Silly question!

> *All my love,*
> *Beth*

The rain slashed the windowpanes as the echoes of my mother's voice faded into the distance. Staring into the fire, I examined my feelings gingerly, the way you explore a cavity with your tongue.

"Isn't it great?" Bill said. "She sounds so happy. It's just blazing off the page. I especially like the part about Reginald. We'll have to go through your mother's photographs when we're back in Boston. Maybe we'll find a picture of the rabbity Lieutenant Lawrence . . ." Bill's voice trailed off.

I glanced at him. "You're right, this is a wonderful find. I never knew that about Reginald."

Bill looked at me for a moment, then got up and cleared the ottoman of boxes. He pushed it over next to my chair and sat on it, waiting for me to speak. I had the feeling that he would wait patiently for hours, if that was how long it took me to find the words.

I pointed to the closing lines of the letter. "My father died of a stroke. He worked too hard, he smoked too many cigarettes. . . ." I shrank from an irony I had been shrinking from my whole life: a man who had survived Omaha Beach had been killed by a briefcase and a bad habit.

"I'm sorry," said Bill.

"I never knew him," I went on. "I was only four months old when he died, and I never . . . asked her about it." I knew so many things about my mother. I knew her favorite color, her shoe size, her thoughts on the French Revolution, but about this central experience in her life I knew next to nothing. Of all the things I had never asked her, this was the one I regretted most. "When she spoke of my father, she spoke of his life, not his death." I brushed a hand across the letter. "I suppose she thought it wouldn't help to dwell on it."

Bill nodded slowly. Then, his eyes fixed on the fire, he asked, "How can you avoid dwelling in the past when the past dwells in you?" He sighed deeply, still gazing into the flames. "Dimity said it to me one night while we were staying with her, when I told her about the way the boys at school had acted. She disapproved. She told me that the past was a part of me, and that trying to avoid it was like trying to avoid my arm or my leg. I could do it, yes, but it would make a cripple of me." Turning to me, he said, "I don't think your mother was a cripple, was she?"

"No," I said, "but I don't know how she managed to get over this." I held up the letter. "Here, she's on top of the world, and four months later her world collapsed. How does anyone get over something like that?"

"Would you mind another quotation?" Bill asked.

"From Dimity?"

"It's something else she said that night. She told me that losing someone you love isn't something you get over—or under or around. There are no shortcuts. It's something you go *through*, and you have to go through all of it, and everyone goes through it differently. I don't know how your mother did it, but I do know that you're wrong when you say that her world collapsed. She still had you—"

"A lot of good I was to her," I mumbled.

"And she still had Dimity. Look around you. What do you see?"

"Her letters." I felt my spirits begin to lift. "Oh, Bill, how could I be so stupid? Dimity must have been her lifeline."

"I can't think of a better person to turn to at a time like that," Bill agreed. He reached over and pulled a box onto his lap. "Let's go on reading. We'll soon find out if I'm right."

**

It was nearing midnight when I put the letters aside, rose to my feet, and left the study, too upset to speak. There had been no phone call from the Harrises, and we had yet to find the unsent letter we were searching for, but that wasn't what bothered me. Bill had warned me of the dangers of digging into the past and I had expected to learn some disturbing truths about Dimity—but I had not expected to learn them about my mother.

Bill caught up with me in the solarium. I stood with my hands on the back of a wrought-iron chair, and Bill hovered behind me, an arm's length away. It was pitch-dark outside and the rain was still falling steadily.

"I know it's not what we expected, Lori, but—"

"It doesn't make sense." My hands tightened on the wrought iron. "My mother wasn't like that."

For four months after the joyful announcement of my birth, the letters from my mother had continued without interruption. Then they stopped cold. She sent one short note informing Dimity of my father's death, and that was it. For three years, not a Christmas card, not a birthday greeting, not so much as a postcard came from my mother. When I realized what was happening, I went back to that brief note in disbelief—I could almost hear the portcullis crashing down, could almost see my mother retreating behind walls of sorrow and self-absorption.

Dimity, on the other hand, had continued to write. And write. And write. For months on end, without response, Dimity sent off at least a letter a week—and I don't mean short, slapdash notes, but real letters: long, lively missives written —it seemed to me—solely for the purpose of letting my mother know that she was not alone.

And how did my mother respond to this outpouring of affection? With silence.

"She wasn't like that," I insisted. "She didn't crawl in a hole when things went wrong. She was strong; she faced things."

"Dimity said that everyone goes through it in their own way. Maybe your mother had to go through it alone."

"But that's why it doesn't make sense. She didn't have to go through it alone. She didn't *believe* in going through things alone. She . . ." Aching for her, I looked out into the darkness, searching for the words that would explain it all to Bill. "She was a schoolteacher, the kind whose door was always open. Her students used to come back to visit her all the time, no matter how old they got. You should have seen her funeral —the church wasn't big enough to hold everyone, and they all stood up and talked about her, told how they wouldn't be where they were if it hadn't been for her." A faint scent of lilacs took me back to that day. "Do you know the one thing they all remembered? That they could bring their problems to her, and she would *listen* to them, really listen, with her heart wide open. If anyone knew how important it was to reach out, it was my mother. So you tell me why, for three of the worst years in her life, she didn't—" I choked on the lump in my throat, swallowed hard, and went on. "And what about Dimity—left out in the cold for all those years?"

"I think Dimity must have understood," said Bill.

"Well, I don't," I said. "I keep thinking of my mom all alone with a crying baby, and the bill collectors banging on the door. There wasn't any Starling House for her, but she could have turned to Dimity." I rubbed my forehead. "God, I never knew."

"Lori," said Bill, "it's late, and a lot has happened to you today. Why don't you go to bed? We can go on with the correspondence tomorrow, when we're fresh."

"I don't know if I want to go on with it."

"Then I'll go on with it for you," Bill said soothingly. "For now, you just try to get some rest, okay? I'll see you in the morning."

I was too tired to protest, but I lay awake late into the night nonetheless, curled forlornly under Meg's blanket, listening to the wind howl mournfully across the rain-slicked slates. I was haunted by my mother's silence, afraid to imagine the kind of pain that would bring it on. The letters had thrown me into a world of hurt I was not prepared to face.

16

As I gazed through the living room windows the following morning, I began to suspect that some local druid had objected to my arrival and conjured this unceasing rain to drive me away. The weather was not what anyone would call auspicious. The storm had continued almost without pause throughout the night and seemed likely, from the look of it, to continue into the next century. As a rule I was very fond of rain, but this kind of endless, cold, driving downpour was enough to put me off the stuff for the rest of my life. Dispirited, I went over to light the fire, hoping that a cheerful blaze would dispel the gloom.

The bedside phone had awakened me bright and early. It had been Emma, returning my calls. She and Derek hadn't gotten home from the vicarage until after midnight, and Derek had returned first thing in the morning to put the finishing touches on his repairs. She asked me to come over later that morning, after she'd dropped Peter and Nell off at school. Bill and I had breakfast, then filled a manila envelope with the items I wanted to show to Emma: the journal, the photo, my mother's letter to me. I threw in the topo map for the heck of it, and Reginald sat atop the envelope, ready to testify on my behalf. Bill stayed in the study to continue reading, while I filled a blue ceramic bowl with oatmeal cookies for the Harrises and killed time watching the storm. I had just finished lighting the fire when Bill called me into the study.

He was sitting on the desk when I came in. "It's occurred to me," he said, "that we haven't asked Dimity about the missing album."

"Why bother?" I replied. "I doubt that she'll discuss anything related to her problem."

"But we don't know for sure if the album's related to her problem," Bill pointed out. "If she evades the question, however . . ." He nodded toward the manila envelope. "It's worth a try."

I took out the journal and opened it to a blank page. "Dimity?" I said. "Hello? It's me, Lori. Do you have a minute?"

I always have time for you, my dear.

Wide-eyed, I glanced at Bill and nodded. "So, uh, how are you?"

As well as can be expected.

"You know, Dimity, Bill and I have been trying to figure out why you're . . . stuck wherever you are, instead of moving on to where you're supposed to be."

It is a very long story.

"I always have time for you, Dimity."

And I would prefer not to discuss it.

"Come on, Dimity, we want to help, but we don't know where to begin. Couldn't you just give us a hint? Like about the photo albums, for instance—"

Lori, I must insist that you drop this line of inquiry.

"You know me too well to think that I'll do that, Dimity."

In that case

Nothing more appeared on the page. I looked up at Bill and shook my head.

"Try again," he said.

I tried again, several times, but not another word was added. Finally I closed the book and put it back in the envelope.

"I guess that answers our question," said Bill.

"Or raises a few more," I said.

"Such as?"

"What if we've gone too far? What if Dimity's gone for good?"

Bill had nothing to say to that. With a pensive sigh, I left him to his reading. I brought Reginald, the manila envelope, and the bowl of cookies to the living room, and as I approached the hall closet to get my jacket, the doorbell rang.

"I'll get it," I called, and went to open the door, wondering who would come visiting on such an awful day.

Evan Fleischer was standing on my doorstep. He shook his greasy locks from his shoulders and sniffed. "Nice little place you have here," he said. "It's a shame about the modernization, but I'm sure that doesn't bother you."

Stunned, I took an involuntary step backward. The door flew past me and slammed in his face. If I'd had any presence of mind, I would have left it that way, but my politeness reflexes kicked in and I opened it again without thinking.

"Strong winds today," he commented as he brushed by me to inspect the hallway. "Yes, yes, very nice. Plebeian, but it suits you. Ooh." He shivered. "Drafty, though."

He was right. The indoor temperature had plummeted. I was at a loss to explain how that had happened, but I hoped against hope that the chill would drive Evan away.

Fat chance.

"I'll keep my coat on, since your heating is so primitive," he said, striding into the living room.

"You'll get everything wet," I protested.

"For heaven's sake, Lori, it's only water." Still bundled up in his sopping wet pseudo-Burberry, he sat and held his hands to the fire.

I stood poised in the doorway for a moment, decided not to hit him over the head with the poker, then marched to the study, which was as toasty as ever. Bill looked up as I entered. "I'll be in in a minute," he said.

"I think your services are required immediately, Mr. Facilitator. Your guest has arrived and I have to leave."

He looked perplexed for a moment, and then the penny dropped. "Evan?"

"Live and in person and dripping all over the—Good Lord, what's he done now?" Loud noises from the living room brought me running. The room was filled with smoke, and Evan was choking and coughing and banging at the windows, trying to get them open.

"Evan, you idiot, stop it!" I shouted. "If you break my windows I'll break your neck!"

I elbowed him aside to open the windows, and the smoke dissipated rapidly. Evan collapsed in a chair, panting and sputtering, while I checked the flue in the fireplace. It was closed. I opened it, then eyed Evan suspiciously.

"Were you messing around with the fireplace?" I demanded.

"I was not," he gasped indignantly. "I was sitting quietly when the room began to fill with smoke. The damned chimney is obviously defective. You should have it replaced at once. I could have suffocated."

"Welcome, Dr. Fleischer." Bill was standing in the living room doorway, smiling weakly. "So you've taken me up on my invitation. Lori said you might."

The arrogant smirk returned to Evan's face. "I wouldn't miss a chance to visit this part of England," he said. "I am, of course, intimately familiar with it. I once wrote a monograph on the Woolstaplers' Hall in Chipping Campden. It was never published—academic publishing is so political, so corrupt—but I should be only too happy to summarize it for you."

"I'd love to hear it," said Bill, "but unfortunately, you've come at a bad time. I'm afraid that Lori was just about to—"

"This piece is quite nice, actually," said Evan, running his fingers along the smooth leg of the table beside his chair. "A Twirley, unless I'm very much mistaken."

"Evan," I said, backing toward the hall, "I really have to be—"

"Aha," said Evan, now on his knees and peering closely at the bottom of the table. "There's his signature, a whirligig, you can see it quite clearly. Nice. Very nice. Augustus Twirley carved only twenty-seven of these tables, and thirteen of them are known to have been destroyed in fires."

"Fascinating," I said, although I was convinced that he was making it up as he went along.

"Not at all." Evan rose, brushed his palms lightly together, and seated himself once more. "Knowledge is a gift that must be given freely. I dare say you knew nothing of the treasure lying under your own nose." He sighed wistfully as he helped himself to a cookie from the bowl I'd left on the table. "It is my considered opinion that Americans have become blind to quality." He was about to dispense more pearls of wisdom when he bit into his cookie and let out a yelp of agony.

"Evan, what's wrong?" I asked in alarm.

"My toof!" he howled, grimacing horribly and gripping the front of his face with both hands. "I broke a toof!"

I raised a hand to my own jaw. If there is anyone for whom I have complete and instantaneous sympathy, it is someone with a broken tooth. The first time I broke one, I was a twenty-six-year-old, independent, and—in most other ways—mature human being, but I was so traumatized that I called my mother in tears, long-distance, right after it happened. I was shocked, therefore, to find myself suppressing a smile at Evan's misfortune.

I was also just plain shocked. Bill and I had both sampled the cookies and none had caused bodily harm. I took one from the bowl and bit into it cautiously. It contained nothing more tooth-threatening than some chewy raisins.

"Would you like me to call a local dentist?" Bill was saying. "It's a little early, but I'm sure—"

"Sod the local dentist!" Evan roared. "No country clown is going to touch a tooth of mine. I'm going back to London. I should never have left civilization in the first place." He pitched the remnants of his cookie into the fireplace and stalked to the front door. Another gust of wind caught it as he crossed the threshold and I think it may have helped hasten his departure with a gentle shove as it slammed shut.

I held my breath until I heard his car speed down the road, then turned to Bill, who was sitting on the couch, looking dumbfounded.

"What did you do to the cookies?" I asked.

"I was about to ask you the same thing."

We stared at each other, then spoke in one voice: "Dimity."

I shook my head, torn between pity and relief. "Poor Evan. Well, she tried to freeze him out, then smoke him out, but he wouldn't pay attention."

"Attending to others doesn't seem to be one of Dr. Fleischer's strong points. All the same, we owe him a debt of gratitude. Thanks to him, we know that Dimity hasn't left us."

"But she still won't talk to us." I fetched my jacket and an umbrella from the hall, then gathered up Reginald, the cookies, and the manila envelope. "Not about the album, at least, and that makes me more determined than ever to find it. You're sure you don't want to come along?"

"One of us should be here in case Father calls," said Bill, opening the door. "Besides, I'm making good progress with the correspondence. Who knows what the next letter will bring?"

*
**

The entrance to the Harrises' drive was less than a mile from the cottage, but the drive itself was a good half mile long, curving between rows of azalea bushes, then skirting the edge of a broad expanse of lawn. Ahead of me and to the left was what appeared to be a very soggy vegetable garden, while to the right stood a rambling three-story farmhouse built of the same honey-colored stone as the cottage. Low outbuildings clustered behind it, and the drive led into an open gravel yard littered with the debris of Derek's profession: sawhorses, a sandpile, bricks, fieldstones, ladders. As I turned off the ignition, raucous barking sounded from the house, and a moment later Emma appeared on the doorstep, wearing a rose-colored corduroy skirt and a pale green cowl-neck sweater. Her long hair billowed behind her as she came to welcome me, sheltered from the storm by a striped golf umbrella.

Clambering out of the car, I began to deliver a string of apologies for my cool reaction to her warning about Dimity, but she stopped me. "No need for that," she said, taking charge of Reginald. "I didn't accept it at first, either."

I cast an admiring glance at my surroundings. "This is an amazing place."

"Six bedrooms and four baths in the main house." Emma raised a hand to indicate the other buildings. "My potting shed, Derek's workshop, the children's lab—much safer to have it at a distance—the garage, and general storage. You never know what you'll find in there." A satellite dish lent an incongruous touch of modernity to the shingled roof of the children's lab, and a two-foot-tall stone gargoyle leered demonically from the half-open door of the storage building. When we reached the doorstep of the main house, Emma stopped. "Do you like dogs?"

"Very much."

"Good. We couldn't have heard ourselves speak if I'd had to lock up Ham. He'll calm down once he's finished saying hello." The low doorway led into a rectangular room with a flagstone floor, where we were greeted by an ebullient black Labrador retriever. He wagged his tail, grinned, and barked exuberantly, while I scratched his ears and told him what a handsome hound he was.

"My daughter found him when he was still a puppy," Emma explained, "trussed up and tossed on the side of the road not far from here. She brought him home, we nursed him back to health, and she named him after her favorite tragic hero."

"Hamlet?" I hazarded.

"As Nell is fond of pointing out, he always wears black." Emma handed Reginald back to me, then put our umbrellas in a crowded stand beside the door and hung my jacket on a row of pegs with many others. Wellington boots, hiking boots, sneakers, and clogs lay in a jumble beneath a wooden church pew that stood against the far wall, and fishing poles, walking sticks, and four battered tennis rackets leaned in one corner. "We call this the mudroom, for obvious reasons. Come into the kitchen. I've just filled the pot."

A brightly colored braided rug covered most of the kitchen floor, burgeoning herb plants trailed over the windowsills, and copper pots hung on hooks near the stove. From a crowded shelf on a tall dresser, Emma took cups, saucers, and a hand-labeled mason jar, placing them beside the teapot on the refectory table in the center of the room. Ham leaned against my leg adoringly as I sat in one of the rush-bottom chairs.

"Oh, Ham, stop flirting." Emma ordered the dog to his blanket by the stove, then sat across from me. Her eyes lit up when I presented her with the bowl of oatmeal cookies. "Derek and the children will be so pleased. They've been after me to make some, but I simply haven't had the time. You don't mind if we talk in here, do you?"

"I can't think of a better place."

Emma handed me a steaming cup of tea, then pushed the mason jar toward me. "Raspberry jam I put up last summer. Try some in your tea."

I stirred in a liberal dollop, took a sip, and sighed with

pleasure. "Yum. Now, about our mutual friend. Would you like me to go first?"

Emma smiled. "Derek says that my orderly mind drives him crazy sometimes and right now I understand what he means. I can hardly wait to hear what's happened to you, but . . ."

"First things first," I said.

"I'm afraid so. And I'm terrible at making long stories short."

"Take all the time you need," I said. "I'm in no hurry."

Emma gathered her thoughts, then leaned forward on her elbows. "Derek and I moved to Finch five years ago. Although we knew of Dimity through a mutual acquaintance, we had met her only in passing. It didn't take us long to learn more about her, though. According to the baker, she had been born and raised in the cottage. According to the vicar, she continued to live there after her parents had died. And according to the greengrocer, she joined up the day war was declared, and served in London until the Armistice.

"That was when Dimity came into her inheritance. It was left to her—according to everyone—by a distant relative, and the money enabled her to return to London, purchase her town house, and become involved in charity work. After that, she rarely returned to the cottage. It was a simple country cottage then: two up, two down, no electricity, and rudimentary plumbing. It must have seemed fairly primitive compared to her digs in London.

"At any rate, I was clipping the azaleas one day when Dimity's Bentley pulled into our drive. Derek had done some restoration work on the church in Finch, so Dimity knew of his skill as a builder, and she'd come to ask him to do some work on the cottage. Derek thought she meant a simple renovation and he jumped at the chance." Emma laughed. "As you can tell, he landed up to his chin.

"Dimity's 'simple renovation' lasted for two years. Derek had to turn down scores of other jobs, and I cut way back on my consulting work in order to do what I love best. Dimity gave me a free hand with everything except the front garden."

So that it would match the cottage in the story, I mused silently, offering Emma another cookie and taking one for myself.

"But the rest was mine," Emma continued, "and it was heaven. Derek was as happy as I was. He loved the challenge Dimity threw at him: rebuild the cottage, expand it, update it, but keep its soul intact. It was the biggest project he'd ever undertaken and it seemed to get bigger as he went along. Dimity would stop by once a month, each time with another suggestion to make. Derek began referring to the cottage as our own private Winchester House.

"But during that whole time, we never knew why Dimity was doing it. We thought at first she might move in permanently, but she just shook her head when we mentioned it. We doubted that she'd ever sell it, so what was the point? There it stood, like . . . like Sleeping Beauty, waiting for her handsome . . . Lori? Are you okay?"

I finished choking on my cookie and took a swallow of tea. "Yes, of course. Please, go on."

"Just before Dimity died, we ran into all sorts of problems with the project. Building materials weren't delivered on time, the ones that arrived were substandard, and some of the workmen decided to disappear when the weather turned ugly. It drove Derek mad. Dimity was quite ill by then and he had his heart set on finishing the work before she died. Dimity called it the ultimate deadline." Emma began to smile, then stopped and blushed self-consciously. "I'm sorry. That must seem heartless. But if you'd known Dimity . . ."

"I can imagine," I said. "It's a good line. I'll bet she thought it was funny."

"She had a wonderful sense of humor. And she never worried about whether the cottage would be finished in time or not. She arranged it so that Bill's father would oversee the financing of the renovation after her death and she told Derek to do the best possible job and not to worry—if she didn't see it then, she'd see it . . . later."

"Little did you know. . . ." I murmured.

Emma nodded. "Her attitude helped Derek cope with the fact that she died before the renovation was complete. But that's not all that helped." Emma rested her chin on her hand, a puzzled expression on her face. "We didn't notice it at first, but gradually everything about the project began falling into place. Derek said he didn't think he could hit his thumb with a hammer if he tried. And the garden!" Her voice was filled with wonder. "I'd drop a seed on the ground and I could almost watch it take root. But, as I said, we didn't notice. We just went along from day to day, feeling very proud of our progress.

"Which may explain why the accident happened. Or rather—didn't happen. Perhaps we had become overconfident and careless. Whatever the reason, Derek dropped his welding torch in a pile of paint-soaked rags. They should have gone up in smoke and taken the cottage with them, and Derek, too." She tightened her hold on her teacup. "But nothing happened! Nothing. Derek ran out into the garden to find me and I went back inside with him to see. There wasn't so much as a scorch mark anywhere.

"We were both shaken up, and as we sat there that afternoon, we began to remember all sorts of things that we had dismissed as they were happening, little things—warped boards that straightened overnight, tools that were always at hand when we needed them, boxes of nails that never seemed to run out—all sorts of things that we could explain in all sorts of ways, except when we added them up. When we did that, we had to admit that, as impossible as it seemed, something—or someone—was . . . helping us. I thought it sounded preposterous, until Derek reminded me of an even stranger experience we'd had in an old chapel in Cornwall. In the end, I was forced to agree that something extraordinary was taking place."

It sounded so familiar; all the little, easily explained happenings that added up to something inexplicable. I realized that I was sitting there with my mouth hanging open, so I closed it, then said, "Well, at least she's a friendly ghost."

Emma laughed. "Yes, we were pretty sure we knew who was helping, but we didn't know why."

"Until Bill's father called you."

"Almost a year after Dimity died, the cottage was as complete as we could make it. Soon after that, Mr. Willis contacted us to ask us to get it ready." Emma stood and rummaged through another shelf on the dresser until she found a tin tea caddy similar to the one at the cottage. Prying off the lid, she sat down again. "The day before you arrived, I went over to the cottage to stock the pantry. In the middle of the kitchen table I found this." She pulled from the caddy a single piece of pale blue stationery. The note read: *Thank you.* By then I knew the handwriting as well as I knew my own.

"I can see now why you wanted to warn me," I said.

Emma put the note back in the caddy and returned the caddy to the shelf, giving me a sidelong look. "Our motives weren't entirely selfless. If all of that had happened to the bit players, we couldn't wait to see what would happen to the star. I take it that there have been further developments?"

"You could say that." I reached for the manila envelope.

*
**

Because of her previous experiences, Emma took the story of Reginald and the journal in stride. She was far more intrigued by my mother's account of Dimity's collapse.

"That's a new one on me," she said. "Dimity never breathed a word about it to us, and if anyone in Finch knew of it, I'm sure we would have heard by now. As for the location of the clearing...I think I may be able to help you there. I discovered orienteering when I moved to England. It's taught me the value of recognizing landmarks." She noticed my blank expression and explained, "It's a kind of cross-country race, using a map and compass."

"Is that what Derek meant when he said you were always off roaming the countryside?" I asked.

"I'm afraid my husband doesn't share my enthusiasm for the sport," she replied. "But Peter and Nell and I belong to a club in Bath. It frequently holds meets in this area." She pointed to one of the distant hills in the photograph. "It's hard to say for sure—places like this change so much over the years—but I think . . . I think that's the ridge Peter fell from last summer. No damage done, but it took a while to get him back up to the top. We came in last that day. Let me get some of my maps and—"

"Will this do?" I offered her the topographic map.

"Oh, yes, that will do nicely," said Emma. "Now, let me see. . . ." Her eyes darted back and forth from the photo to the map, as her finger moved along the curving lines. "They have contests like this in the orienteering magazines," she commented. "I must say that I never expected to . . ." Her finger stopped. "I think . . . yes, that has to be it. I should have recognized it right away. It's much steeper and more heavily wooded than most of the hills around here. It's called Pouter's Hill."

"It's right behind the cottage?"

"It's part of the estate," Emma explained. "I've never been up there myself, but it's the correct orientation to give you this view of those hills."

"Is that a path?" I asked, touching a broken line that ran up the hill.

"Yes," said Emma. "It starts on the other side of the brook out back." She pointed. "Here. From the way it's marked I'd say that it was pretty rough going. I wouldn't try it today if I were you."

"Just knowing where it is is enough for now." I started as a cold nose nudged my hand. Ham had come to claim a reward for his good behavior and he'd certainly earned it, curled patiently on his blanket while the humans had chattered end-lessly. "Hello, you sweet thing." I scratched behind his ears and glanced at Emma for permission to give him a treat from the table.

She shrugged. "Why should you be any different?" Ham approved of my oatmeal cookies, too, and wolfed down three of them before Emma called a halt. "Would you like to have a look round the place?" she offered.

By then I was glad of a chance to stretch my legs, and Ham was more than ready for a romp. He frisked at our heels as Emma took me from room to room. "The house was badly run-down when we bought it—a handyman's dream, as we say in the States, and therefore an ideal home for Derek. We've battled dry rot and mildew, but our worst enemy has been our predecessors' bad taste. Please don't ask me to describe the wallpaper we found in the parlor. It took us a whole summer to get rid of it."

The parlor walls were now plain whitewashed plaster, but the furnishings were eccentric, to put it mildly. The television sat atop an antique and worm-eaten altar, and the coffee table was an intricately carved wooden door overlaid with glass. A pair of elegant Louis XIV chairs faced a plain-as-dirt horsehair sofa, and a Chinese black-lacquered desk held a Victorian globe lamp, a brass pig, and a human skull. "Derek comes home with all sorts of things," Emma explained, "and we thought that the family room should be furnished by the family." She pointed to the television. "That's Derek's little joke, and the chairs were Nell's idea. I don't know who brought the skull in here, but Peter chose the desk."

The parlor reflected an active family life. It was littered with books and magazines, a forgotten shoe peeked out from under the couch, and a bowl half-filled with cherry pits graced a marquetry chest beneath the windows. When I saw the chest, I realized that I had forgotten to ask Emma about the missing photo album. When I put the question to her, she nodded thoughtfully.

"Nell was working on a project for school last spring, something about the role of women in the Second World War. Dimity loaned her some pictures for it, but I thought she'd returned them." She glanced toward the hall. "But let's make sure." With Ham galloping ahead, we went upstairs to what I thought was a second-floor bedroom. When I hesitated, Emma said reassuringly, "We're not about to invade my daughter's inner sanctum. This is the children's study."

In marked contrast to the parlor, the study was sparely furnished and orderly, with heavy-laden bookshelves, filing cabinets, and a pair of desks facing opposite walls. "I'm happy to say that the children take their schoolwork very seriously. They may make a shambles of the rest of the house, but they're neat as a pin in here. Nell's half is on the left." Emma scanned the bookshelves on that side of the room while I went through the drawers in her daughter's desk. Five minutes later, Emma came up trumps.

"Is this it?" She handed me a brown leather photograph album labeled *1939–1944*.

Too excited to speak, I nodded, then opened the album on Nell's desk and flipped rapidly through it. There were three or four pictures on each page, all of them affixed with black paste-on paper corners. Dimity had written brief captions beneath each of them: names, dates, places. I turned past pictures of Dimity posed alone or with groups of other women in military uniform, catching my breath when my mother's young face appeared in the crowd, until I came to the end.

"Damn," I muttered, "there's nothing missing."

"What do you mean?"

"If the photograph from Pouter's Hill came from this album, there'd be an empty space somewhere. But there isn't."

"Oh, I see." Emma half sat on the edge of the desk, her arms folded. "What a shame."

"No, wait. Maybe I'm just jumping the gun again." Sitting in Nell's chair, I switched on her desk lamp, reopened the album, and began going through it slowly, spreading it flat at every page. "I used to work with rare books, and one of the things I had to check for was vandalism—theft, really. There's a big market for old woodcuts and engravings."

"Like those framed botanical illustrations you see in antique stores?" Emma asked.

"Right. Some come from books that are too far gone to salvage, but some . . ." I turned the fifth page, spread it flat, and stopped. "Some are razored out of perfectly sound volumes. Like this." Emma bent low for a closer look as I thumbed a series of quarter-inch stubs, all that remained of twelve black pages.

"You don't think—" I began, but Emma shook her head decisively.

"Not Nell. Not in a million years."

I sighed, closed the album, and brought it back downstairs to the kitchen, where Reginald eyed me sympathetically and Emma looked once more at the photograph of the old oak tree.

"There's still hope," I said wistfully. "Maybe Bill's father will find the missing pages."

"I wonder who could have given this to your mother," Emma mused. "The couple we bought this place from passed away several years ago, and I don't know of any other . . . May I read your mother's description?"

I had told her about it earlier. Now I dug out the letter and handed it to her. She read it intently.

"But this doesn't say anything about a couple," she murmured. "It only says 'two of Dimity's neighbors.' 'Elderly . . . not terribly coherent . . .' " Suddenly she looked up, her eyes sparkling. "I think I know who you're looking for."

17

"The *Pym sisters?*" I exclaimed. "The sock-knitting Pym sisters? Are they still alive?"

"And kicking," Emma replied. "Decorously, of course." She went on to say that Ruth and Louise Pym were the identical twin daughters of a country parson. No one knew how old they were, not even the vicar, but most guesses placed them over the century mark. They had never married and had spent all of their lives in Finch. "I think they know more about what goes on in the village than most people would like to believe," Emma concluded. "I'm sure they're the ones who gave the photograph to your mother, and if they didn't, they'll know who did."

"How do I get to meet them?"

"Invite them to tea, of course. They'll be dying to meet you. I'll ask them for you, if you'd like."

"Yes, please. And you'll come, too, won't you?"

"Why don't I come early to help you set up?"

"That would be terrific."

Emma accompanied me to the mudroom, where I donned my jacket and gave Ham a last few pats.

"You'll have to come over when the sun is shining so I can show you the grounds." Emma held Ham's collar while I opened the door. "Be sure to let me know if you find out anything about those missing pages, and I'll call as soon as I've set things up with Ruth and Louise."

I unfurled my umbrella, then reached out to clasp Emma's hand. "Thank you. I don't know if you realize how much this means to me, but—"

"I think I do." She smiled. "Derek and I loved Dimity, too."

*
**

Bill was asleep in the study when I got back, his feet up on the ottoman, the date-filled notebook dangling from his fingertips. I woke him up by dropping Reginald in his lap, then sat on the ottoman and repeated everything Emma had told me that morning. I showed him the stubs in the photo album and he shared my disappointment, but agreed that Willis, Sr., might come through for us yet. He was delighted by the thought of meeting the Pym sisters, but the mention of tea made us both realize that we were ready for lunch. Greatly daring, I tried a spinach soufflé. It was flawless.

I couldn't bring myself to face the correspondence after lunch. The things I had learned about my mother had spooked me and I shied away from learning any more. True to his word, Bill soldiered on in silence while I returned scattered archive boxes to their proper places on the shelves. I was sitting at the desk, paging through the photo album when he spoke up.

"Listen!"

"I don't hear anything."

"That's what I mean. It's stopped raining!"

I could scarcely believe my ears. The steady drumming of the rain had been replaced by a stillness as heavy as Devonshire cream, and when I leaned forward to look through the windows I saw that a dense fog had settled in the storm's wake.

Bill closed the notebook and put it in his pocket, then walked over to have a look for himself. "Ah, the glories of English weather."

"I'll bet it's a big relief to Derek and the vicar. You think it'll clear by tomorrow?"

Bill shrugged. "Something tells me that we're going up that hill tomorrow even if it snows. You have many virtues, my dear Miss Shepherd, but patience is not one of them."

"I'm always halfway up the block before I know where I'm going," I admitted. "My mother used to say—" I broke off and looked out at the fog again. "I've been meaning to thank you, by the way."

"For what?"

"For believing me when I told you about the journal, even before you'd seen it with your own eyes. If you had come to me with a story like that, I would have—"

"Wait," said Bill. "Let me guess." He put his hands on his hips and his nose in the air and launched into what I feared was an accurate imitation of me at my indignant worst. " 'Bill,' " he said with a sniff. " 'What kind of a fool do you take me for? I don't believe in ghosts!' " He relaxed his stance, then raised an eyebrow. "Did I come close?"

"A direct hit." I winced. "I've been pretty impossible, haven't I?"

"No more than I," said Bill, "and you had a much better excuse. Finding yourself alone in a very strange situation, I can understand why you'd be on guard."

"On guard, maybe, but not hostile," I said. "I don't know—maybe I acted that way because I was confused. I didn't understand why you were being so . . . friendly." I dusted an invisible speck from the edge of the desk. "To tell you the truth, I still don't understand it."

"Can't you just accept it?" he asked.

"It's hard for me to accept something I don't understand," I said.

"Like your mother?" he said gently.

I planted my hands on my hips and shot a fiery glare in his direction, then realized what I looked like and sank back in the chair, deflated. "Yes, like my mother." I pointed to a picture in Dimity's album. "That's her. That's my mom."

Bill put one hand on the back of my chair and watched over my shoulder as I paged through the rest of the album. It was filled with pictures of my mother, in uniform and in civilian dress, her dark hair pulled back into a bun or braided in coils over her ears. "She wore it that way to keep her ears warm," I said. "She said that coal rationing in London during the war meant chilly offices. She had beautiful hair, long and silky. She used to let me brush it before I went to bed, and every night I prayed that my curls would straighten out and that I'd wake up in the morning with hair just like hers." I ran a hand through my unruly mop. "It didn't work."

"You have her mouth, though," said Bill. "You have her smile."

"Do I?" The very thought brought a smile to my lips. It had been a long time since I had talked to anyone about my mother, and now it seemed as though I couldn't stop talking about her. "Yes, I guess I do. See this one, where she's making a face? She used to make that same face at me, wrinkle her nose and cross her eyes, and it killed me every time, just laid me out flat, giggling. We used to have pillow fights, too, and she'd chase me all over the apartment until Mrs. Frankenberg banged on her ceiling with a broom handle. She'd made up this whole set of holidays. I was in kindergarten before I realized that no one else celebrated Chocolate Chip Tuesday." I turned the page. "Other mothers seemed like cardboard cutouts compared to her."

"Were you in any of her classes?" Bill asked.

"Never. She knew what kids could be like, so she enrolled me in another school entirely."

"PTA nights must have been tricky."

"Tricky? Try being in two places at once sometime. But she always managed to take care of everyone." I closed the album and sighed. "Everyone but herself."

"Lori—" Bill began, but the telephone cut him off. He snatched it up before it could ring again.

"Yes?" he said. "How are you, Father? Good, good. Of course I'm behaving myself. You don't think I want to go through *that* again, do you? Yes, in some ways she's very much like my old headmaster, though she lacks his little mustache, of course. . . . Yes, she's been hard at work on the correspondence." Bill glanced at me, then turned away. "I'm sorry, Father, but I don't think she can come to the phone right now. Would it be possible for you to call—"

"It's all right, Bill," I said. "I'll take it."

"One moment please, Father." Bill covered the receiver with his hand and said to me, "This can wait."

"I know. But I'm all right. I'll talk to him."

Bill gave me a measuring look, then spoke into the phone again. "You're in luck, Father. She's just come down. Here, I'll give you to her now. Yes, I will. Good to speak with you, too." He passed the phone to me.

"I'm so glad to have caught you, Miss Shepherd," said Willis, Sr. "I looked into the matter we discussed yesterday, as you requested. There are photographs with Miss Westwood's papers, but I regret to say that none of them were taken before the year 1951. They are official portraits, having to do with her role as founder of the Westwood Trust."

"That's a shame," I said, shaking my head at Bill, "but thanks for checking it out."

"You are most welcome. My son tells me that you've made great progress in your reading. Since that is the case, I wonder if I might trouble you to answer a few of Miss Westwood's questions?"

"Questions? Oh—you want to ask about the letters," I said,

tapping Bill's breast pocket. I had forgotten all about our question-and-answer sessions. If I'd been attending to my research, it wouldn't have mattered, but as it was, I was relieved to see Bill pull out his notebook and open it, poised for action. "Why, certainly, Mr. Willis. Fire away."

"The first concerns the letter in which Miss Westwood's cat is introduced. Have you run across it in your reading?"

"Aunt Dimity's cat?" I said. Bill consulted his notebook, ran his hand along the rows of archive boxes, and took one down. "Yes, that one appeared fairly early on."

"Excellent. Miss Westwood wished for you to explain to me the ways in which the original anecdote differs from the finished story. Would it be possible for you to do so?"

"The differences between the story and the letter," I said. "Let me see, now. . . ." Bill located the letter and handed it to me. I scanned it, then closed my eyes and ran through the story in my head. "The story is more detailed, for one thing. The letter doesn't mention the cat overturning the knitting basket or spilling the pot of ink on the window-seat cushions."

"Yes," said Willis, Sr., with an upward inflection that suggested I wasn't off the hook yet.

"And in the letter, the cat is named Attila. In the story, he's just called 'the cat.' "

"Very good," said Willis, Sr., but I got the feeling that I was still missing something. I put the letter down and tried to concentrate.

"In the story," I said, "the cat is a monster. Honestly, he has no redeeming qualities. He's played for laughs, but he's— Just a moment, please, Mr. Willis. *What?*" This last was to Bill, who was waving wildly to get my attention. He had opened the manuscript of the stories and was now pointing urgently to a page.

"Wrong answer," Bill whispered. "Look—right here."

Still holding my hand over the phone, I bent down to skim the page. It was the conclusion of the *Aunt Dimity's Cottage* and as I read through it I realized that I had gotten it wrong. Confused, and a little shaken, I straightened and spoke once more to Willis, Sr.

"That is to say . . ." I cleared my throat. "What I meant to say is that the cat has no redeeming qualities *at first*, but then, when you get to the end of the story—and the letter— he turns out to be kind of a sweetie. I mean, he still does all sorts of awful things and he still makes Dimity lose her temper, but he also amuses her, and he . . . he keeps her feet warm in bed."

"Thank you, Miss Shepherd," said Willis, Sr. "If you have no further commissions for me, I shall ring off. I have no wish to impede your progress."

"No, no further commissions. I'll talk to you again soon." I hung up the phone and looked down at the story. "I don't understand this. . . . I thought I remembered every word."

"Did Dimity change the ending?" Bill asked.

"No. That's what's so strange. As soon as I began reading it, the words came back to me, exactly as they're written on the page."

"So your memory slipped up a bit. I wouldn't worry about it."

But I was worried. I had been utterly convinced that I knew these stories inside out, but it seemed as though I had been wrong. I felt disoriented, bewildered. What else had I forgotten? I turned to the beginning of the manuscript and began reading.

18

We were fogbound for three days.

Emma swore she had never seen anything like it. She dropped by to let me know that Ruth and Louise Pym had accepted my invitation to come to tea on Saturday, and to reiterate her warning about Pouter's Hill. "It may not be Mount Everest," she said, "but it can be just as hazardous in weather like this." I confounded Bill's expectations by agreeing with her, and confounded them further by postponing the trip for another twenty-four hours after the sun finally appeared on the morning of the fourth day. I figured it wouldn't hurt to give the hill a chance to dry out—a path mired in mud would be no easier to climb than one covered in fog.

Our time wasn't wasted, though. Bill finished a first read-through of the correspondence and handed me a complete index of letters that related in one way or another to the Aunt Dimity stories. I was amazed at the speed with which he had completed his reading, but he shrugged it off, saying that it was a breeze compared to reading contract law.

He failed to find so much as a hint about Dimity's problem, but he set to work compiling a list of the people mentioned in her letters, everyone from Leslie Gordon of Starling House to Mrs. Farnham, the greengrocer's wife. If Ruth and Louise Pym didn't pan out, we would go down the list until we found someone who did.

While Bill was busy with the correspondence, I continued to pore over the manuscript, testing my memory against the written text. All too often, my memory fell short, and the ways in which it did were disturbing. I clearly remembered the very large man who had stepped on Aunt Dimity's foot at Harrod's, for example, but what happened next had somehow been edited from my recollection.

> *With profuse apologies, the very large man turned to Aunt Dimity and offered her his very large arm. "I am so very sorry, Madame," he said, in his very large voice, "but the crush is quite impossible today. Won't you take my arm? Perhaps we can make better progress if we face the crowds together."*

And Aunt Dimity did take his arm, and they did face the crowds together, and he escorted her to the train afterward and said a cheery farewell. And, although she left without the torch, the bright memory of the kind man lit the way home.

All I had remembered was her squashed foot. It was as though I had twisted the story to fit an entirely different view of the world, one which was harsher and more harrowing, and the same was true of almost every story in the collection. Disquieted, I said nothing of it to Bill, but I wondered—when had I grown so bitter?

When I had finished the stories, I made a careful search of the cottage, starting with the utility room and going from there through every cupboard, cabinet, drawer, and shelf, looking for the missing photographs, a personal diary, anything that might help us figure out what had happened to

Dimity. I went so far as to try tapping walls and floorboards to discover hidden recesses—a procedure that amused Bill no end—but my hunt proved fruitless.

I used Bill's index to cull from the correspondence all of the letters related to the stories, then used them as an excuse to drive into Bath. I told Bill I was going there to find a photocopy shop, and he agreed that it made sense to work with copies of the letters rather than the originals. It was a plausible story—I believed it, too, until I found myself browsing through the dress shops. That's when I decided that I had *really* gone to Bath to find something to wear to tea on Saturday. After all, it was my duty as a hostess to show up in something more presentable than jeans and a sweater.

So, after wandering through the splendid arcades and elegant crescents of the prettiest of Georgian towns, and after duly copying the letters, I did a little shopping. Maybe more than a little. Once I'd found the dress—a short-sleeved blue silk one, with a dainty floral print—I had to find the shoes to go with it, and then came all the bits in between, and by the time I was finished, I had squeezed my supply of personal cash dry. Why I didn't ask Bill for an advance was a question I avoided like the plague.

I tiptoed upstairs to stash my new clothes in the master bedroom, then floated innocently back down to the study, photocopies in hand. When Willis, Sr., called, late in the afternoon on the fourth day of our hiatus, I greeted him with the self-assurance of someone who knows that all the bases are covered.

"What's it to be this time, Mr. Willis? Do you want to know about Aunt Dimity's adventures at Harrod's? Or maybe we'll stick closer to home—Aunt Dimity setting aside a patch of garden for the rabbits."

"I am heartened to hear the enthusiasm in your voice, Miss Shepherd," said Willis, Sr. "It is reassuring to know that Miss Westwood's wishes are being carried forward with such zeal. My question, however, has to do with Aunt Dimity's experiences at the zoological gardens. Can you recount for me the original version of that story?"

"*Aunt Dimity Goes to the Zoo*," I murmured, leafing patiently through the photocopies. "Let's see. That should be here somewhere. . . ." But it wasn't. I double-checked Bill's index, but the end result was the same: there had been no reference to the zoo in any of Dimity's letters. Reluctantly, I admitted as much to Willis, Sr. "I don't know what to say. There doesn't seem to *be* an original version of that story."

"Precisely, Miss Shepherd. Thank you very much. Have you had an opportunity to look about you yet? Though your work comes first, of course."

"As a matter of·fact, we've been having some pretty wet weather since we arrived," I said. "It's cleared up a bit today, though, and I think I may get a chance tomorrow to use the map you gave me."

"I envy you, Miss Shepherd. England in the springtime is not a thing to miss. I would suggest a longer outing, but, alas, the work needs must be done." And with a pleasant good-bye, he hung up.

I put the receiver back in the cradle, then turned to Bill, who was still laboring over his list of names. "Why didn't Dimity write to my mother about the zoo?" I asked. "She talks about Berkeley Square and that rabbit-faced lieutenant, but in all her wartime chatter there's not one word about the zoo."

"Another uncomfortable memory?" he suggested. "Your mother did find her there, wandering about in a daze."

"As though whatever happened had happened recently," I said. "And Dimity went there . . . why?"

"Because she'd been happy there? Because it reminded her of better days?"

"What a shock it must have been to find it deserted, boarded up. . . . Yet she used it as the setting for one of her most cheerful stories." I riffled through the manuscript. "You know, Bill—Dimity said she wrote these for me and for my mother. I'm beginning to wonder if she wrote them for herself as well."

*
**

I rose early the next day, showered, then put on a pair of shorts, a T-shirt, heavy socks, and my hiking boots. I tied the arms of a sweater around my waist, in case the sun decided to hide its face again, and tucked the topographic map and the photograph in my back pocket. After a light breakfast, I was ready to face the great outdoors.

Bill, on the other hand, didn't look ready for anything more strenuous than a stroll across a putting green. He met me at nine o'clock in the solarium dressed in his usual tweed sport-coat, button-down oxford shirt, and corduroy trousers. The only thing out of the ordinary was the absence of a tie.

"Don't you have any other clothes?" I asked.

"You sound like my father," he said, shifting impatiently from foot to foot.

"You should listen to your father. But I'm not talking about matters of taste at the moment. I'm talking about survival." I looked doubtfully at his smooth-soled leather shoes. "Even a pair of sneakers would have better traction than those, and I think you're going to swelter in that jacket. Didn't you ever climb any hills when you were in Africa?"

"I had a Land Rover," Bill replied evenly. "Besides, Emma said there was a path."

"A rough path, in a roughly vertical direction." I poked the bulging canvas bag he'd slung over one shoulder. "What's in there?"

"A few necessities. Let's see. . . ." He opened the bag and rummaged through it. "A bottle of water, a loaf of bread, some cheese, a few bars of chocolate, the emergency lantern from the car, a throw rug, a trowel from the utility room, a camera—"

"We're not going on safari," I protested. "Trust me on this, Bill—that bag is going to weigh a ton before we get to the top. You're going to wish you'd left some of that stuff behind."

"You let me worry about that." Throwing open the solarium door, he strode out into the garden. "What a glorious day!"

He was right about that much, at least. It felt so good to be outside that I had to restrain myself from taking off at a run. A sheep meadow stretched green and serene to the west, the oak grove stood to the east, and ahead of us rose Pouter's Hill.

We crossed the sunken terrace of the back garden, then went up the stairs and through the gate in the gray stone wall and out into a grassy meadow. A graveled path led us between the pair of redbuds I had seen from the deck, to a willow-shaded brook that ran along the foot of the hill. The rustic bridge that spanned it practically pointed to an opening in the trees. We consulted the map, decided it was the path Emma had pointed out, and started up. I fell silent, saving my breath for the climb, but Bill spent enough for both of us.

"Birdsong, bluebells, and bracken," he rhapsodized. "Soft breezes to speed us on our way. Good, honest sweat, the heady scent of spring, and a winding path beneath our feet." He paused to take off his sportcoat and mop his brow. "Ah, Lori, it's wonderful to be alive."

"Right," I said, and kept on walking. As the good, honest sweat began cascading down Bill's face, his lyric interludes grew fewer and farther between. Halfway up, there was no sound from him but labored breathing, and he began muttering something about chainsaws when the pretty, soft little plants that had invaded the lower part of the path were replaced by great hulking thornbushes.

Three-quarters of the way up, I had mercy and took the shoulder bag, but by the time Bill had dragged his scratched and aching body up the last stretch of path, he was muddy, sweaty, and pooped and seemed to have a very clear idea of why it was called Pouter's Hill. He looked ready to sulk for a week.

Until we saw what lay before us.

The path had deposited us in a glade that overlooked the land beyond the hill. A wide valley opened out below, a patchwork of bright yellow and pale green and deep, rich brown; of freshly planted fields and newly turned earth crisscrossed with low stone walls and woven together by the meandering course of a stream which glinted silver in the sunlight. Sheep grazed on distant hillsides and a pair of hawks soared in wide, sweeping arcs across the flawless blue sky. It was the clearing in the photograph, come to life.

"My God," Bill murmured, his voice hushed with awe.

The scene below looked as though it hadn't changed for a hundred years. I sensed a stillness in the clearing, in myself, that I had never felt before, a tranquillity as timeless as the hills that rolled away to the horizon. I knew as surely as I knew my own name that whatever terrible thing had happened to Dimity hadn't happened here.

I took the photograph from my pocket and held it up, glancing at it as I moved slowly across the open space. "This is where the picture was taken," I said, coming to a halt.

Bill came over to where I was standing, looked down at the photograph, and pointed. "There's the ridge Emma's son fell from. And there's the tree."

The gnarled old oak tree stood by itself at the edge of the clearing, and we walked over, drawn to its cool circle of shade. I set the bag gently on the ground, not wishing to disturb the stillness, and Bill dropped his jacket on top of it, then gazed out over the land below. He turned, startled, when I uttered a soft cry.

A heart had been carved into the old tree. It was darkened with age, and the bark had grown back over some of it, but the initials it encircled were still plainly visible.

"*RM & D*—" I looked at Bill. "RM and Dimity Westwood. RM. Who's RM?"

"Someone who came up here with her," Bill guessed, "and took pictures to commemorate the day? Maybe someone who went to the zoo with her as well?" He traced the heart with a fingertip. "Clearly someone she loved."

I sank to the ground at the foot of the tree, and Bill sat beside me. He took the water bottle from the bag and we each had a drink. Pouring some water into his cupped hand, he cooled his face, then recapped the bottle and put it away. He sat with his back against the rough bark while I watched the hawks glide gracefully through the air.

Whose hand had carved that heart? What had happened to him? I closed my eyes and sensed . . . something. A dream of distant laughter, a memory of voices, a whisper of sweet words echoing down through time; the stillness at the center of a raging world.

"Lori?"

Bill's voice came to me from a long way off. Closer, much closer were those other voices, low voices murmuring, whispering, echoing, then snatched away by a roaring wind. I strained to hear them, but the roar of the wind was followed by silence. I felt a sadness, an intense longing, a sense of loss so powerful that it struck me like a blow. Who had come with Dimity to this still and peaceful place? Whom had she lost to the chaos that surrounded it?

Bill put his hand on my shoulder.

"A soldier," I said, unaware that I was speaking the words aloud. "RM was a soldier, a boy Dimity loved, who joined up early and was killed."

"Was he?" said Bill.

"I . . . I don't know." I opened my eyes and put a hand to my forehead, squinting against the sun's sudden glare. "I don't *know,* but I thought I heard . . . Did you hear it?"

"All I hear is the wind in the trees."

"The wind . . ." The wind of death had silenced the voices

in the clearing, as it would one day silence all voices. I rubbed my eyes and tried to shake the cobwebs from my mind.

"RM—a soldier?" Bill mused. "It makes sense. There was a lot of dying being done in those days, and a lot of hearts were broken. It would explain why Dimity was so shaken when your mother met her. It might even explain why she never married. But why would she get rid of the photos? If she loved him, why would she try to erase his memory?"

I ran my fingers along a twisted root, still touched by a sorrow that was, and was not, my own. "Sometimes it hurts to remember."

Bill let the words hang in the air for a moment. "It hurts worse to forget. Because you never really do, do you?"

"No," I murmured, "I suppose you don't."

"Dimity didn't. If we're guessing right, she may have tried to forget, but . . ." He looked up at the heart on the tree. "RM wouldn't leave her alone. She's still hurting, still in pain over . . . something that requires forgiveness. I don't understand why she would need to be forgiven for the death of someone she loved."

"I do," I said, in a voice so low that Bill had to lean forward to catch my words. "Sometimes you feel guilty after someone dies."

"For what?"

"For . . . all sorts of things. Things you did and things you didn't do."

"Like suspecting a perfectly innocent man of playing ghost?" said Bill archly.

"Something like that." I glanced at him, smiled briefly, then plucked a blade of grass and wound it around my finger. "My mother used to do that—say silly things to pull me out of a lousy mood."

"Did she?"

"She used to tease me all the time, the way you do. I was pretty impossible with her, too."

"I find that hard to believe," said Bill.

"It's true, though. She never said anything about it, but . . ." I shook my head. "I don't think I grew up to be the daughter she had in mind."

"Who do you think she had in mind?"

"Someone who wasn't stupid enough to study rare books, for one thing." I began to shred the blade of grass into tiny pieces. "Someone who could manage to keep a marriage together. Someone who wasn't so damned pigheaded. But I've always been that way. That's why . . ."

"That's why what?" coaxed Bill.

"Nothing." I tossed the bits of grass to the wind. "We're supposed to be talking about Dimity."

"We'll come back to Dimity. Right now we have to talk about something else. That's why *what*, Lori?"

"That's why . . ." The wind had ceased, and not a leaf was stirring. It was as though the old tree were holding its breath, waiting for me to go on. "She asked me to come home, Bill. She pleaded with me to come home. But I was too proud, too stubborn, too set on proving . . . I don't know what. And that's why . . . that's why I wasn't there when . . ."

Bill put his arms around me and pulled me to his side. He held me quietly, caressing my hair, then murmured softly, so softly that I could scarcely hear his words, "Did your mother ask you to come home for her sake or for yours?" I stiffened, but he tightened his hold, waiting for the tension to ease from my body before going on. "You shouldn't have stopped reading those letters when you did. You might have learned a thing or two." His fingers feathered lightly down my cheek. "You inherited more than your mother's mouth, you know. You have her chin, too, and it's a very determined one. That's how your mother described it, at any rate. I don't recall her ever using the word 'pigheaded.' 'As strong-willed as I am,' were the words she used."

I shook my head in protest, but Bill continued on, regardless.

"Do you think your mother joined the army because it was

a good career move? Do you think she sat down and weighed the pros and cons? She didn't, Lori. She saw the war as a grand, romantic adventure, and she saw the same romantic streak in you. Why else would you study something as impractical as old books? She didn't think you were foolish, though. She would've supported anything you did, as long as you were following your heart. You know that, don't you?

"As for your marriage—she understood that, too. She had doubts about it from the beginning, and she was proud of you for discovering your mistake. Yes, she wanted you to come home then, but it was because you seemed lost. She thought *you* needed *her* help. She never wanted yours."

"Because she knew I was useless," I said bitterly.

Bill's fingers dug into my arm. "Stop it. You know that's not true."

"But—"

"Your mother, Lori Shepherd, was just as pigheaded as you are. She never asked *anyone* for help. That's why she clammed up after your father's death. It took Dimity a long time to knock some sense into her."

"And did she?" I sat up, my heart racing. "Did she talk about it?"

"Yes, after Dimity did everything but send a brass band through the mail." Bill pushed a stray curl from my forehead. "Yes, your mother finally came out with it, all of it, all of the pain and the loneliness she'd gone through, along with the joy she'd found in you. She told Dimity all about it, eventually. But she would have saved herself a lot of heartache if she'd spoken of it sooner."

"I wish she'd told me about it," I whispered.

"She should have. She should have explained what a nightmare it is to lose someone you love. She should have told you that it took her a long time and a lot of work to wake up from it."

"Maybe she was trying to protect me," I said loyally.

"I'm sure she was. But she ended up hurting you. Dimity

warned her about it—I'll show you the letter when we get back. She said you'd grow up thinking that your mother was the Woman of Steel, that you'd want to be just like her. Dimity said there'd be trouble when you found out you weren't as tough as you thought you should be."

"When my mother died . . ."

"You found out that you weren't made of steel. You had no way of knowing that *no one* is made of steel. How could you? You had no one to tell you otherwise."

"You had Dimity."

"And your mother had Dimity." Bill raised his eyes to the distant hills. "But who did Dimity have?"

I followed his gaze. Bill's words had fallen like balm on my wounded spirit, but the thought of Dimity's unnamed sorrow reawakened the sense of anguished longing I had felt upon seeing the heart. The clearing itself seemed to change when he spoke her name, as though something were missing, or out of place. The sunlight had become harsh and a cool breeze chilled me. The ground felt rough against my legs and when I searched the sky for the soaring hawks, I could not find them.

Bill reached for the bag and stood up, then stretched out a hand to pull me to my feet. "It's time to go back to the cottage."

*\
**

I spent the rest of that day in the study, catching up on the correspondence.

Bill spent it in the Jacuzzi.

19

I would have made a fortune if I'd had the foresight to sell tickets to *Tea with the Pym Sisters*. It was better than anything playing in the West End.

It helped a lot to have Mother Nature as set designer. It was another sunny day and when Emma showed up it seemed only natural to suggest tea in the solarium. With the aid of Dimity's cookbook and my ever-growing self-confidence in the kitchen, I baked an array of seedcakes and meringues and strawberry tarts. While Bill set out Dimity's best china and linen, Emma decked every nook with freshly picked flowers, even seeing to it that Reginald's ears were adorned with a diminutive daisy chain. By the time she announced the arrival of my guests, the solarium looked like something out of an Edwardian novel.

As did the Pym sisters. They were identical, from the veils on their hats to the tips of their lavender gloves. They looked so tiny and frail that I wondered how on earth they had managed the walk from Finch to the cottage, until I noticed a car parked behind the one we had leased. Like them, it was both ancient and pristine.

As remarkable as the Pym sisters were, I was pleased to note that Bill found me even more distracting. His jaw dropped when I descended the staircase, dressed in my teatime finery, and Emma had to introduce him to the Pyms twice before he remembered to say "How do you do." Even then, he said it without taking his eyes from me. I, of course, gave my undivided attention to my guests.

"Thank you so much for your kind invitation," the one on the right said.

"Yes, indeed. Such a lovely day for a drive," the other added. Even the voices were identical—not just the tone, but the rhythm as well.

Emma had cautioned me not to tackle the subject of Dimity head-on. The sisters' sense of propriety would not permit them to gossip. They were, on the other hand, perfectly willing to *reminisce* for hours if given half a chance, so I invited them to take a look around the cottage. I hoped that a tour would spark memories of their longtime neighbor.

"How kind."

"How lovely. Emma tells us . . ."

". . . it has changed quite a bit . . ."

". . . since our last visit."

It was like watching a tennis match. As I led the way through the ground-floor rooms, the Pyms kept up a steady flow of point-counterpoint commentary in my wake. After a while, I was able to distinguish one voice from the other: Louise's was softer, and she seemed more timid. The minute they closed their mouths, however, I couldn't tell one from the other.

After we had seated ourselves around the wrought-iron table in the solarium, Emma excused herself to make tea. The Pyms chatted on about the weather and the garden and the vicar's new roof, and just as I'd begun to think my memory-sparking tour had fizzled, both sets of eyes came to rest on the heart-shaped locket which still hung on its chain around my neck.

"Oh, my . . ." said Ruth softly.

"How very curious. Might we ask . . ."

". . . how you came by this piece of jewelry?"

"I found it upstairs," I replied. I held the locket at the length of its chain for the sisters to examine more closely. "It was in a little blue box. I think it belonged to Dimity."

"Indeed it did," said Louise. "She acquired it in London, during the war, and she wore it . . ."

". . . always. We never saw her without it. We had been given the impression, in fact . . ."

". . . that a young man had given it to her."

My heart leapt and Bill leaned forward eagerly, but the Pyms seemed unaware of the impact of their words.

"Dimity was always a very kind . . ."

". . . very generous . . ."

". . . very good-hearted girl. And a great . . ."

". . . judge of character."

"Yes, indeed. She was quite a . . ."

". . . matchmaker and not one of her matches . . ."

". . . ever failed."

"Yes," I said. "I know about that. She introduced my mother to my father, didn't she, Bill?"

"What?" He looked up from what appeared to be a minute inspection of his teaspoon. "Oh, yes." He cleared his throat. "She did."

"And were they happy together?" asked Ruth.

"Extremely happy," I said.

"Well, there you are," said Ruth, and beamed with pleasure. "Dimity grew up in this cottage, you know."

"And she never left . . ."

". . . until the war."

"A most tragic affair. Here, dear, let me help you with

that." When Louise turned her attention to helping Emma pour, Ruth took up the narrative thread on her own—more or less.

"She was engaged to a young officer very early in the war." I held my breath. "Young Bobby MacLaren." I looked at Bill with exaltation and he gave me a covert thumbs-up.

"Did you ever meet Bobby?" he asked.

"Indeed, we did." Ruth accepted her cup of tea with a distracted air, her face reflecting a long-forgotten sadness. "Such a fine boy, and so courageous. We lost so many. . . ." Her voice trailed off.

I took my cup of tea from Emma and placed it on the table, wondering how many young boys Ruth's old eyes had seen march off, first to one war and then to another. She sat motionless, and I could almost see their faces as she saw them, the faces of boys who would never grow old, who would always be young and fine and courageous. A memory flickered at the back of my mind, but a jay's angry chatter from the back garden extinguished it.

Ruth drew herself up and went on. "Dimity brought him to visit us once when they came to Finch on leave. He was such a lively boy, so energetic, and he had such lovely manners." She sipped her tea. "When he died, Dimity was . . ."

"Devastated." Louise had finished helping Emma.

"Quite devastated. She would have worked herself to death in London. But her commanding officer saw what was happening and ordered her to rest up for a month. She returned here, to the cottage, looking like a . . ."

"Ghost."

"A pale ghost, a shadow of herself. Louise and I thought it would be best if we came over regularly, to sit with her and look after the garden. We didn't like to leave her alone, you see . . .

". . . not after the first time."

"The first time we stopped by . . ." Ruth paused and her

eyes widened. "My, but these seedcakes are lovely," she said. "Did you make them yourself? Might I ask for the recipe?"

"Y-yes, of course," I stammered, startled by the abrupt change of subject.

"I'll copy it out for you," Emma offered, and went into the kitchen to pull out the dog-eared cookbook. I sent a silent blessing after her.

"Oh, that is most kind of you. It is so difficult these days to find *real* seedcake." For a second it looked as though Ruth might stop there, but after a sip of tea, she continued. "The first time we stopped by, we found Dimity curled up on the couch, as cold as ice, staring and staring at that lovely photograph. It didn't seem healthy to leave it with her. We don't think she noticed . . ."

". . . when we took it. And she didn't seem to miss it. We brought it home with us and kept it safe. We thought that one day . . ."

". . . it might be precious to her." Ruth looked up as Emma returned, recipe in hand. "Thank you so very much, dear. Tell me, are you still having trouble with your *Alchemilla mollis?*"

Emma was halfway through her reply before I realized they were talking about a plant. I'm not sure if Bill actually saw me gripping the edge of my seat, but he seemed to sense my agitation because he decided to lead the witness for her own good. He waited for a pause, then leaned slightly toward Ruth. "Can you tell us about Bobby?" he asked.

"So full of life," mused Ruth in reply. "He wasn't a local boy, you know, but he loved it here at the cottage all the same. He said that he could imagine no place more beautiful than Pouter's Hill, and he could think of nothing more wonderful than to return there after the war. He and Dimity spent hours up there, the way young lovers do. A valiant young man, and so proud of his wings."

"So very proud," Louise echoed. "I believe the bluebells

are out on Pouter's Hill." Ruth and Louise turned their bright eyes upward. "What a lovely sight."

*
**

The fact that I survived the afternoon is amazing, but it's nothing compared to the fact that the Pym sisters emerged unscathed. After the initial burst of information, their progress was sporadic at best. They'd move toward adding another tidbit about Bobby and then meander onto some wholly unrelated topic, usually having to do with food or flowers, and every time they did, I was torn between having an apoplectic seizure or committing Pymocide. Now I knew why my mother had described them as not very coherent. But Bill and Emma kept their cool and guided the conversation with admirable dexterity. By the time the Pyms took their leave—in stereo—we had learned quite a lot about the sequence of events following Bobby MacLaren's death.

When Dimity was strong enough she'd returned to active duty, but she remained dazed, heartbroken, and inconsolable. The next time Dimity came down, a year later, it was as though a cloud had lifted from her soul. The reason became clear when she introduced them to her new friend: my mother. Seeing at once how close the two women were, the Pyms entrusted my mother with the photograph, knowing that she would give it to Dimity when the right time came.

They were worried that they might not live long enough to do it themselves. No matter how lighthearted Dimity seemed, the Pyms saw a darkness in her eyes that showed she was grieving still. Unlike the other villagers, they were not surprised by the fact that Dimity seldom came back to the cottage after coming into her fortune.

Shortly after we had pieced the story together, Emma left for home, carrying my heartfelt thanks and a selection of goodies for her family. Bill and I loaded the dishwasher, then sat in the solarium, watching the dusk settle. Reginald sat in the center of the table, his daisy chain lopsided and wilting.

"Your mother was a remarkable woman," Bill commented. "It sounds as though she turned Dimity's life around completely."

"Not completely," I said, "but enough to get her back on her feet again and moving forward. My mother was a great believer in moving forward, in looking on the bright side of things." I plucked a red rose from a vase and leaned it between Reginald's paws. "I suppose . . ."

"What do you suppose?" Bill asked.

"Give me a minute, will you? This isn't easy for me to say." I got up and opened the door. The sound of crickets wafted in on a soft breeze. "I've done some thinking about what you said up on the hill—some thinking and some reading, too."

"You went back to the correspondence?"

"Yes, while you were soaking your . . . sore muscles in the Jacuzzi. Well, after all those things you said, I had to. I was up pretty late last night, reading through letter after letter, and I noticed something. My mother never says anything that isn't cheerful. Even when she's talking about things that must have bothered her tremendously—like taking ten years to have a baby, for instance—even when she's talking about that, she's cracking jokes, as though it didn't *really* bother her. And that's how I remember her—happy all the time." I turned and held a hand up. "Don't get me wrong. That's not a bad way to be. I mean, look at what it did for Dimity." My hand dropped and I looked back out into the garden. "But I'm not sure it was all that good for me. It's not . . . human. As you said, she didn't teach me how to be *un*happy." I shook my head. "And that's hard for me to handle. I didn't think she had any weaknesses."

"Do you mind finding out that she did?"

I sat down again, leaning toward Bill with my elbows on the table. "That's the strangest part, Bill. I don't mind at all. It's a relief, in fact. It's not easy being the daughter of a saint."

Bill smiled ruefully and nodded. "Being the son of one is no fun, either. That's why I constantly remind myself of each and every one of Father's faults. It's a depressingly short list, but it helps. Did you know, for example, that he has a secret passion for root beer?"

"Is that a fault?"

"For a man raised on Montrachet? One might even call it a serious character defect. He'd be drummed out of his club if word got around. Please don't let on that I told you."

"I wouldn't dream of it." We shared a smile, then I lowered my eyes to the wrought-iron tabletop. "You know, Bill, I might not have gone back to the correspondence if it hadn't been for you. Thanks for giving me a shove."

"You're welcome." The sound of the crickets rose and fell as the dusk turned into darkness. Bill took the rose from Reginald's paws. "Excuse me, old man, but you don't mind if I . . ." He handed the rose to me. "I didn't get the chance to tell you how beautiful you look. The color suits you."

I couldn't be sure if he was referring to the cornflower blue of my new dress or the blush that had risen to my cheeks, so I changed the subject. "Ruth and Louise were very helpful, weren't they?"

"Yes, indeed." Bill sat back in his chair. "RM. Robert MacLaren."

"More commonly known as Bobby—an airman who was killed in action late in the year 1940, just before my mother met Dimity. A call to the War Office would confirm all of that, I suppose."

"But they wouldn't be able to tell us about this." My heart did a flutter step as he reached over to touch the locket. "The War Office doesn't keep track of that sort of thing. Whatever is tormenting Dimity, it's not just grief over losing Bobby. Something must have happened between them, something terrible." Bill stood up. "What we need is someone who knew Bobby and Dimity." He strode off down the hallway.

"Where are you going?" I asked, scrambling after him as fast as my brand-new pumps would allow.

"Upstairs to pack," he called from the stairs.

I followed him up. "To pack? Why?"

"I'm going to London." At the top of the stairs, he turned to face me. "Lori, think about it. Bobby was an *airman*." He went ahead into his room.

"So?" I stood frowning on the stairs, then hit myself in the forehead, feeling like a complete fool. "Of course! The Flamborough!"

Bill stuck his head out of his door. "Bingo."

"I thought of the Flamborough when we were talking with the Pyms, but then it slipped away." I climbed the last few stairs, then stood in Bill's doorway while he tossed a few things in a bag.

"I'm going to pay a visit to the redoubtable Miss Kingsley," said Bill, pulling a shirt off a hanger in the wardrobe, "to find out if anyone still knows how to operate the Flamborough Telegraph. They might be able to put us in touch with some of Bobby's friends or fellow airmen." He folded the shirt and placed it in the bag, then opened a drawer in the dresser.

"Why do you keep saying 'I'? You mean 'we,' don't you?"

Bill pulled a pair of socks out of the drawer and shook his head. "Not this time. You have to be here to field calls from Father." The socks went into the bag.

"Oh. Right." Bill's plan made perfect sense. I could trust him to ask the right questions, to discover all there was to discover. There was no need for me to accompany him. So why did my heart sink when he zipped the bag shut?

He left the bag on the bed and came over to where I was standing. "I'll call as soon as I find anything out," he said.

"I know," I mumbled, looking at my shoes.

"I'll call even if I don't find anything out."

"Fine."

"I'll give you the number at the Flamborough, Miss Kingsley's private line, so you can reach me night or day."

"Okay."

He bent slightly at the knees and peered at me through narrowed eyes. "So what's the problem?"

I couldn't stand it any longer. Scowling furiously, I grabbed hold of his lapels and planted a kiss firmly on his lips. "There, all right? I don't want to stay here. I don't want to be away from you. I'm packing my own bag and coming along and that's final, end of discussion, no debate. Okay? Satisfied? Does that answer your question?"

He closed his eyes and stood very still for a moment. Then he released a long breath. "Yes, thank you."

Looking somewhat dazed, he made his way back to the bed, bumped into the nightstand, knocked the lamp to the floor, picked it up, dropped it again, then left it where it was and came back to the doorway to pull me into his arms.

"I just want to be sure I understood you correctly," he said. "You know how lawyers are. . . ."

By the time we were both ready to leave, everything was clear enough to satisfy the Supreme Court.

20

We didn't lose our heads entirely. I took the precaution of calling Willis, Sr., before we left. It was the middle of the night in Boston, so I left a message informing him that I was so far along in my reading that I had decided to spend a few days exploring the countryside, with Bill in tow to look after things. I added that we would telephone him the minute we got back to the cottage.

Bill phoned ahead and Miss Kingsley responded with characteristic efficiency. Our rooms were waiting for us when we arrived, and a late supper was ready in one of the Flamborough's private dining rooms. At Bill's invitation, Miss Kingsley joined us, and she lived up to her redoubtable reputation by remaining undaunted even by the vague nature of our quest.

"Robert MacLaren?" she said. "Well, the name certainly doesn't ring any bells, but I'm a relative newcomer. I've only been at the Flamborough for fifteen years. I'm sure we'll be able to find someone who can tell you something about the old days, though. Retired military gentlemen are our mainstay. I shall make some inquiries, and I should be very surprised if I have nothing to tell you by tomorrow evening."

Miss Kingsley's inquiries took a little longer than that—two days, to be precise—but the results were spectacular. Archy Gorman was worth a whole army of retired military gentlemen. He was a stout man with a magnificent head of wavy white hair and a drooping handlebar mustache, and before opening his own public house, he had spent seventeen years as the bartender at the Flamborough—including the war years. Archy had long since retired from bartending, but Paul had kept in touch with him, and Miss Kingsley had been able to reach him at his flat in Greenwich. Paul drove the limousine round to pick him up, and the two of them met us in the Flamborough lounge two hours before opening time. The polished dance floor shone in the light from the fluted, frosted-glass wall lamps as we gathered at one of the round wooden tables near the bar. Paul sat with us, but Archy immediately made his way to the taps and began pulling pints for the assembled group.

"Have to keep my hand in," he explained, with a wink at Miss Kingsley, "and I never was a stick-in-the-mud about the licensing laws, was I, Paul?"

"No, you weren't, Archy. And there's many an airman who thanked you for it."

"Here you are, now." Bill got up to carry the tray of drinks to our table and Archy joined us there, puffing slightly with the effort. "To happier days," he said, and raised his glass. I watched over the top of my own as he expertly avoided dipping his mustache into the foam.

"Now, you might be wondering why I was here at the Flamborough for the duration instead of out there doing my duty," Archy began, folding his hands across his ample stomach. "The plain and simple fact is, they wouldn't have me. Rheumatic fever and a heart murmur and no-thank-you-very-much said the board." He thumped his chest. "But here I am, closing in on seventy and never a day's bother with the old ticker. Never understood it, why they sent the healthy lads off and left the tailings at home, but there you are. You can't expect common sense from the military, can you, Paul?"

"Not a bit of it, Archy."

"What was it that Yank told us that one time? Snafu, he called it—you remember, Paul?"

" 'Situation Normal, All Fouled Up,' " Paul recited dutifully.

"That's your military, the world over." Archy took another long draught, then set his glass on the table. "Now, tell me again about this chap you're looking for."

When I had recounted the little we knew about Bobby, Archy pursed his lips. "He must have flown during the Blitz," he said. "The Battle of Britain, they called it. Not many survived to tell the tale, did they, Paul?"

Paul shook his head soberly. "After a while, it was hard to strike up friendships with the lads. They were gone so fast, you see."

"Here today, and gone tomorrow, that's the way it was, eh, Paul?"

"A truer word was never spoken, Archy."

"You don't happen to have a snap of this MacLaren fellow, do you?" asked Archy. "The old memory is sharp as a tack, but there were so many boys through here . . ."

"No," I replied, "but I do have some pictures of his girl-friend." I handed him several photographs from Dimity's album. "This is Dimity Westwood," I said.

"Dimity Westwood, you say? Well, there were a lot of girlfriends coming into the old Flamborough in those days. It was a lively place back then, not the museum piece it is now—begging your pardon, Miss K."

"That's alright, Archy, no offense taken," said Miss Kingsley. "Things are rather quieter around here nowadays."

"Dull as dishwater," Archy muttered, with a conspiratorial wink at Paul. Stroking his mustache, he looked carefully at each picture. "I couldn't say that I recognize . . ." He paused. "Wait, now . . ."

The rest of us craned our necks to see what had caught his eye. He had come to one of my favorite pictures, a shot of Dimity standing in front of a shop with shattered windows. She had reached inside to touch the dress on a toppled mannequin, and was grinning mischievously at the camera. Archy contemplated the photo for a moment; then his eyebrows shot up and he slapped the table with his hand. "The belle of the ball," he exclaimed. "You remember, Paul—the beautiful belle of the ball—that's who she is."

"By heavens, you're right, Archy. That's who she is," said Paul. "The sweetest girl you'd ever want to meet . . ."

Archy cupped a hand to his mouth and in a stage whisper explained, "Paul took a fancy to her."

"Look who's talking," Paul retorted. "I seem to remember you being rather fond of her yourself."

"So I was, so I was," Archy conceded. "But who could help being fond of her? She was . . . something else. Something you don't find every day, I can tell you. You may know her as Dimity Westwood, but we called her Belle. She came in here all the time, on the arm of that Scottish fellow. Frightful accent, mind you, but how he could dance. Bobby . . . yes, Bobby and Belle. What a pair."

"Lit up the whole place when they came in," said Paul.

"I kidded them about spoiling the blackout—you remember that, Paul?"

"I do, Archy."

Archy put his arm around Paul's shoulders and the two men gazed, misty-eyed, at the photograph before Archy returned it to me. They emptied their glasses, and stared stolidly into the middle distance.

"It's easy to remember the happy times," Archy said. "No one likes to think of the rest, but it was there all the same, wasn't it, Paul?"

"It was, Archy."

"I remember the last time Belle came in here. She was on her own that night and I could tell just by looking at her what had happened. I'd seen it so many times before, but my heart broke for her all the same. I gave her the message and off she went, without saying a word. She never came back after that."

"That's how it was in those days," said Paul. "Dancing one minute, and the next—"

"There was a message?" I said.

"Oh, yes," Archy replied. "The chaps were always leaving messages with me here at the Flamborough, billets-doux for their sweethearts and the like."

"That's why they called it the Telegraph," said Paul.

"Do you remember what the message was?"

Archy was taken aback. "I never opened it," he said. "It wouldn't have been proper."

My face must have fallen, because he pushed his chair back and lumbered to his feet. Raising a crooked finger, he said, "Now, you come over here, and I'll show you something. It's not something I show to everyone, mind you. You can be sure I didn't show that young bloke who came in after me. He got very snippy when I tried to show him the ropes—you remember him, don't you, Paul?"

"A regular Mr. Know-All," said Paul.

"So I said to him, 'Fair enough, Mr. Know-All, figure it out for yourself.' But seeing as you have a personal interest in all of this . . ."

I followed him to the bar, and the others drifted over from the table. Archy lifted the hatch and motioned for me to go inside, then closed it behind him as he came in after me. He spread his hands flat on the smooth surface of the serving counter, looking very much at home.

"They called it the Telegraph," he said, "but in point of fact, it was more like a post office. It was a sight more efficient than your official post office, and Paul here will vouch for that."

"It was," said Paul, "especially in those days, with so many house numbers disappearing, thanks to Mr. Adolf-bloody-Hitler—oh, excuse me, miss." He covered his mouth with his hand and looked a good deal more shocked than anyone else in the room.

"No need to excuse yourself," Archy declared. "Now, about the Telegraph . . ." Archy ran his hand lovingly up one of the pillars that supported the decorative woodwork overhead, every square inch of it covered with scrolls and flourishes. "I was the postman, you see, and this"—he pointed up to a knob that had been camouflaged by the elaborate carving—"was the postbox. That's where I used to put all the messages the boys left with me. Didn't want them getting wet, so I had Darcy Pemburton—where's old Darcy got to these days, Paul?"

"Living in Blackpool with his sister."

"Blackpool? What's he want to live in Blackpool for?"

"Says he likes the donkey rides."

"The *donkey*— You're having me on, Paul."

"That's what he says."

"Then he's having *you* on. But never mind. . . . Darcy was a fine cabinetmaker in his day, and I had him fit this little box up for me to keep the notes and such out of harm's way. You see, you just give the knob a twist and the door swings—" Archy's mouth curved into an unbelieving grin as a cascade of papers rained down on his leonine head.

*
**

It took us a while to gather them all up, and a little while longer to persuade Archy to let us read them. Piled neatly on the bar were folded note-cards, sealed envelopes, and slapdash notes scrawled on scraps of napkins, train schedules, betting cards, whatever had been at hand, it seemed. Most were brief ("Pru: Bloody balls-up at HQ. Can't make our date. Will call. Jimmy.") and not all concerned romance ("Stinky: Here's your filthy lucre, hope you lose your ration book"—unsigned, but accompanied by a faded five-pound note). A few were cryptic ("Rose: You were right. Bert.") but some were all too clear ("Philip: Drop dead. Georgina.").

"I can't understand it," Archy muttered, twirling one end of his drooping mustache. "I might have left one or two behind, but never this many."

"Archy?" Paul said softly.

"Doesn't make sense," Archy continued. "The new man didn't know about the Telegraph, so how could he manage it, eh? Tell me that."

"Archy?" Paul repeated, a bit more loudly.

"Not as though he'd do a favor for—"

"I did it!" Paul declared.

Archy turned to Paul, shocked. "You, Paul?"

"I did it for the lads, Archy." Paul's eyes pleaded for understanding. "The notes kept coming in after you left, and someone had to look after them, so I did. Then Mr. Know-All caught me behind the bar one day and booted me out of the lounge, and after that I . . . I must've lost track of time."

"I'll say you did." Archy looked from Paul to the notes and back again. "Poor old Stinky went short five pounds because of you."

"I know, Archy," Paul said miserably.

"And let's hope this one hasn't caused more serious mischief." Archy bent down to retrieve a white envelope that appeared to have a raised coat of arms on the flap. Archy examined it closely, then, without saying a word, handed it to me.

"It's addressed to Dimity." I locked eyes with Bill. Archy came up with a polished breadknife, and I used it to slit open the envelope. The others clustered around me as I pulled out a single sheet of paper and read:

Miss Westwood,
   It is my duty to inform you that I recently came into possession of a certain object that belonged to my late

brother. Please contact me immediately, so that we may discuss its disposition.

A.M.

"It's dated July 15, 1952," noted Miss Kingsley. "Imagine, it's been sitting here all these years."

"Have I caused a terrible mess?" Paul asked in a low voice.

I leaned across the bar to squeeze his arm. "You were doing your best, Paul, and it wasn't your fault that that jerk kicked you out of here. You've helped us enormously today, and we really appreciate it." Bill echoed my words, but it wasn't until Archy reached across to pat Paul's shoulder that the smaller man finally perked up again.

"There's no return address," I said, looking once more at the white envelope.

"If we assume the writer to be *A. MacLaren*, that and the coat of arms should be enough," said Miss Kingsley. "Let me check my files." She reached the door of the lounge in time to head off the Flamborough's current bartender, a slender man with flowing blond hair.

"Having a party?" he asked.

"We are having a private conference," replied Miss Kingsley tartly, "and I'll thank you to wait outside until I call for you."

The man clucked his tongue at the empty glasses on the table, but he was no match for Miss Kingsley and left without further comment. Archy leaned on the bar and watched as the door closed behind the two. "A fine figure of a woman," he said, his voice filled with admiration. "Now, would anyone say no to another round? Bring those empty glasses over here." While Paul gathered up the letters and Archy was busy at the tap, Bill and I walked over to look at the framed snapshots arrayed upon the wall.

"I wonder if Bobby's here," I said. "It's so strange to think that we might be looking right at him and not know it." I called over to the bar, "Archy—do you know if Bobby MacLaren's picture is here?"

" 'Course it is. His chums brought it in and I hung it there myself. Let me see, now." Pint of stout in hand, Archy came over, with Paul at his heels. "That's Jack Thornton," said Archy, as his large hand moved slowly across the wall. "Brian Ripley. Tom Patterson. Freddy Baker. He was a wild one, old Freddy. Always getting himself put on report."

"They never found fault with his flying, though," Paul pointed out.

"No, Paul, they never did. Ah, it brings 'em all back, this wall does. They were none of them saints, but they were there when we needed them. Here, now, here's Bobby." Archy unhooked one of the pictures and handed it to me, and the four of us looked down upon a young man in flying gear, standing beside a fighter.

"That's his Hurricane," said Paul. "Proud of it, he was. Said it streaked through the sky like a falcon. The picture doesn't do him justice, though."

"Hard to do that in a snap, but you're right," Archy agreed. "His eyes were brighter, and his smile . . ."

"Yes," said Paul. "His smile."

Sighing, the two men returned to the bar. Bill took Bobby's picture from me and stared at it for a long time before hanging it back in place. "So many of them, and each one of them left someone behind." He took a deep breath, then cleared his throat and looked down at the letter. "I think our next step is to contact A.M., if Miss Kingsley can discover who he is. I'd be interested to know if Dimity ever received word about this"—he tapped the letter— " 'object' that belonged to Bobby."

"Me, too, but what are we going to say to A.M.?"

"You leave that to me."

Archy had not quite topped off Paul's glass when Miss Kingsley returned, a piece of paper in her hand and a gleam in her eye.

"Mr. Andrew MacLaren is sixty-six years old, unmarried, and still living on the MacLaren estate in the mountains west of Wick," she informed the table. "Quite far north, actually. He had only one sibling, a brother, Robert, whose death made Andrew the sole heir to the family fortune, which is extensive—wool, whiskey, and, lately, North Sea oil. He's something of a recluse, apparently, seldom sets foot off of the estate. I have his telephone number, if you'd like it."

"Bless you, Miss Kingsley. Where would we be without you?" said Bill, as Miss Kingsley handed him the number. "I'd love to have a look through those files of yours someday."

"I'm afraid they are held in the strictest confidence," she replied with a smile. "Would you like to come into my office to place the call? Yes, Archy, you and Paul may stay here and enjoy your drinks, but I'll have to allow Bjorn to open the doors to the rest of our patrons as well."

Archy snorted in disgust. "I might have known," he said. "What's a chap named Bjorn doing at the Flamborough, that's what I'd like to know. Sign of the times, eh, Paul?"

"Yes, Archy, a sign of the times."

Bill and I left them there and went with Miss Kingsley into her office. Bill sat at the desk, dialed the number, then began to speak in a voice that was businesslike, mature, authoritative—in short, completely unrecognizable. Listening to him, I began to understand how he had gained access to the Imperial War Museum archives.

"Good morning," he said. "This is William A. Willis speaking, of the law firm of Willis & Willis. I am calling in regards to a certain matter pertaining to the disposition of the Westwood estate—yes, the Westwood estate. I am the estate's legal representative and I would like to speak with Mr. Andrew MacLaren, if he is available. Yes, William A. Willis. Thank you, I'll wait." Bill covered the phone with his hand. "Don't look so astounded," he said to me. "This is my professional manner. Or did you think I didn't have one?"

"I was just wondering if the 'A' stood for—"

"Admirable? Astute? Articulate? Modesty prevents me from saying, 'All of the above.' "

Andrew MacLaren must have come on the line at that moment because Bill turned his attention back to the telephone. As he did, Archy Gorman came into the office. "Don't bother your young man," he said. "I just popped in to say I'd be on my way." He held up the assembled notes. "Have to go home and sort this lot out. My duty as the postman, you know."

"Paul's driving you, isn't he?" I asked.

" 'Fraid not," he said. "Has no head for lager, our Paul. He'll be asleep in the lounge if you need him."

"You wait out front, Archy," said Miss Kingsley. "I'll have another driver for you shortly. As for Paul . . . will you excuse me, Lori? I think my presence is required in the lounge."

I turned to Archy and thanked him for all his help.

"Don't give it a second thought," he said. "You've given me a chance to finish up a job I should have finished years ago. I'm the one who should thank you." He nodded in Bill's direction. "You tell your young man I said cheerio, will you? He's a nice fellow and the two of you make a fine couple. I'm very pleased to have met you both. You be sure to stop and visit if you're ever passing through Greenwich." He shook my hand, winked, and was gone.

Bill hung up the telephone.

"Well?" I asked.

"MacLaren invited us both to come up to his estate." When my eyes lit up, he raised a cautioning hand. "It was a strange invitation. He was ready to hang up on me until I mentioned the long-lost letter. Apparently he doesn't share Archy Gorman's enthusiasm for chatting over old times."

"He did lose his brother," I said. "It must be a pretty painful memory."

"Yes, but . . ." Bill stroked his beard. "No, never mind. Let's wait and see if you get the same impression." He stood up as Miss Kingsley returned.

"If anyone had told me that one day I would see our Paul dead drunk before noon . . ." She shook her head.

"He's a lot smaller than Archy," said Bill. "I suppose it goes to his head faster. And now, Miss Kingsley, I have another favor to ask of you."

By seven o'clock that evening, Bill and I were on board a private jet bound for Wick.

21

Andrew MacLaren was at the airport to meet us. As tall as Bill and broader across the shoulders, he walked with a pronounced limp and used a cane, yet he seemed surprisingly agile. Certainly he was more fit and trim than I'd have expected for a man of his age, not to mention a man with a handicap.

He must have read the question in my eyes, and it must have been a familar one because he tapped the cane lightly against his leg. "Polio. Grew up with it. Doesn't slow me down." His nonchalant manner put me at ease and by the time we had reached the parking lot, Andrew's lopsided gait seemed as unremarkable as Bill's steady stride.

He led us to a dilapidated Land Rover. Uh-oh, I thought as we climbed in, an aristocrat on the skids. I wondered if that might explain his reluctant invitation; perhaps he was ashamed to have houseguests. But that theory went out the window as we approached MacLaren Hall. When the road narrowed from a one-lane gravel drive to a rutted track,

I realized that Andrew's choice of transport was merely practical.

"I'm sorry about the road," he said. "We have a perfectly usable drive, of course, but this is faster and, as it's getting late, I thought you might be in need of supper."

There was no need for him to apologize. We were far enough north and it was still early enough in the year for there to be a good deal of daylight left even at that late hour, and the scenery more than made up for the jouncing, jostling ride. We were surrounded by some of the wildest, most desolate country I'd ever seen, with mountains looming on all sides, barren, craggy, majestic. They took my breath away, but also left me feeling uneasy. This was a harsh, unforgiving place. I suspected it would not deal kindly with weakness and, given half a chance, it would kill the unwary.

MacLaren Hall did nothing to soften that impression. It was an enormous, intimidating old place faced in weathered red brick, with dozens of chimneys and deep-set, shadowy windows. It stood on a rocky hillside above a loch—magnificent, but terribly lonely, overlooking the black water in bleak isolation.

As if to compensate for the somber surroundings, Andrew had ordered his housekeeper to lay on a huge spread, including venison from a deer he had bagged himself and whiskey from the family distillery. While we ate, he regaled us with the history of MacLaren Hall. He was obviously proud of his ancestral home and he seemed to have a story about every family member who had ever lived in it. Except for Bobby. It wasn't until we had retired to the library, whiskeys in hand, that Bill was able to broach the subject. On the flight up I had agreed to leave the questioning to him.

"As I mentioned on the telephone, Mr. MacLaren," Bill began, "we found something in Miss Westwood's papers that piqued our curiosity." From his breast pocket he took the letter we had found at the Flamborough and handed it to Andrew. "The envelope was still sealed when we found it. We were wondering if the matter you mentioned was ever resolved."

Andrew glanced briefly at the letter. "It was settled long ago," he said. Then he crumpled it into a ball, and with a flick of the wrist, threw it on the fire. I started up from my chair, aghast, but Bill motioned for me to remain seated and continued on as though nothing had happened.

"Might I ask what it concerned?" he said.

"Some property. It's unimportant now. As I say, the matter was settled years ago."

"You relieve my mind," said Bill, seemingly unconcerned. He raised his glass to the light. "This is from the family distillery? It's marvelous. Tell me, do you use oak barrels for the aging process or do you prefer . . ." With unshakable aplomb, Bill led the conversation on a circuitous route. By the time he got back to Bobby, Andrew had tossed back three glasses of whiskey in quick succession and his mood had mellowed considerably.

"Was Bobby your elder brother?" asked Bill.

"By two years," Andrew replied. "There was only the pair of us."

"You must have been very close."

"We were." Andrew stared moodily into the fire, as though mesmerized by the dancing flames.

I wondered how long it had been since he had spoken of his brother. I wondered if it came as a relief to him to say Bobby's name aloud, or whether it fell like a hammerblow every time. How much more whiskey would it take before he could say the name without flinching?

"I worshiped him," Andrew went on. "You might think I'd feel a dram of jealousy or envy, with Bobby being the elder son and healthy to boot . . ."

"But you didn't?" said Bill.

"Never crossed my mind." Andrew emptied his fourth glass, then set it on a table beside his chair. "What you must understand is that Bobby treated me as an equal. When I couldn't walk, he carried me up into the hills to see the falcons' nest, or out to fish in the loch. He taught me how to track, how to use my eyes and my brain to compensate for the weakness in my legs. I'd have been bedridden for years longer if Bobby hadn't lured me out to explore the world."

"He must have been a fine young man," said Bill.

"They come no finer," said Andrew. "The curious thing was that he made me love the place much more than he ever had. He was so full of life himself that our barren crags left him feeling hungry for . . . something kinder, less austere, I suppose, something more like himself." Andrew picked up the empty glass and held it out to Bill.

"It must have been very hard on you when he joined up," said Bill. When he handed the glass back, it was filled only halfway.

"He was too young, much too young," Andrew said with a note of bitterness. "But they didn't question matters too closely in those days. There was a great demand for air crews and he was keen as mustard, so . . ."

"They took him on."

"They did. He was stationed at Biggin Hill. God help me, I was so proud of him. It never occurred to me that he could be killed. My brother was young and strong and invulnerable. He was . . ." Andrew's voice faltered, but another swallow steadied it. "He was shot down over the Channel on the ninth of September, 1940. His wingman saw the plane hit the water, but there was no parachute, and Bobby . . . The body was never recovered," he finished gruffly.

"My God," I whispered.

Andrew raised a hand to smooth his thinning gray hair. "It was a common enough occurrence during the war," he said, bowing his head to stare into his glass, "but I'll admit that it was an uncommon blow to me. It may sound foolish, but I sometimes go into the chapel to be with him."

"The chapel?" Bill asked. "But I thought . . ."

Andrew looked up. "It's a family tradition," he explained. "A family as old as ours has left its share of unburied sons on many battlefields. When Bobby died, we added his name to the memorial tablet. I like to think I can sense his presence down there. MacLarens are canny that way." Andrew was silent for a few moments. Then he asked: "Would you like to see it?"

"Thank you," Bill replied. "We would be honored."

Carrying a lantern to light the way, Andrew led us to the family chapel, a narrow Gothic structure attached to the west wing of the hall. Generations of MacLarens were entombed there, and I'd never seen a darker, damper place in all my life. The weeping granite walls seemed to close in upon us, and the chill air made me wish I'd worn something warmer than my short-sleeved tea-party dress. I couldn't imagine how anyone could rest in peace there. I could almost hear their bones rattling from the cold.

Footsteps echoing on the uneven stone floor, we wound our way past recumbent lords and ladies to the far side of the chapel, where a large bronze plaque had been set into the wall. Many names had been inscribed on it, and many dates, and down in one dim corner Bobby's name and birth date appeared above the words: LOST IN DEFENCE OF THE REALM, 9 SEPTEMBER 1940.

"My brother had just turned twenty," Andrew said. His voice rang hollowly in the chamber. On impulse, I bent down to touch the inscription, and when the locket slipped from the neck of my dress to hang glinting in the lantern light, I heard a sharp intake of breath and felt Andrew's eyes on me.

"I'm sorry," I said, straightening quickly, "I didn't mean to—"

He passed a hand across his face and seemed to shrink in on himself. "If you will excuse me . . . I have had a very tiring day." Slowly, painfully, all agility gone, he made his way back to the entrance. His valet and the housekeeper were waiting there, as though Andrew's visit to the chapel were a nightly ritual. Andrew leaned heavily on the strong arm of his valet, a stocky young man with broad shoulders.

"I will show you to your rooms now," said the housekeeper. She was a sharp-eyed older woman in a starched black dress, and her words seemed to be a statement of fact, not a suggestion.

"Yes," said Andrew. "You go ahead with Mrs. Hume. We'll speak again in the morning." He started off, then hesitated, and turned to Bill. "There's good fishing nearby, if you're up early enough."

"I wouldn't want to impose—"

"It's no imposition," said Andrew. "Colin and I are usually up at first light. We'll find a rod for you, young man, and a pair of waders."

"In that case, Bill would be happy to accept your invitation," I said, treading lightly on Bill's foot.

"Uh, yes," he said. "Yes, thank you, I'd be delighted."

"Good," said Andrew, with a wan smile. "Colin will rouse you bright and early, and perhaps we'll have fresh salmon for breakfast." With one hand on Colin's shoulder and the other on his cane, Andrew made his way slowly down the hall.

The housekeeper led us up the dark-paneled main staircase to adjacent second-floor bedrooms overlooking the loch. She indicated the location of the nearest lavatory and bathroom, then added, in a cold, unfriendly voice, "Mr. MacLaren sometimes has difficulty sleeping. It would be appreciated, therefore, if you did not disturb his rest while you are here. Should you require assistance during your visit, you may use the bellpulls in your rooms to summon one of us." She paused, and her brown eyes narrowed to slits. "There is always someone awake in MacLaren Hall. Good night."

We nodded obediently; then Bill went into his room and I entered mine. I half expected to hear a key turn in the lock, shutting me in for the night. Mrs. Hume's words had sounded more like a warning than an offer of hospitality: you are being watched; don't stray from your rooms. Creepy, but also tantalizing. Someone was afraid to let us roam MacLaren Hall unattended.

My room had a funereal charm to it, with shoulder-high wainscoting, a single dim brass lamp, and grim Victorian furniture. Dark green velvet drapes blocked the view, and a green brocade quilt covered the rock-hard bed. Everything was spotless, though, and well maintained. Museum pieces, I thought, fingering the black tassel on the bellpull. When enough time had elapsed for Mrs. Hume to go back downstairs, I tiptoed over to knock at Bill's door. He opened it, grabbed my arm, and pulled me inside. He seemed somewhat peeved.

"*Waders? At dawn?* What have you gotten me into?"

"Keep your voice down." I steered him over to sit on a low, burgundy plush couch at the opposite end of the room. "I have a feeling that Mrs. Hume's hearing is excellent."

He glared belligerently at the door, but lowered his voice. "Lori, I'll make a fool of myself out there. I don't know the first thing about fishing."

"I have complete confidence in your ability to fake it," I said cheerfully. "Playing fisherman can't be all that much harder than playing chauffeur."

"Are you still mad about that? Lori—"

"I'm not mad about anything. You'll do fine. Just take your cues from Andrew and let Colin bait your hook. And while you're out there, suggest a walk around the grounds, maybe a hike up to the falcons' nest."

"More hiking?" Bill groaned and buried his face in his hands. "I still have blisters from Pouter's Hill."

"Then put on an extra pair of socks," I said sternly. "Listen, Bill, do whatever you can to keep Andrew and Colin away from the house tomorrow."

"Don't tell me." Bill raised his head from his hands. "While I'm out there drowning, you'll be in here searching for whatever it was that Bobby left to Dimity."

"You saw what Andrew did with the letter," I said. "Why would he destroy it if he was telling us the truth? It was an incredibly stupid thing to do, don't you think? Like shouting

'I'm innocent' before we'd even accused him of anything. He must have known it would arouse our suspicions."

"I don't think MacLaren's thinking very clearly," said Bill. "That's why I kept a certified copy."

"*What?*"

"Keep your voice down," said Bill, his good humor fully restored. "Remember Mrs. Hume."

"You rat," I whispered. "Why didn't you tell me?"

"I wanted one of us to have an authentic reaction. I'm a lawyer, so he wouldn't expect one from me, but—"

"But authentic reactions are my specialty. Thanks a lot."

Bill stretched his legs out and tucked a fringed throw pillow behind his head. "I thought something might be up when I talked to him on the telephone. He wanted nothing to do with us at first, but as soon as I mentioned the letter, he couldn't invite us up here fast enough. It seemed odd to me. There's a photocopy machine in Miss Kingsley's office, and Miss K counts among her many talents those of a commissioner for oaths. That's a notary public, to you."

"Then you agree with me? You think he's hiding something?"

"I do. What's more, I think it might be out in the open and he must think it's something we'd recognize on sight. Otherwise, Mrs. Hume wouldn't have dropped her leaden hint about staying in our rooms."

I nodded slowly, then got up and walked over to the windows. Pulling the drapes aside, I looked into inky darkness. Not a glimmer of starlight reflected from the lapping waves of the loch. With a shiver, I turned back to Bill. "Why'd he invite you to go fishing, then? You'd think he'd want us out of here as soon as possible."

"Who knows? Maybe he's lonely. Maybe he's tired of hiding. Or maybe he feels safe with the dragon lady to watch his back. How do you plan to get around her?"

"Mrs. Hume doesn't know it yet, but she's going to give me a tour of the hall."

"Is she?"

I returned to the couch. "You heard the way Andrew talked about the place—he's bound to want to show it off, and if you persuade him to take you on an excursion, he'll have to deputize someone. My guess is that it'll be Mrs. Hume. If she's going to be breathing down my neck anyway, I might as well make use of her."

"Thus, by a process of elimination . . ."

"Whatever she doesn't show me tomorrow must be what we want to see. That's why I need you to keep Andrew away as long as possible. This is a big place and I'm going to insist on seeing all of it." I paused for a moment in silent thought, then asked, "What did you think of the chapel?"

Bill snuggled his head deeper into the pillow and shuddered. "Pouter's Hill it most certainly is not."

"No. No light, no warmth, no open space." I frowned. "It doesn't seem right, somehow, that Bobby's only monument should be a plaque in the damp corner of a mausoleum in the middle of nowhere. I find it very hard to believe that Andrew can sense his presence down there. Everyone we've talked to—his brother included—remembers Bobby as bursting with life, vibrant."

"Dancing, laughing, lighting up the room."

"Exactly. Bobby's name seems out of place in that cold hole. And did you notice that Andrew never once mentioned Dimity? Not once. Do you suppose he was jealous of her? Afraid she would steal Bobby away from him? Is that what this is all about?"

"I've got a better one for you. Why doesn't Dimity take care of it herself?"

I looked at him blankly.

"Lori, if she can fix Reginald and write in journals and send Evan packing, why can't she just swoop in here and get whatever it is Bobby meant for her to have? For that matter, why can't she just fly straight into Bobby's arms?"

"I—I don't know."

Bill tented his fingers and looked thoughtfully at the ceiling. "I think it's because she loves you."

"But she loved Bob—"

Bill's hand shot up. "Hush. My theory, such as it is, requires patience." Folding his arms, he went on. "Dimity loves you. You're her spiritual daughter, so to speak. Every single manifestation of her supernatural power has been for your benefit, from lending a hand in the kitchen to helping Derek finish the cottage on time. This much we know for sure."

"Yes, but—" Bill gave me a sidelong glare and I subsided.

"We also know that she loved Bobby, probably as much as she loves you, if the Pym sisters are to be believed. Regardless of that, her . . . spirit . . . is unable to connect with his. Why? If she loved both of you, why can she make contact with you but not Bobby?"

I shrugged.

"I think it's because her bond of love with you was never broken."

"But her bond with Bobby was?" I ventured.

"In a way that required forgiveness." Bill took off his glasses and rubbed his eyes. "A theory. Only a theory. One step at a time, and I don't know about you, but my next step is going to be toward the bed." His head moved from the pillow to my shoulder. "Now, about the sleeping arrangements . . ."

"They will stay as they are." I nudged his head back onto the pillow and got to my feet. "We don't want to scandalize Mrs. Hume."

"I think Mrs. Hume could use a nice juicy bit of scandal."

"Be that as it may," I said, heading for the door, "you need your rest. Your fishy friends will be waiting at the crack of dawn." Halfway out the door, I said over my shoulder, "Besides, Bill, we're *hardly* a pair of teenagers, are we?"

I ducked as the throw pillow sailed past me into the hall.

22

There was fresh salmon at breakfast, but Andrew and I had to start without Bill. He was up in his room, changing into dry clothes.

"I warned him to watch his step," said Andrew, "but he became overexcited when he saw the falcons. I don't suppose he sees many in America."

"No, I suppose he doesn't," I said, accepting another cup of tea from Mrs. Hume. She hovered silently between us, filling cups, removing plates, and generally overseeing the meal.

The night's sleep and the morning's outing had done little to refresh my host. His eyes were shadowed, his face drawn, and his thoughts seemed to wander at times, yet he seemed oddly bent on helping us to enjoy the rest of our stay.

"He asked if we could go up to the nest after breakfast," Andrew continued. "He seemed so keen on it that I didn't have the heart to refuse. I've loaned him some clothes, as his aren't particularly well suited to our Highland terrain, and we'll be starting up directly after breakfast." He addressed the housekeeper. "Mrs. Hume, will you please see to it that a picnic lunch is prepared? It may take us some time to complete the expedition." Mrs. Hume gave him a curt nod and left the room. "With Colin's help, I can still clamber up there and back," Andrew added, "but not as speedily as I once did. You're welcome to join us, if you like, Miss Shepherd."

"Thank you, but I think I'll stay here. I'm not nearly as outdoorsy as Bill." I cast an admiring glance around the room. "And it's not often that I find myself in a place like MacLaren Hall. We don't have anything like this in America, either."

"Then you must have a look round while you're here," Andrew offered.

"Really?"

"You're more than welcome. Mrs. Hume is nearly as well versed in the hall's history as I am. I'm sure she can take some time off from her morning duties to escort you." When he put the proposition to Mrs. Hume, she agreed to it with her usual economy of words.

Bill entered the dining room a short time later, and I had to hand it to him—he was much better at concealing his emotions than I was. He must have been ready to throw me into the loch, but his greeting was as genial as ever. He made light of his dunking, waxed rhapsodic about going up to the falcons' nest, and graciously expressed his gratitude to Andrew for his new apparel—a pale gray cashmere turtleneck beneath a navy pullover, and heavy wool knee socks tucked up into a pair of tweed plus-fours. He even dared to call a cheery good-morning to Mrs. Hume.

"Mr. MacLaren has promised me a pair of hobnailed boots for the climb." He displayed a stockinged foot. "It's going to be a while before my own shoes are dry enough to wear. Coffee, if you please, Mrs. Hume. I don't think the tea is quite strong enough to take the chill away." When he bent his head over the steaming cup, I noticed that his hair was curling in damp tendrils behind his ears. "Tell me, Lori, how do you plan to spend your time while the menfolk are away in the hills?"

"Mrs. Hume is taking me on a tour of the hall."

"What a splendid way to spend the day," said Bill, with more heartfelt sincerity than either Mrs. Hume or Andrew could have realized. "How I wish I could be here with you."

*
**

MacLaren Hall was massive, but it seemed to grow even larger as I trailed behind Mrs. Hume, who was impervious to small talk and met any attempt at humor with a stony stare. More like a dour professor than a tour guide, she plodded methodically from room to room, giving a set speech about the contents of each, and achieving with ease the remarkable feat of turning a Scottish lilt into a monotone. If she expected to dull my wits, she was in for a disappointment. She took me past smoky oil portraits and marble-topped pedestal tables, rosewood étagères and musty tapestries, from the dim and dusty attics to the spotless kitchens—she even showed me the linen closets—but there were three places in which we did not set foot. As we passed by Andrew MacLaren's private suite and the staff apartments, Mrs. Hume merely gestured at the closed doors, as though no more needed to be said on the subject.

But one closed door, the fourth one up the hall from my bedroom, won neither gesture nor comment. We had passed it several times on our way to and from the main staircase, but Mrs. Hume acted as though it were invisible. I dutifully kept my eyes front and center.

After a late afternoon lunch, Mrs. Hume escorted me to the library, where she left me with a selection of dusty books about the history of the MacLaren family. At any other time they would have intrigued me, but at that moment my mind was on other things—such as breaking and entering. I sat for fifteen minutes by the ormolu clock on the mantelpiece, then opened the door to see if the coast was clear.

Mrs. Hume looked up from polishing the time-darkened

oak wainscoting that lined the hallway. "Yes, Miss Shepherd? May I help you?"

I gave her a frozen grin, then managed, "I wonder if I might trouble you for a cup of tea?"

"Of course." Mrs. Hume put down her cloth and walked off in the direction of the kitchens, while I closed the door and thought fast. If I went up to my bedroom she'd probably move her polishing operation right along with me. There were miles of wainscoting to polish in MacLaren Hall. What I needed was a diversion. I scanned the room, spied a telephone, and a plan clicked into place. Hurriedly, I dialed, and began speaking the moment I heard Willis, Sr.'s voice.

"It's Lori," I said in low, urgent tones. "I can't explain now, but I need you to do a favor for me. A really big favor, right away. Do you have a pen and paper?"

"Yes, Miss Shepherd."

"Then write this down." The phone number of MacLaren Hall was printed on a small card affixed to the phone. "Did you get that?" I asked, glancing at the door. He read it back to me and I raced on before he could ask any questions. "I need you to call that number in about twenty minutes and ask for a Mrs. Hume. That's *H-U-M-E*. She's a housekeeper at a big old place way up in northern Scotland. Keep her on the line for as long as you possibly can, and don't mention my name or Bill's or anything about Dimity Westwood. Don't tell her who you are, either. Can you do that?" Every muscle in my body tensed as I waited for him to give the matter his due consideration.

"I suppose I could present myself as an American relation," suggested Willis, Sr., finally. "I could, perhaps, be in the midst of conducting an investigation into the genealogy of my family."

"Perfect!" I said. "You're a genius, Mr. Willis—and thanks. I'll explain soon and, remember, give me twenty minutes. I have to go now." I hung up the phone and was back behind the pile of dusty books in plenty of time to assume a suitably studious appearance. When Mrs. Hume arrived with the tea trolley, I closed the book I had opened at random, and yawned languorously.

"Gosh," I said, rubbing my eyes. "I'm sorry, Mrs. Hume, but I don't think I'll have that tea after all. To tell you the truth, what I really need is a nap. I believe I'll go up and stretch out until the men come back."

Mrs. Hume's lips tightened, but she conducted me up the main staircase without comment, pausing only to pick up her basket of polishing supplies.

"Is there anything else you require, Miss Shepherd?" she asked when we arrived at my room.

"Thank you, Mrs. Hume, but I think I've bothered you enough for one day." I yawned again, and hoped I wasn't overdoing it. "Thanks again for the tour. This is a marvelous place."

Mrs. Hume's head turned at the sound of footsteps on the staircase. A red-haired girl in a maid's uniform approached, then proceeded to astonish me by dropping a curtsy to the housekeeper.

"Please, ma'am," said the girl, "there's a telephone call for you. A trunk call."

"A trunk call?" Mrs. Hume queried sharply. "For me? You're certain?"

"Yes, ma'am," said the girl. "And Mr. Sinclair has come about the stove."

"Very well." Mrs. Hume's knuckles went white on the handle of the basket. "Tell Mr. Sinclair to wait in the kitchen. I will attend to him presently." The girl bobbed a curtsy once again, and left. Mrs. Hume turned back. "I trust that you will have a restful few hours, Miss Shepherd. I shall be up again shortly, to make sure you have everything you need. You will excuse me."

"Of course, Mrs. Hume. Good luck with the stove." When both sets of footsteps had faded into the distance, I sprinted up the hall. I placed a trembling hand on the doorknob, sent a quick prayer to the god of locks, and followed it with thanks when the knob turned. Slipping into the room, I closed the door gently behind me, then leaned against it to catch my breath. I felt so much like a little kid playing hide-and-seek that I wanted to giggle, but when I turned to view the room, the laughter died in my throat.

It was a boy's room, still and silent, washed in the golden light of the late afternoon sun. A stuffed badger peered down from the top of the wardrobe, and the shelves above the bed were crowded with clockwork tanks, lead soldiers, and gleaming trophies. A battered leather binocular case dangled from the gun rack in the corner and schoolbooks were arranged in ranks upon the bookshelves. Above my head a squadron of model airplanes hung at dramatic angles. An unfinished one, made of balsa wood and tissue paper, sat on a table against the wall, still waiting for its wings. I turned a slow circle to take it all in, then crossed the room.

The desk was covered with pencil drawings of gentle hills, a patchwork valley, a rose-covered cottage with a slate roof. The smiling face of Dimity Westwood looked out from a graceful silver frame that had been placed to one side. I looked from the portrait to the softly shaded drawings and knew that this was Bobby's room, preserved in amber. The center drawer of the desk held pencil stubs, bits of eraser, a broken ruler—and a tattered exercise book that bore the name ROBERT MAC-LAREN. Burning with a sudden flush of shame, I closed the drawer and turned away.

This was no game. Blinded by my own cleverness, I had forgotten that we were dealing with death and loss and wrenching grief. I had betrayed the trust of my host, and I had invaded what must have been, for him, a shrine. My very presence felt like a desecration. If this was what it took to help Dimity, then I would have to fail her. I got up from the desk and headed for the door.

I was halfway there when it opened.

23

Andrew MacLaren stood erect in the doorway for a moment; then his shoulders drooped. I feared for a moment that he would collapse, but he called upon some inner reserve of strength, pulled himself to attention, and entered. Bill followed, closing the door behind him.

"I see that you have found my brother's room," Andrew said in a soft, tired voice. "When I saw Mrs. Hume, I suspected . . . but no matter. Had you waited, I would have brought you here myself." He pulled the chair from the desk and sat down, gesturing for us to sit in two others. He raised his eyes to the model airplanes overhead. "I have tried to keep it the way it was during his last visit. The last time before . . ." Andrew rubbed a hand across his weary eyes. "Perhaps I have tried to keep too much unchanged."

He reached over to pick up the photograph of Dimity, and the words he spoke were spoken to her. "I have tried to keep my anger unchanged, but it has been hard, so very hard. You cannot warm yourself at the fire of anger without chilling your soul. I am an old man now, and it seems that the fire has died. All that is left is sorrow, and guilt, and the cold and certain knowledge that I was wrong." He pulled a silk handkerchief from his pocket, gently dusted the frame, then returned it to the desk, taking care to place it in exactly the same position. He twisted the handkerchief absently for a moment; then his hands relaxed and he folded them calmly on top of his cane.

"You wish to hear of Dimity Westwood," he said. "Dimity, my brother's bonny Belle. He met her at the Flamborough and, for Bobby, one meeting was enough. He knew at first sight that he had found all that his heart desired. He told me he'd proposed to her on a hill overlooking heaven, that he planned to return there after the war, to the place he had first discovered love. He asked me to look after his beautiful Belle if anything should ever happen to him, and I promised, upon my oath as a MacLaren, that I would do as he wished.

"It was such an easy promise to make. His love for Dimity enveloped him in a—" Andrew passed a hand through the dust motes dancing in the sun, "a golden haze. I had never seen such happiness before, and I have never seen it since. It was exquisite, the kind of love that admits no envy, no jealousy. I was dazzled and warmed by it and felt sure that Dimity would feel as I did, that it would be worth any sacrifice to keep that golden aura glowing."

Andrew placed his cane on the floor, opened the bottom drawer of the desk, and withdrew a bundle of papers bound with a pale blue ribbon. Untying the ribbon, he took out a single photograph. He gazed at it for a long time before handing me a picture of a handsome young man in uniform, sitting in the shade of a gnarled oak tree. He nodded at the bundle of papers.

"It was in among Bobby's personal effects at Biggin Hill," he explained. "I was mistaken about Dimity, you see. The night before his final mission, Bobby called me from the base, saying that she had broken off their engagement." With a shaking hand, he raised the papers toward me. "She'd returned his letters, his pictures, his ring, everything that might remind her of their time together. She'd told him that they must stop seeing one another. I was outraged, incensed. I couldn't understand how she could be so blind, so willfully cruel. But Bobby remained undaunted.

" 'She thinks she's being practical,' he told me, without a trace of rancor. 'She thinks it's foolish to make plans in such uncertain times.' He laughed then. 'She's wrong,' he said. 'This is when you need to make plans, dream dreams. This is when you need to believe that there will be a tomorrow to fly to. I'll convince her of it, I know I will. She's returned the ring to my keeping, but she and I both know that it's hers forever. As I am.' "

Andrew picked up the ribbon and tied it once more around the papers. He gave the bundle to me, then let his hand fall limply to his knee. "It was the last time I ever spoke with my brother. He was shot down the following day.

"I could not comprehend it. I could not accept that his death had been a mere twist of fate, a misfortune of war. My brother had always flown like a falcon. What had tripped him up? The question tormented me night and day, until, finally, I knew the answer." Andrew's hand closed into a fist. "I kept my promise to him. I deposited his share of our inheritance in Dimity Westwood's account. I cannot be accused of betraying that trust.

"But I . . . I also wrote her a letter. Bobby had told me that, should I ever need to communicate quickly with Dimity, I should write in care of the Flamborough. He said that everyone there knew who Belle was.

"When I got word of his death, I wrote to her, telling her that the money was hers to do with as she pleased, but that if she tried to return it, we would throw it to the winds because my family wanted nothing more to do with her. I told her that Bobby's mind had been clouded by thoughts of her betrayal, that his reflexes had been dulled, and I . . . I accused her of being responsible for . . ." Andrew pressed his fist to his mouth.

A chill went through me. What must Dimity have felt? She must have been half-mad with grief, consumed with guilt, all too willing to believe Andrew's vicious accusation. The words must have seared into her soul, and she had carried that great and secret sin with her to the grave.

"She never touched the money," Andrew went on, "not until she began her work with Starling House. She invested it, then, on behalf of the children, as though seeing to their welfare would right the wrong she had done. She was a canny businesswoman and she made a tidy sum, I'll grant her that. But how I hated her for it.

"I wrote to her once more, a letter I hoped she would never receive. Although the war was over, I sent it to the Flamborough, with no return address, and I used her proper name, hoping no one would recognize it. I knew that I was breaking faith with Bobby, but I did not care. When the years passed and I received no reply, I felt well satisfied.

"That was when the nightmares began." Andrew bowed his head and touched his fingers to his temples. "They did not come every night, but often enough to make me afraid to sleep. You cannot imagine their vividness, their power. They always begin with the same hellish vision. I am spinning out of the clouds toward an iron-gray sea. I watch as the waves grow closer and closer, but I can do nothing to stop myself. Sometimes the impact awakens me, and I cry out, gasping for breath, terrified. And sometimes the gray waves pull me under, and that—that is the true nightmare, when I am pulled down into the chill, black depths of the sea and left there, alone and wandering, searching for, but never finding, my way home." A shudder racked Andrew's body, and when he opened his eyes, his face was haggard.

"I lied when I told you that I sensed my brother's presence in the chapel. It is in these visions that Bobby comes to me. For years I've told myself that he came to keep my rage alive, to remind me of the horrible way he had died. But in the chapel last night, my certainty began to crumble." He raised his eyes to mine. "The locket you're wearing—it was Dimity's, was it not?"

"She treasured it," I said. "She was never without it."

"It was my grandmother's. Bobby gave it to Dimity. She must have worn it the day she broke off their engagement, and that's why Bobby knew . . . She didn't return everything, you see; she kept back one token of their bond, and when I saw it last night, I knew that Bobby had been right, that, regardless of her actions, she had never stopped loving him." Andrew bowed his head and moaned softly. "If I'd been wrong about that, was it not possible that I'd been wrong about everything else? My brother was not given to anger— why would his visions encourage it in me? Perhaps he sent them for another reason. Perhaps they were sent to tell me that, as long as Dimity suffered, my brother's spirit would find no peace."

He faced the desk once more, opened a narrow side drawer, and withdrew a small box. He gazed at the box, turning it between his fingers as he spoke.

"Shortly after my brother's plane was shot down, a member of the Home Guard was patrolling the waterfront in the coastal village of Clacton-on-Sea. He found a map case that had floated ashore. In it, he found this." Andrew passed a gentle finger over the lid of the box, then handed it to me and gestured for me to open it. It held an elaborately carved gold ring.

"The man who found it must have been scrupulously honest," Andrew continued, "because he turned it in to the local constabulary. It took some years, what with the war and all, but they eventually traced it back to its owners by identifying the MacLaren crest.

"The ring belonged to Bobby," he said. "He had it with him when he died. He sent it back to her, not to me. He must have known what was in her heart."

I stared at the ring wordlessly, knowing that the last piece of the puzzle had finally fallen into place. Bobby had known what was in Dimity's heart. He'd sent the ring home to reassure her, to comfort her, to show her that he had never lost faith in her love. He'd sent the ring home, but it had gone to the wrong home, waylaid by a brother's misguided love. MacLaren Hall had been Bobby's birthplace, and the birthplace of his ancestors, but it was not his heart's home. He had been struggling desperately ever since to find his way back to that place where he had been most vibrant, most alive.

The aching loneliness that filled Andrew's nightmares had been Bobby's. It had been Bobby's voice I'd heard on Pouter's Hill, his longing I'd felt, a longing to return to the place where he had spent the most precious moments of his brave, brief life, to return to the woman he loved and convince her to take his love and keep it, believe in it, no matter what the odds, no matter how short the time.

Andrew seemed to read my mind. "Bobby trusted me to get the ring to Dimity, but I betrayed him. I did what I could to deprive her of this token of my brother's love. Can you imagine what I feel, knowing that, by keeping the ring from Dimity, I have prolonged my brother's suffering? I should have celebrated Bobby's memory by living as he would have lived, with honor and kindness and greatness of spirit. But I have spent my life on the pyre of anger, and now there is nothing left but ashes. I make no excuse. And now it is too late. . . ." Andrew covered his face with his hands.

I couldn't take my eyes from the ring. The light from the setting sun glinted off the gold, making it look warm and alive. I closed my hand over it.

"It's not too late," I murmured. The old man raised his head and I repeated, more loudly: "It's not too late, Andrew. Bobby's been out there all this time, searching for a beacon to bring him home. I promise you, Andrew, I'll bring him home."

24

Andrew allowed us to help him to bed, where he fell into what may have been the first sound sleep he'd had since the ring had come into his possession. Looking down on his peaceful face, I knew that his nightmares were at an end, and I was glad for him. I couldn't be angry. There had been too much anger already.

When we came downstairs, Mrs. Hume was still on the telephone in the library, diligently recounting the ill-fated marriage of a couple named Charlie and Eileen. She seemed to be enjoying the conversation—it was the first time I'd seen her smile. I murmured a brief explanation of the scene to Bill.

"Why did you bring my father into it?" he asked in a low voice. "I would have thought Miss Kingsley—"

"Bill," I said, "can you think of anyone more capable than your father of charming Mrs. Hume?"

Bill called Mrs. Hume away from the phone for a few moments, and I picked up the receiver. "It's me again," I said quietly. "You can wrap up your conversation when Mrs. Hume comes back."

"Did I fulfill my commission, Miss Shepherd?" he asked with an air of mild curiosity.

"Admirably. I'll tell you all about it as soon as I get a chance."

"I look forward to your explanation."

*
* *

Colin was kind enough to drive us to the airport. The moon was rising when we left MacLaren Hall and it was nearing midnight by the time we landed in London. Bobby's ring was tucked safely into a deep pocket in my jacket, and we flew in silence for a time, sorting through the bundle of papers that Andrew had given to us. The missing pages from the photograph album were there, folded with care so as not to damage any of the pictures. The photos were of Bobby, and all but five had been taken atop Pouter's Hill. The rest showed him with his Hurricane and his fellow airmen at Biggin Hill. The bundle contained some handwritten notes as well, the kind that would have fit easily into Archy Gorman's "postbox" at the Flamborough. Bill picked one up, but I stopped him before he opened it, murmuring, "These aren't for us to read."

It was Bill who found the pictures I'd been searching for. Cut from a larger photograph, the two small heart shapes bore two familiar faces. Dimity's dark hair was swept back and up off her face, held in place with a ribbon that might have been pale blue. Bobby was smiling his warm, engaging smile, and wings gleamed on the collar of his uniform shirt. As I fitted them into the locket, I said, "Remember the marking on the blue box? The *W* for *Westwood* was really an *M* for *MacLaren*."

"You read it upside down," Bill said with a wry smile. He held up a page from the album and pointed to one of the captions. "Did you notice this? Their first date. Just over a month before Bobby's plane went down. He must have proposed right after they met."

"My dad proposed to my mom on their second date," I said, "and she accepted on their third. Things happened faster in those days. I guess they had to." Gathering the pages together, I laid them flat on the seat across the aisle. "When we get to the cottage, we'll put them back where they belong. We'll put back the picture my mother gave me, too." I put the folded notes into a pile, tied the ribbon around them, and put them in my carry-on bag.

Bill gazed pensively out of the window at the star-filled sky. "Poor Andrew," he said. "Barricading himself in his mansion on the hill, all alone with his anger and his grief."

"And his love," I said, "his terrible love for his brother. That was at the root of everything that followed."

"Mmm." Bill nodded absently, and when he looked at me, his eyes were troubled. "Did Dimity really believe she'd killed Bobby?"

I switched off the overhead light and looked past him at the stars. "You were right when you said that it had to be something pretty drastic to cause her this much grief. Dimity must have convinced herself—with Andrew's help—that Bobby had died because of her cowardice, and she never forgave herself."

"Cowardice?" Bill said in surprise. "What cowardice?"

"She chickened out of the engagement, Bill. It's my guess that she didn't want to end up like the women at Starling House, married one minute and widowed the next, so she tried to play it safe. She was so afraid of things ending that she never let them begin."

Bill shook his head. "I hate to think of her that way, leading a life filled with secret misery."

"I don't think there's any way around it." I put a hand on the ring in my pocket. "If Dimity had let herself off the hook for a minute, Bobby's spirit would have touched her, his ring would have gotten to her, somehow, and she would've known that everything was all right."

"As it was . . ."

"Bobby never stood a chance. Dimity's guilt blocked him like a brick wall. She never talked or wrote about him, she only went back to the Flamborough once, and she rarely went back to the cottage. She probably wore the locket to remind herself of the pain she'd caused him. We'll never know for sure if Bobby 'visited' her the way he 'visited' Andrew, but even if he tried—"

"She'd have misinterpreted his message," Bill said. "She'd have filtered it through her guilt, the way Andrew filtered it through his anger."

"And twisted its meaning as badly as he did."

Bill stroked his beard, then asked doubtfully, "Then guilt can be stronger than love?"

"I didn't say that." I let go of Bobby's ring and took Bill's hand. "Oh, Bill, haven't you figured anything out? You're just too sane, I guess. It might help if you were a bit more neurotic."

"I'll work on it," he said, "but in the meantime, I'll defer to an expert." He made a half bow in my direction.

I ducked my head sheepishly. "Yeah, so I have been sort of . . . crazed. So was Dimity. So was Andrew, for that matter. Grief can make you believe things that never happened and forget things that you know for sure."

"The way you forgot your mother's pride in you?"

"And a lot of other things as well. You remember what I did with Aunt Dimity's cat? I did the same thing with the rest of the stories. It wasn't until I had them shoved in my face that I began to remember the way things really were, the whole of it, not just the disappointments. Dimity handled it a lot better than Andrew and I did, though. She didn't let pain cut her off from the world."

"She had your mother to help her," Bill reminded me.

I squeezed his hand. "Let's say they helped each other."

Bill nodded thoughtfully, then scratched his head. "So guilt can overwhelm you—"

"But love is stronger. It's in the process of triumphing, remember? It just took a little time for the right messenger to come along."

"Dimity's spiritual daughter."

I nodded. "There's nothing between Dimity and me but love, and I think I know a way to bury her guilt, to get Bobby's message through to her once and for all. That's what we were sent here to do."

"Who sent us? Bobby?"

"Yes." I reached into the bag at my feet and pulled from it the battered old photograph of the clearing. "We were sent by Bobby, and by my mother, and Ruth and Louise, and your father, and Emma and Derek—even Archy and Paul helped. We were sent here by everyone who ever loved Dimity."

Bill nodded slowly. "So what do we do now?"

"Wait and see," I said. "And in the meantime, help me think of something to tell your father."

**

I had called Emma and Derek from MacLaren Hall to give them an update and they were waiting for us at the cottage, flashlights in hand, when we drove up. I fetched the one I had purchased at Harrod's and Bill took the emergency lantern from the car. The three of them exchanged looks, but asked no questions as I led them through the back garden to the path up Pouter's Hill.

The woods had been dim in full daylight; now they were black as pitch. We had to stop frequently to search for the path and the beams from our flashlights danced like will-o'-the-wisps as we swung them from side to side. I could hear Bill puffing behind me, and the faint rustling noises of night creatures running for cover. I wondered what they made of our peculiar expedition.

As we reached the top of the hill, the gray predawn light was beginning to filter through the swirling mist that had settled in the clearing. When I pulled up short at the eerie sight, Bill walked into me and then Derek and Emma bumped into him, so our entrance was more in character with the Marx Brothers than the Brontë sisters, which was okay by me.

I led the way to the old oak tree and swung my carry-on bag to the ground. Kneeling, I pulled out a trowel and began to dig between two gnarled roots. Emma and Derek and Bill switched off their lights and watched in silence, and when the hole was deep enough, I paused to look up at the heart Bobby had carved so long ago. They followed my gaze and, one by one, knelt beside me, eyes alight with understanding.

I took from the bag the folded notes, still tied with the pale blue ribbon, and placed them at the bottom of the hole. From a pocket I took the blue box, then unclasped the chain from around my neck. I slipped Bobby's ring onto it; it clinked softly as it touched the locket. I placed them together in the blue box and set it gently atop the bundle of notes. Bill troweled the dirt back in and as he patted the last scattering into place, the sun rose.

The clearing glittered with dew-diamonds and a lark sang out the first sweet song of morning. The mist rolled back from the valley floor, and the fields and hills emerged, flushed pink and peach and golden. It may have been a trick of the light, and I've never confirmed it with the others, but I'm willing to swear that the heart on the old tree shimmered as I stood up.

The scene was complete now; nothing was missing or out of place, and I knew that when the sun was high, the hawks would rise again to ride the thermals.

25

I'm not sure if the mind at work was that of a son or a lawyer, but Bill managed to come up with a fairly convincing story for me to give to Willis, Sr. It had to do with running into old friends during our country ramble, being invited to visit them at their home in northern Scotland, and getting drafted into arranging a surprise party. It sounded farfetched to me, but Willis, Sr., seemed willing enough to accept it. I figured that sort of thing must be routine in their circle.

Much to my surprise, Willis, Sr., was also willing to go along with my request to end our question-and-answer sessions. He seemed to understand when I told him that they weren't needed anymore, that I was ready to begin writing. I called Bill into the study to say hello, and when he had hung up the phone, I pointed to the door. "Now go away," I ordered. "I have an introduction to write."

From that moment on, Bill was like a second ghost haunting the cottage. Sandwiches and pots of tea mysteriously appeared and the empty plates and pots seemed to vanish on their own.

At one point, a cot showed up in the study, then an electric typewriter, with Reginald perched jauntily on the keys. Needless to say, my memory of those days is hazy at best, but nine drafts later, with a week left to the end of the month, the introduction to *Lori's Stories* was finished.

I slept for fourteen hours straight, then typed it up and went looking for Bill. He was upstairs on the deck, luxuriating in the sun. He squinted up at me, then waved. "Hello, stranger. I've been meaning to ask you, have you talked to Dimity lately?"

"Yes, but there was no reply. I didn't expect one. She had a lot of catching up to do. Have a look at this, will you?" I handed the pages to him, then stood by the railing to wait while he read them.

I had put into them all that I had learned since I had come to the cottage. I wrote about pain and loss and disappointment; about splendid plans going tragically awry. And I wrote about courage and hope and healing. It wasn't hard to do— it was all there already, in the stories. There were no names mentioned, of course, and the sentences were simple, and that had been the most difficult part: to say what I needed to say, in a voice that would speak to a child.

I also tried to speak to the adult that child would one day become. I urged her not to let the book lie dusty and forgotten on a shelf, but to keep it nearby and to reread it now and again, as a reminder of all the good things that life's trials might tempt her to forget.

I had added a final paragraph, one that I would not include in the next and final draft because it was intended for one pair of eyes only. In it I wrote of the terrible, wonderful power of love; how it could be used to hold someone captive or to set someone free; how it could be given without hope of return and rejected without ever being lost. Most of all, I wrote of how vital it was to believe in the love offered by an honest heart, no matter how impractical or absurd or fearful the circumstances. Because all times were uncertain and the chance might never come again.

Bill seemed to take forever to finish reading it, but when he did, the look in his eyes told me that it had done what I had hoped it would do. "It's good," he said. "It's very good. I think the critics will be writing about this instead of the stories."

"As long as the children remember the stories."

"If they pay attention to what you've said here, they'll remember them all their lives." Bill left the typed sheets on the deck chair and came over to me. "That last part might be a little tricky for them, though. It's beyond the scope of the assignment, isn't it?"

"It's not part of the assignment."

"I see." Bill's hand reached out to cover mine, where it rested on the railing. "And did you mean what you wrote?"

"Every word."

"In that case . . ." He got down on one knee and looked up at me. "Lori Shepherd, I have nothing to offer you but . . . well . . . the family fortune and a slightly warped sense of humor. And my heart, naturally. Will you marry me?"

"An interesting idea," I said judiciously, "and one to which I have given much thought. After due consideration—"

"You're enjoying this, aren't you," Bill grumbled, shifting his weight from one knee to the other.

"After due consideration," I repeated, "I have decided that I will accept your proposal, with two conditions."

"Name them."

"First, that you tell me what the 'A' stands for in William A. Willis. Does it really stand for Arthur or am I just imagining a family resemblance?"

"I prefer to think of it as an affinity with a great, imaginative mind," Bill said haughtily, "but yes, you're right. Quick now, before my leg falls asleep—what's the second condition?"

"That we spend our honeymoon here at the cottage."

Bill's face fell, and this time there was nothing theatrical about it. "Lori, you know I'd arrange it if I could, but it's impossible. The cottage has already been sold. The new owner is moving in at the end of the month."

My gaze swept out over the back garden. Emma's skillful hands had woven a glorious tapestry of colors, textures, scents, and I hoped that whoever lived here next would pause to savor its loveliness. Every petal seemed to glow, every leaf fluttered spring-green and shining. The shallow pond reflected clouds of roses in a crisp blue sky, and tiny purple blossoms cascaded over the gray stone walls. The oak grove loomed cool and inviting, and the meadow beyond the sunken terrace was awash in daffodils. I looked from their bright yellow trumpets to Bill's anxious face.

"In that case," I said, "I guess I'll have to accept your proposal without any conditions at all."

"You will?"

"Of course I will. Rise, Sir Knight, and claim your lady." I reached down to take his hand, but he stayed where he was.

"Then you accept?" he asked.

"Would you like me to write it in blood?"

"I would like you to say yes."

"*Yes*, William Arthur Willis. I will marry you."

I expected him to rise to his feet and sweep me into a passionate embrace. Instead, he sat back on his heels and let out a whooshing sigh of relief. "Thank God," he said. "I thought I'd never pry it out of you."

"You didn't seriously think I would refuse, did you?"

"No, but you had to say yes. You had to say that particular word, and I didn't think you would ever say it." He stood up and began to put his arms around me, but I held him off.

"Wait a minute," I said. "Why that particular word? Why do I get the feeling that there's something you're not telling me?"

"Because you're right. I couldn't tell you before, but now I can." He leaned forward on the railing. "You remember those stories I told you about, the ones Dimity told me when Father and I were staying at her town house in London?"

"Yes."

"I never told you who the heroine was. She was a feisty, irrepressible, entirely enchanting little girl, and her name just happened to be . . . Lori."

"You're not saying—"

"All I'm saying is that I never got her out of my mind, especially after Dimity promised that I'd get to meet her one day. She said I'd meet her and fall in love with her and that she would fall in love with me, too, though it would take her a while to realize it. And she said that I couldn't tell her anything about any of this until I'd won her heart and hand."

"*Dimity?* Dimity was *our* matchmaker?"

"Now, Lori, you said yourself that you have nothing against matchmaking. And we have it on the very highest authority —that of the inestimable Pym sisters and the experience of your own parents—that Dimity was the best."

"But . . . but . . ." I gave up and shook my head. "No wonder they call twelve an impressionable age."

"I'm sorry for pushing all those clothes on you, by the way. I should have known it would be too much too soon. But I'd waited so long and I was so happy. . . . And, uh, there's one other thing I should probably clarify as long as I'm at it." He pulled a small box from his pocket. It was covered with dark blue leather. He held it out to me and said, "*Ngee oot sanzi, Lori.*"

I blinked up at him in confusion and searched my memory. "Let's get back to work? But I've finished—"

"Wait. That's not what it means. What it actually means is what I've wanted to tell you all along. It means, I love—"

Before he could get the last word out, the sound of tires on gravel wafted through the air from the front of the cottage. He grimaced. "What a perfect time for Emma to bring the kids over to meet the Cookie Lady."

"Oh, come on," I said, tugging his arm. "I've been wanting to meet Peter and Nell. It won't take long."

"It'd better not," he said, but he allowed himself to be dragged to the front door.

We swung it wide, and to our mutual astonishment beheld none other than Willis, Sr., climbing out of the limo with the ever-helpful Paul at his elbow. Paul waved and tipped his cap at me, unloaded Willis, Sr.'s luggage, then backed the limo onto the road and sped off. Willis, Sr., meanwhile, stood on the flagstone walk, his eyes fixed on the cottage, deep in thought.

"Father! Why didn't you call? I would have come to pick you up."

"Mr. Willis, if I'd known you were coming early, I'd have—"

"Curious," Willis, Sr., said, half to himself. "Most curious." He became aware of our dumbfounded presence and shrugged helplessly. "I assure you that I share your surprise at my early arrival. I am not at all certain that I can explain it."

"I think I can," Bill muttered as he went to get his father's luggage. I had to bite my lip to keep from laughing out loud.

By the time we were settled in the living room—Bill beside his father, and me perched on the window seat—Willis, Sr., had given us as much of an explanation as he could. It wasn't much. He had simply canceled all of his appointments for the day, boarded a Concorde, and come straight to the cottage, drawn by an urge as irresistible as it was inexplicable. "Whatever will Mrs. Franklin think? And Mr. Hudson? Two of our most valued clients. Oh, dear me . . ."

"Father, I think that Lori and I will be able to explain this to you." Bill put a reassuring hand on his father's impeccably tailored shoulder.

"Will you?" Willis, Sr., asked doubtfully.

"Yes, though you may find our explanation a little difficult to believe," I said.

"It could scarcely be more incredible than the present circumstances. To change one's routine so abruptly is really quite . . ." His gray eyes focused on me. "My dear, please forgive this inexcusable intrusion. I beg of you, do not interrupt your own work on my account."

I dismissed his apology with a wave. "I'm always glad to see you, Mr. Willis. As a matter of fact, I was going to call you today to let you know that I've finished the introduction. If I had to, I could leave right now."

"Now, Miss Shepherd? You wish to depart today?"

If I had been honest, I would have admitted that there was nothing I wished less. My eyes wandered from the fireplace, with its neat pile of fine white ash, to the lilacs, still fresh and fragrant in their bowls. I touched the inkstain in the corner of the window seat, and looked through the diamond panes at the rose petals fluttering in the breeze. I would miss this place, I would cherish it in my memory, and I didn't want to leave it. But I knew that I could. It was better, much better, to leave now, with my head up, than later, looking back over my shoulder.

"Yes," I said decisively. "I don't need to stay here any longer."

"I see." Willis, Sr., regarded me in silence, then added, "Your mind is quite made up on that point?"

"It is."

"I see." Willis, Sr., pursed his lips, raised his eyebrows, then seemed to reach a decision. "Well, in that case, I see no reason to delay carrying out Miss Westwood's final instructions."

"There's no need to do that, either, Mr. Willis," I said. "I'd feel guilty taking a penny of the commission. My work has been a labor of love."

"That is a very noble sentiment, Miss Shepherd, and I shall honor it, if you so desire. But I am not speaking of the commission."

"You're not?"

Willis, Sr., asked Bill to fetch his briefcase from the hall. When Bill returned with it, Willis, Sr., withdrew a leather portfolio and examined its contents soberly. He nodded once, then closed the portfolio and folded his hands on top of it.

"My dear Miss Shepherd," he said, "there is one last question I must put to you. Would you please tell my son and me the story entitled *Aunt Dimity Buys a Torch?*"

I folded my legs beneath me on the window seat and told the story again, the correct version this time, with the bright memories as well as the trodden-on foot. As I told it, I seemed to travel back in time to the night I had arrived at the Willis mansion. I saw myself standing on the doorstep in the dark, cold and alone and angry at the world, and it was like looking at a stranger. That person could never have believed in ghosts or happy endings. That person could never have fallen in love with the Handsome Prince. I felt a great tenderness for her, and when the door opened and the warm light drove away the darkness, I wished her well.

". . . and Aunt Dimity went home to warm herself before the fire and feast on buttered brown bread and a pot of tea, smiling quietly as she remembered the very large and very kind man she had met that day at Harrod's."

Willis, Sr., let the silence linger for a time, then nodded slowly. "Thank you, Miss Shepherd. Most beautifully told." He opened the portfolio and cleared his throat. "I am now empowered to inform you that the cottage, the land surrounding it—in fact, the entirety of Miss Westwood's considerable estate, are to come into your sole possession at the conclusion of the allotted month's time. I am afraid there is no way to speed that along, my dear, but I am certain that such a delay will not—"

"Mine?" I whispered, afraid to say the word aloud. "The cottage is mine?" My astonishment was mirrored in Bill's eyes. Apparently his father had not discussed with him this detail of the case.

"Yes, Miss Shepherd. Your answer to Miss Westwood's final question was more than satisfactory. In fact—"

"Mine?" I repeated faintly, as the full beauty of the scheme unfolded before me. Dimity and Beth, those two remarkable women, guiding each other through rocky terrain, then reaching out to pull me from my isolation and show me another way. They had seen my downward spiral; they had brought me to the cottage to open my closed mind; and they had given me a month to read their words, to hear what they were trying to tell me, so that I would not use Dimity's considerable estate as a shield, a fortress, a lonely mansion on a hill.

Dazed, I rose from the window seat and walked out of the room. Bill started to follow me, but Willis, Sr., must have restrained him, because I left the cottage alone. Without quite knowing how I got there, I found myself in the clearing at the top of Pouter's Hill.

The words I exchanged with the gnarled old oak tree must remain between the tree and me. Suffice it to say that the tree proved to be as good a listener as Bill.

Epilogue

Emma planted flowers there later that summer, and according to Willis, Sr., they bloom all year round. He sits beneath the old oak tree for hours whenever he visits and he visits as often as he can. He nearly gave *me* a heart attack the first time he tackled the climb, but it seems to have done him good. His heart hasn't bothered him since.

I have to depend on his reports about the clearing because I don't get up there as often as I'd like. Between unearthing rare books for Stan, visiting Uncle Andrew in Scotland, and shuttling the little Willises between cottage and mansion several times a year—and they say that D day was a big deal! —I'm kept pretty busy.

Not one single person was surprised by the news of our engagement, least of all Willis, Sr., who had placed a special order with his tailor immediately after hearing of my first visit to Arthur's dome. "It has been a long-standing dream," he explained, "to see my son married in a morning coat, and I thought that perhaps you, Lori, might be able to persuade him. . . ." I did.

Miss Kingsley chartered flights to bring our Yankee guests over for the wedding, I baked the three-tiered cake from page 265 of the dog-eared cookbook, and the reception was held under the vicar's new roof amid hundreds of blue irises. Reginald took it upon himself to preside over the bouquet of fragrant white lilacs that had arrived without a card. And I only wanted to smack Bill once the whole day, when he announced in stentorian tones that he was marrying me for my cookies. Archy Gorman's interpretations of his remark sent Paul into paroxysms of glee and confused the Pym sisters no end.

Meg and Doug commissioned a portrait as our wedding present, which Meg unveiled with a flourish and a sneaky grin. The oil painting of the bearded knight in shining armor hangs above the fireplace in our living room now, and hardly anyone notices that he's wearing glasses. And on our first anniversary a new blanket arrived, made from the finest Scottish wool and big enough to cover two.

Oh, and I guess I forgot to mention it, but instead of giving me an engagement ring when he proposed, Bill gave me a heart-shaped locket. Two different faces smile up at me when I open it, and the feelings they engender are about what you'd expect from perfect happiness.

Beth's Oatmeal Cookies

1 cup butter (or margarine)
1 cup granulated sugar
2 jumbo eggs
5 tablespoons raisin water
 (see below)
2 cups all-purpose flour
1 teaspoon baking soda
1 teaspoon salt

1 teaspoon cinnamon
1/2 teaspoon nutmeg
2 cups old-fashioned rolled oats
1 cup raisins
2 cups water
1/2 cup chopped walnuts
 (optional)

Preheat oven to 350 degrees.

In small saucepan, combine raisins with water and bring
to boil; lower heat and simmer uncovered for 5 minutes.
Set aside to cool. When cool, reserve 5 tablespoons
raisin water, then drain raisins in colander.

In large mixing bowl, cream shortening and sugar. Add
eggs and raisin water and mix well. Blend dry ingredients
into creamed mixture. Add nuts, if desired. Add raisins
and combine well.

Drop by heaping teaspoonsful, 2 inches apart, onto greased
baking sheets. Bake 10-15 minutes, or until golden brown
and firm on top when touched with your finger. Cool on
racks.

Makes approx. 6 dozen cookies.